"You little devil," he sai~~~~~~~ ~~~~~~~~~~~
to leave a playful bite o~~~~~~~~~~~~~~
wasn't fair!"

She giggled with pure joy. "Yes, it was. It was so cute, listening to you persuade me to dance."

"I get even," he threatened.

"Oooh," she teased. "I can't wait!"

He laughed, shook his head and pulled her close for a minute. "I go to this place in San Antonio on Friday nights—Fernando's. They're famous for flamenco and the tango. We'll show the audience how the tango is done."

"Is that a promise?"

He drew back enough to see her face. She could feel his black eyes probing hers, feel his breath on her lips. "It's a promise," he said in a deep, husky tone, and he didn't smile.

It was a moment out of time, one of those moments when things are so sweet, so poignant, that it seems they can last forever. Of course, they don't. Ever.

Dear Reader,

I've had Cal Hollister's story on a back burner for years, but it wasn't until I wrote *Wyoming Strong* that I finally connected Amelia with him. The problem was how to tell their story. The only way to do that was in flashbacks. You may think that it ends too abruptly. But it's an affirmation of a love that survived the worst efforts of twisted people to kill it. And when the truth came out, so did all the anger and pain.

It was while I was working on this novel that my German shepherd, Dietrich, was diagnosed with Lou Gehrig's disease. Yes, dogs get it, too. It's progressive. There is no cure. So I enjoy each day I have with him to the fullest, and I try not to look ahead. It's a reminder that life comes with no guarantees. And a reminder not to take one single hour of it for granted.

I send my warmest regards to the University of Georgia's Small Animal Clinic, where tests revealed Dietrich's disease. The personnel there—our own Dr. Cecily Nieh, my friend Chris especially and the staff—have been so kind to us both. I support research into this terrible disease. And I thank all of you for your kindness and patience if my books are a little more spread out while I care for my lovely fur child.

Diana Palmer

RANCHER'S LAW

DIANA PALMER

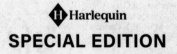

Harlequin

SPECIAL EDITION

Harlequin®
SPECIAL
EDITION™

Recycling programs
for this product may
not exist in your area.

ISBN-13: 978-1-335-59470-9

Rancher's Law
Copyright © 2024 by Diana Palmer

Guy
Copyright © 1999 by Diana Palmer

Harlequin Enterprises ULC
22 Adelaide St. West, 41st Floor
Toronto, Ontario M5H 4E3, Canada
www.Harlequin.com

Printed in Lithuania

MIX
Paper | Supporting
responsible forestry
FSC® C021394

Author of more than two hundred books, **Diana Palmer**
lives with three Maine coon cats and a German shepherd
in Habersham County, Georgia. She was married to
James Kyle for forty-eight years, before losing him to
Covid in 2021. They have one son, a daughter-in-law and
two grandchildren. Her main hobby is gaming (PC and
Xbox). She graduated summa cum laude with a BA in
history in 1995. She loves hearing from her readers. She
can be found online at Twitter (under cehntahr, her gamer
handle), also on Facebook and at dianapalmer.com.

Also by Diana Palmer

For additional books by Diana Palmer,
visit her website, dianapalmer.com.

To all the researchers trying valiantly to find a cure for Lou Gehrig's disease. It is a human disease, but it can also affect canines, like my poor German shepherd, Dietrich. One day, there will be a cure. I contribute to the cause.

CONTENTS

RANCHER'S LAW

Chapter One

Cal Hollister nursed his piña colada, only half watching the flamenco dancers on the dance floor at Fernando's in San Antonio. He wasn't sure why he kept coming here, except that she'd enjoyed the music back in the days when they were friends. Before the big blowup that had left him reeling with shock and fury.

He was drop-dead gorgeous. Tall, broad-shouldered, with thick blond hair and black eyes. Women noticed him. He never even looked up.

He sipped his drink, his mind far away. It had been seven years. All that time. He'd married a San Antonio socialite only two days after the woman from his past had brought the world down on his head. His socialite had herded him, drunk and in anguish, to a justice of the peace. And he'd texted the woman who betrayed him with bitter, shaming words and the news that he was now married. At the time, it had seemed exactly the right thing to do.

She, the socialite—Edie Prince by name—had always said that the other woman was too young and carefree to settle down. She'd convinced him that revenge was his best bet, and he'd said it was justified.

But the breakup was bad timing. He'd just come home from a devastating mission that had left him sick of his own hopeful new career and aching all over for Amelia. Her grief had led to an unforgettable night in bed, one that led to tragedy.

Guilt had ridden him hard afterward. At her grandfather's

funeral, he'd taken Edie with him, just so he wouldn't have to face Amelia alone. He knew it had hurt and confused her. But then, he was confused, too. He'd thought mercenary work was right up his alley, with his background in police work. Well, it wasn't. He'd seen things, done things, that haunted him still.

He'd stayed away from Amelia for weeks while he got counseling, put his life back together, changed jobs and became settled. He'd finally come to terms with his feelings for her. He even had a set of rings in his pocket. He'd been looking forward to starting a new life. Then Amelia's great-aunt, in a fit of rage, had called him to say that Amelia had solved their little problem and now there were no complications, so he was free to seduce another innocent woman, wasn't he?

He took another swallow of the drink. That news had started him on the downward spiral that led him right into marriage with his worst nightmare. So long ago. So much pain. He'd given Amelia hell, not allowing her to even get a word in edgewise, not giving her a chance to defend herself, explain herself. And to complicate matters, a few days later, at the end of a drinking binge that had almost landed him in jail, he'd married Edie. Biggest mistake of his life.

It was a shame that he'd sobered up soon afterward. Because Edie had faults that he hadn't known about when he'd put that ring on her finger. He hadn't known that she was a blatant alcoholic; that she used drugs; that she was a habitual liar. He'd found all those things out one by one.

She'd said they could have children, but that was before he found out that she'd had a hysterectomy some years before, and that she'd never wanted children.

They were a nuisance, she told him, and she wasn't risking her figure to add another squalling brat to the world.

It had only taken him a few days to realize that what he really felt for her, when he wasn't drunk, was contempt. He'd married her out of spite, to rub it in that Amelia meant nothing to him, that he'd never cared for her.

It had been a lie. His life had been hell for three long years before Edie finally drank too much one night and, after adding narcotics to the mix, had put herself in the morgue.

Cal, who'd given up mercenary work to hire on with the San Antonio Police Department, had climbed from patrolman to sergeant, then to lieutenant. He was now captain of the detective squad, a testament to his ability to manage cases and get along with politicians and protesters alike. Promotions that usually took years had taken him far less time, through a series of lucky breaks and ability.

But his job, although satisfying, was just a job. He went home to an empty house on his Jacobsville ranch, where he lived alone. He'd given Edie's house to a distant cousin of hers, who promptly sold it. Cal hadn't wanted it. The place held too many memories of his drunken wife making his life hell. He moved into an apartment and then, not long afterward, bought a small ranch in Jacobsville, where he and Amelia had first met.

People in his department noticed that he never dated. They assumed it was because he was still mourning his late wife. Nothing was further from the truth. He'd hated Edie with a passion. When he was finally cold sober, he slowly came to realize that he might not have had the whole story about what had happened in the past. But after he married Edie, he hadn't done any checking. He didn't want to know. Amelia was out of his life, and he could never trust her again, even if they met again someday.

He didn't know where she was, or what she was doing. He'd heard rumors that she was involved in some covert work, but that didn't sound like the young girl who'd listened, fascinated, to his stories about his mercenary years. She was soft and gentle, not at all the sort of person to involve herself in violence.

He grieved for the young girl she'd been when they'd first

known each other. He never should have touched her in the first place, but he'd wanted her so desperately, for so long, until she was all he thought about. What happened was…inevitable, he supposed. But what came after had destroyed him.

Why hadn't she told him about the child? Didn't she realize that he'd have married her at once? He'd planned it even before he knew there was a child. He adored her. When he'd gone on that last mission, he'd almost ended up shot because he was thinking about her instead of the danger he was facing.

Only to be presented with evidence that she'd gotten rid of his child. She'd gone to a clinic. She hadn't wanted him, or the baby, and she hadn't even bothered to tell him. He'd been bitter. So bitter. He'd called her names, raged at her, damned her for what she'd done. But here he sat, after all these years, in Fernando's. Hoping she might walk in some day, because he'd brought her here at least twice to introduce her to the addictive tango. And he'd taught her to dance it.

It was stupid. She'd never come back. Her life was elsewhere, somewhere. Hell, she might even be married by now.

That thought depressed him even more. He finished his drink just as he spotted his friend Clancey sitting with her little brother, Tad, and her new husband, Colter Banks. Clancey had worked for him several years ago. He was fond of her and Tad. They were like the family he didn't have. He'd looked out for them until Banks came along. Well, he liked Banks, and it was good to see Clancey and Tad settled. But he was alone again. He didn't have friends, unless you included Father Eduardo, a fellow merc who'd taken the collar. He had a church in San Antonio smack dab in the middle of gang territory. But Los Serpientes had learned the hard way not to attack this priest. He'd put them in the hospital. Seven armed men, and he'd put them all down. Two had joined his church afterward. He chuckled silently. Father Eduardo was a local legend.

He paid the check and walked over to the table where Clancey was sitting with her family.

Clancey invited him to sit down after introducing her cousin from Chicago. The woman was nice-looking, but she was a brunette. Cal wouldn't have been interested even if she'd been a blond, though. He was still buried in thoughts of the past, in misery and anguish for what he'd lost.

Just as he started to excuse himself and go home, he saw her. There, at the counter, picking up an order. She hadn't aged a day! It had been years, and she was just the same as he remembered her.

He murmured something, unaware that his companions were staring at him. Amelia. His heart tried to climb into his throat. Same pretty figure, same pretty face, same blond hair in a bun atop her head. He'd have recognized her in a crowd of thousands.

She turned with her purchase, still smiling, until she spotted Cal. The smile was suddenly gone, wiped away like magic, to be replaced by a look of such anger that he felt those eyes making holes in him.

Amelia, he thought in anguish.

But if she felt anguish, it didn't show. She glared at him, turned and walked out of the restaurant. He murmured something to the people at the table and went out after her. He got to the sidewalk, and she was just gone, just like that.

He shoved his hands into his pockets and stared out at the misting rain with dark eyes that mirrored his misery. So many years without a sight of her, and here she was, back in San Antonio. But where? Doing what? He was going to have to do some digging. He had to find a way to talk to her. Somehow.

Amelia Grayson had darted around the corner of Fernando's and hailed a cab back to her new apartment.

Her heart was going like a fast watch, and she could barely

catch her breath as she told the cab driver where to take her.
She hadn't expected to see Cal. But, of course, she knew that
he'd always gone there on Friday nights when he was in town
to watch the flamenco dancers. And the tango.

He was a past master at tango, one of the few men she'd ever
known who could dance it. In fact, he'd taught her, in the days
when they were like one person, when the world began and
ended with him in her life.

That was over. He'd never given her a chance to explain what
had happened. It no longer mattered, anyway, she told herself.
If somebody cared for you, they wanted an explanation. They
wanted your side of the story. It wasn't like that with Cal. He'd
attacked her verbally the minute he saw her. Accusations, blame,
hatred, in the space of seconds, after they'd been so close that
they almost breathed together.

He'd gone out of town on police business for two weeks.
She'd been living with a hateful great-aunt here in the city, one
now long dead and forgotten. After a tragic loss, and two days in
the hospital, she'd left her great-aunt's house and gone straight
to Eb Scott with her bags packed and her heart encased in ice.
He'd always said he wouldn't train women, but she changed his
mind. She told him what had happened. She lost her job, her
home, her child… Cal. Everything. She had no place to go. So
how about training her?

And he had.

Amelia hailed a taxi to her apartment. She just sat there,
after giving the driver her address, in the back seat, staring into
space. Seeing Cal so unexpectedly had opened gaping wounds.

The woman he'd married seven years ago was a socialite she
knew. The woman had been a pest. She came down from the
city on weekends to pester Cal, who seemed to find her amusing. At least, he never sent her away. Amelia had been furiously
jealous, but he'd only laughed and said the woman was harm-
less; just bored and flamboyant. He'd known a dozen like her.

So Amelia hadn't fussed. But the woman, Edie Prince, didn't like her and made a point of trashing her clothes, her accent, anything she could find to pick on. Cal didn't seem to notice. He said she was just kidding, and Amelia shouldn't take her seriously.

That must have included not believing her when she said that Cal was just playing with Amelia because she was a novelty in his life, but he was going to marry Edie, so Amelia might as well enjoy Cal's company in the little bit of time left to her.

Amelia didn't believe her. The socialite had just laughed. She'd see, she'd replied. And soon. Then, Amelia's grandfather had died. She and Cal had grown quickly intimate, but he'd backed off at once. She hadn't understood what had happened to him in Africa, not until she joined Eb Scott's counterterrorism unit. She did now, too late. Cal had been coping—rather, not coping—with trauma from what he'd seen and had to do in Ngawa. He'd been confused and upset, and she hadn't understood that it was just too much too soon.

But the baby was a fact. Her great-aunt, with whom she'd lived up in Victoria after her grandfather's sudden death, had been a fanatic about the family name never being soiled. And here was her great-niece, living with her, pregnant out of wedlock! Worse, Amelia was planning to keep the baby! Everyone in town would know. Great-Aunt Valeria was horrified. She'd acted out of that horror and caused a much worse tragedy.

When Amelia got out of the hospital, she had an aide go and pack her things and bring her suitcase to the hospital. The pain was too raw to allow her to even speak to the woman who'd done so much damage. From the hospital, she went to Eb.

So much pain. So much anguish.

And the worst was yet to come. Cal called her and she wasn't able to get one word in about what had really happened. He'd made his opinion of her known, railed at her, raged at her. He'd been drunk out of his mind, but she didn't know that. And he didn't know that Edie had phoned her earlier to thank her for getting rid of that little complication that Cal didn't want anyway.

Not three days after the accident, Cal married the flamboyant socialite. Everybody in town knew because Cal had put the announcement in the local newspaper. Amelia had lunched at Barbara's Café in Jacobsville on her way to Eb Scott's place, with sympathetic glances making her uncomfortable. It was a small town, and most people knew that she and Cal had been close. When couples broke up, it was food for gossip. Especially when one partner married someone else after the breakup. They thought of Amelia as family, and they were protective of her. It wasn't until much later, when she was doing jobs for Eb, that she'd learned Cal had bought a ranch in Jacobsville. But he had to shop for it in San Antonio. The owner of the feed store wouldn't trade with him. Through the anguish, it was one of the few things that amused Amelia in between jobs.

There wasn't much in-between time. She mostly worked as a bodyguard and traveled with her clients. Right now, she was between assignments, or she wouldn't have been around San Antonio. She had an apartment there because she wasn't living in the same town with Cal. She'd had enough of gossip. Even kindly gossip. She'd never forgotten that last day in the hospital. While she lay awake that night, she had a thought. Cal had worked for Eb Scott, who had a counterterrorism school in Jacobsville. He trained mercs and did jobs for many governments including, it was gossiped, ours. She'd heard that he'd trained at least one woman from overseas who was going to work for a foreign government. That meant that he might take on Amelia, if she could convince him. She wasn't afraid of much, and her grandfather had taught her to shoot a gun. It wasn't much, but it might get her foot in the door.

* * *

So the next morning, quaking inside, she'd phoned Eb and got an appointment to talk to him. She'd hitched a ride with an orderly at the hospital who lived in Jacobsville. He dropped her off at Eb's huge compound.

He'd given her a strange look when she told him why she was there.

"I can do it, Mr. Scott," she said quietly. "I may look like a wimp, but I'm not. And," she added quickly, "I have an undergraduate degree in chemistry."

That had raised both his eyebrows. "Chemistry?"

She nodded. "Plus, one of the guys auditing my class had done demolition work while he was in the service." She smiled slyly. "He taught us how to make deadly substances out of common household chemicals." She leaned forward. "I can make bombs," she added.

"Well, damn." He burst out laughing. "I have to confess, this is the most interesting interview I've conducted recently."

She grinned. "I learn fast, study hard, and I won't run under fire."

"Why do you want to do this sort of work?"

She sighed and sat back in the chair. "I've just been thrown over by the only man I ever cared about, because of something he thought I'd done that I didn't do. He wouldn't listen when I tried to tell him the truth."

"You might try to make him listen," he began.

"He got married two days ago," she said flatly.

Eb drew in a breath. He knew Cal Hollister, and his temper. The man was like a stone wall when he made up his mind. And if he'd married someone else, he was through with poor Amelia. Everybody already knew.

"It's not really a life for a woman," he began.

"I have nothing left to lose," she said simply and without self-pity. "There are lots of roofs. I only need to step off one of them."

He grimaced. He'd misjudged the level of her desperation. She kept her emotions under tight control, but she was in deep pain, and it showed.

"So it's you or Australia."

He stared at her. "Australia?"

"It's what the mob guys call it. Down under? Hint, hint?"

He got it and shook his head. "You're so young," he began.

"Misery doesn't have an age limit. I need to get out of Texas and do something with my life, while I still have one." Her dark eyes were quiet. "I know about the work you do. It's not only important—it saves lives. I know what your agents have done over the years. It's a record anyone would be proud of. I'd like to be a part of that. I'm good at chemistry, top of my class. I'll bet you've got somebody on staff who can teach me how to do demolition work for real."

"In fact, I do, part-time. I've got Cord Romero."

"I've heard about him," she recalled. "Stuff of legends."

"He is. He's with the FBI and gets antsy from time to time, but he's not risking his wife, Patricia, to try and slide back into merc work. So when he's climbing the walls, he comes down here to teach for a day or two a month."

She grinned. "I'd be a good student. I promise."

He shook his head and sighed. "Okay. But there will be lots of rules."

"I love rules," she said.

"And the work will be dangerous."

"I love dangerous, too."

"Are you sure?"

"I'm sure that if I don't find something challenging to do, that I'll mourn myself to death, Mr. Scott," she replied, and just for a few seconds, the depth of her anguish was visible.

He hesitated, but only for a minute. "All right."

She smiled. "Thanks. So, when do I start?"

"Tomorrow morning, at eight. You'll live in."

"Thank you. I was hoping I wouldn't have to pitch a tent on Victoria Road."

"You've got a house…"

She shook her head. "It's already on the market," she said, and her face hardened to stone. "I'd dig ditches before I'd live in a house with my great-aunt again, after what she did. And I was let go at my place of employment day before yesterday."

"Why?" he asked.

Her eyes met his. "Because I was in the hospital unconscious and didn't call to tell them that." She sighed "It's been a pretty harsh week."

"We all have those," he replied. "We get through them."

"That's what I'm counting on. A new job. A new life."

"It will be hard," he cautioned.

"Life is hard."

"Point taken." He stood up. "Welcome aboard, Amelia." And he smiled.

The first two weeks were the hardest. Amelia had never had to learn a martial art. She was out of shape, because the job she'd had in San Antonio was working in a warehouse doing inventory and putting up stock. That wasn't hard. Martial arts was.

Fortunately, she loved it at once, and excelled at it. Decked out in her new kit, she performed the katas with grace and energy, enjoying the feeling it gave her to learn something new and potentially lifesaving.

Guns came harder. She was a dead shot with a light pistol, but she couldn't cock the .45 auto she was given, so Eb switched her to a Glock. It was a lighter weight and fit her hands perfectly. She spent a lot of time on the firing range, using both hands, as she'd been taught, along with the different stances that were common to police department protocol.

"Not bad, Amelia," Eb said on her third week at it as he

studied the placement of bullets in the target. All, every one, was dead center.

"I love it. Shooting is fun!"

He chuckled. "It is, here, because the targets don't shoot back!" he reminded her.

"Not to worry, sir, I can duck with the best of them!"

"Lies," a deep voice drawled from nearby.

She grinned at Ty Harding, who was also taking Eb's courses. He was tall and good-looking, with long dark hair, dark eyes and a handsome face. They'd graduated high school together. Ty had had a crush on her, but she never felt that way about him, so he'd settled for friendship.

"You think so?" she chided. "Okay, shoot at me. Go ahead. I'll show you how to duck and make it look graceful!"

"You do it and I'll send you to Guatemala to hunt narco lords," Eb threatened him.

Ty made a face. "You let her get away with murder."

"Not yet," Eb chuckled. "Okay. Back to work!"

She learned martial arts and gun safety. And within the first two months, Cord Romero showed up to teach her demolition.

"My wife made me give it up," he grumbled as he taught her how to assemble an IED—an improvised explosive device. "Just because a bomb went off once, only once!"

"A bomb…?" she exclaimed, all eyes.

Cord was gorgeous. He had a wife that he rarely talked about, but most people knew that he'd been a merc before he joined the FBI. Tall, dark-eyed, dark-haired, olive complexion. His foster sister, Maggie, was also gorgeous. Eb Scott was engaged to her, although Ty Harding said that it was mostly just friendship. Maggie and Cord had been foster children, both adopted by the same woman. Maggie, so he said, went out of her way finding things to irritate the man she truly loved, which was Cord.

"I had my mind on something besides what I was doing," Cord explained. "So pay attention. When you defuse a bomb, there's nothing in the world except you and the bomb. Got it?"

"Got it," she promised.

"Okay. Now, this is how you connect the wires..."

She knew already how to combine chemicals to produce toxic substances, so adding that to ordnance in bomb-making was second nature. Cord had lots of experience at the art, and she paid close attention. As he explained to her, that knowledge might one day save her life, or someone in her group.

"Why chemistry?" he asked as they went on to a new project.

"I don't know," she said honestly. "I've always loved it. One of the first presents my parents ever gave me was a junior science chemistry set." She made a face. "I blew up the coffee table."

He chuckled. "I blew up a snake."

"A snake?"

"I improvised some fireworks. Mamie, my adopted mother, had no idea that I knew any such thing. One day while she and Maggie were out shopping, I bundled together some gunpowder and other substances in the outbuilding. I accidentally dropped the device right onto a rattlesnake." He grinned. "I didn't mourn much."

"Neither would I!"

He laughed. "When Mamie saw the damage to the yard, she started to fuss, but Maggie said that it was a great way to get poisonous snakes out of the way and she should encourage me to use my skills." His eyes sparkled. "Mamie gave in. I learned demolition mostly the hard way until much later, when I trained in it."

"Was your dad really a bullfighter?" she asked.

"Indeed he was, and very famous. So was my grandfather." He shook his head. "Bullfighting has a bad rep these days, but in the early nineteenth century, it was the mark of a man, to be able to walk into an arena armed with only a cape and fight a bull that could weigh half a ton. And you only had a cape and courage to do that. The bull had the advantage. They were huge, and their horns weren't blunted."

"I read about them," she said. "I got library books about Manolete."

"Yes, one of the most famous of them all. They called him El Monstrou, and it wasn't an insult. He was magnificent, they say. There's a monument to him, a statue, where he's buried."

"He got gored in the ring," she recalled.

"He did, but it wasn't the bull that killed him. It's said that he was given a blood transfusion with the wrong blood type." He shrugged. "There was a lot of gossip about his death."

"That's so sad."

He nodded. "The world was a different place in the late 1940s, just after the war. The bulls who killed matadors were as famous as the men who died in the ring," she added. She glanced at him. "They say it was that way with men who sang opera, back in the same period of time. They were treated like royalty in Italy, even in America!"

"Now, don't tell me you like opera," he teased.

"I love it. Anything Puccini wrote," she sighed. She glanced at him and chuckled. "I know. I'm a Texas girl. I should love country-western music. And I do. But I've rarely met any sort of music I didn't like."

"That's good," he said. "There's nothing worse than a music bigot."

She burst out laughing.

"And don't you forget it," he added. "Now, back to work!"

She went to bed tired every night, but her new life was exciting, and she loved every facet of it. She still mourned Cal, though. It seemed some days that she'd dreamed the brief period of time she'd had with him when they'd been so close.

* * *

The cab driver spoke again as he pulled up at her apartment building. "Miss, we're here," he said, a little louder, interrupting her thoughts about the past.

She caught her breath. She'd been lost in flashbacks and hadn't heard him. "Oh. Sorry!"

He laughed. "I do the same thing. I drift off into the past. Sometimes it is good to look back and remember good times."

"These weren't so good," she said as she paid him. "But life is all lessons."

"Indeed it is. Have a good night."

"You, too."

Her apartment was one of the newer ones, very homey with all her little touches, and it had a great view of the River Walk. She had a small balcony. She liked sitting out on it and watching the boats go up and down with tourists on them while mariachis played nearby. San Antonio was a fascinating place to live. She never grew tired of it, although she'd been away for some time guarding ex-merc Wolf Patterson and his new wife.

Now that Wolf's enemies had given up or been killed, she wasn't really needed there anymore. She'd checked in with Eb Scott, but he had nothing at the moment, so she was taking a well-deserved vacation for a couple of weeks.

It had been going well, until tonight. She hadn't expected that she'd walk into a bad memory in Fernando's. A very bad memory.

She made herself a cup of coffee and ate her supper on the balcony, while her stubborn mind climbed back into the past in Jacobsville. She remembered the first time she'd seen Cal Hollister...

Chapter Two

Seven years ago, Amelia was in her last year of high school in Jacobsville. It was a hot summer and she and her maternal grandfather, Jacob Harris, had been sitting on the front porch, fanning with old-timey funeral home fans like they handed out in churches.

Her grandfather turned his head. A tall, blond strikingly handsome man was out in the front yard of his rental house watering flowering plants. "There's that man again," Jacob teased his grandchild, watching a faint flush come to her cheeks. "Why don't you ever talk to him?"

"Are you kidding?" she squeaked. She was painfully shy and there were rumors about their neighbor. He worked for Eb Scott, the former mercenary who'd founded an internationally known counterterrorism school. He and his educators taught all sorts of dangerous things, from defensive driving for chauffeurs to martial arts and weaponry to all sorts of people. Foreign governments kept his doors open. But then, rumor said, so did our own government. Eb had the very best, experienced people teaching for him. He also had plenty of people he could send on missions when asked. It was rumored that Cal Hollister was one of them.

"He likes flowers," her grandfather remarked. "It's almost a character reference."

"He carries a gun and shoots people," she said under her breath.

"That would depend on why he shoots them," he said. "I

heard that Eb Scott was loaning operatives he trained to a foreign government in Ngawa, an African country, to get the legitimate president back in office. There have been hundreds of murders of innocent people, including children."

"How do you know all this stuff?" she asked, trying not to feed on the sight of Hollister in khaki pants and a yellow pullover shirt. He was incredibly handsome.

"I go to the post office every day and sit on the bench outside while I go through the mail," he said simply, and grinned. "Sooner or later, every gossip in town sits beside me, anxious to share juicy news."

"I'm not living right," she murmured.

He chuckled. "Your day will come. Hollister there is formidable on the firing range, they say."

"It's still sort of an illegal occupation."

"Not so. He works for Eb Scott, and Eb never deals under the table. If he sends men to help fight, it's always for a good cause. In this case, it's a noble one. Ngawa has survived so many uprisings," he added sadly. "It's a beautiful place, with good, openhearted people. I hate seeing conflict there."

"How do you know so much about Ngawa?" she asked.

"I was stationed there years ago," he said, "in one of the southern states. And don't ask why. A lot of operations that take place overseas are classified. Mine was, too."

She shook her head. "I'll never understand why we're always sending troops over to other countries, when our own is in such a mess."

"We call it patriotism," he said. "Our enemies call it imperialism. It's all politics, sugar. The rich guys in Congress declare wars and poor people die fighting them."

"There should be a law that any politician who votes for foreign wars that aren't a direct threat to us should be first in line to sign up for combat," she muttered. "That would sure limit the number of wars. It's easy to declare them when you don't have a personal interest in them."

"All too true," he agreed, rocking.

The blond man had spotted them on the porch. He set down his watering can and sauntered down the street toward them.

"Oh my gosh, he's coming here!" Amelia almost squeaked. "Is my hair combed? Do I look okay? Darn, I'm wearing a T-shirt with holes...!"

"He's not going to be trying to date you, sugar," he said under his breath, chuckling. "You're barely eighteen. He's in his mid-twenties."

That stung, but she didn't take him up on it. She drew in a breath and forced a shaky smile.

"Hi, neighbor," she said, fanning for all she was worth.

"Morning," he replied. He had a nice voice, deep and smooth. His dark eyes studied them. "I'll bet you knew the guy who owns the house I'm renting," he told Harris.

He chuckled. "Yes, I did. He had a Friday night poker game. I was always the first one over."

"He said that. He's a sweet old guy. My sergeant at San Antonio PD introduced us before I quit and sighed on with Eb Scott. I didn't want to live in the city."

"You didn't want to be a career man?"

Hollister made a face as he perched on one of the wide stone balustrades leading down the steps. "Policing isn't what it was," he said. "And I'm notoriously politically incorrect. Eb Scott's operation is more my style."

"Eb's one of a kind," Harris replied. "I thought about asking him for a job. Then I got in a car wreck. Hurt my back. I can walk, after a fashion, but I'll never be agile again, I'm afraid." He chuckled. "I just became eligible for social security. It's made all the difference in the world."

"Tell me about it," Hollister sighed. "So many people would die without it."

"True. You used to live in Houston, didn't you?" he added.

Hollister nodded. "I grew up there. My mother was a nurse, and my dad was a cop."

"Was?" Harris asked gently while Amelia hung on every word.

He sighed. "She and Dad went on vacation. They stopped in at a fast-food joint to get a meal and there was a guy with an automatic weapon and a suicidal attitude."

The look in his eyes was terrible. "Such a pity that the perp took the easy way out. I'd have enjoyed being at every parole hearing. Assuming that it wouldn't have been the needle," he added with a taut expression.

"Amelia lost her parents in a car wreck," Harris told him. "Also, both at once."

"It's hard to get through that," Amelia said quietly. "At least I had my grandfather," she added, with a warm smile at the old man.

"And I had you," he replied, smiling back. "Doris and I only had one child, a girl—your mother, Mandy. And your dad was also an only child," he added.

"So was I," Hollister said, and smiled gently at Amelia. "Families used to be larger when people lived on the land. These days, it's only one or two kids. And one is more common."

"Are you going to stay in Jacobsville?" Harris asked.

"I plan to. I don't have any relatives left and this is a nice place," he added, glancing around. "Notable citizens, as well," he said on a chuckle. "A population that seems to be half ex-mercs. It must be the safest town in America."

"We like to think so," the older man replied.

"What are you studying in college?" he asked Amelia. "I heard that you were enrolled at our local community college."

Her heart jumped. It was so fascinating that he'd even mention that. "I'm studying chemistry," she said.

Both eyebrows arched. "Chemistry?"

Her grandfather rolled his eyes and shook his head. "I encouraged her. She blew up half the dining room with a junior chemistry set Christmas present when she was ten. I bought her some books from a science website, and then she studied it in high school, as well. It seemed a natural choice. Besides," he added with a grin at Amelia, "she can blow up the school lab instead of my dining room!"

"I only blew it up a little," she protested. She laughed. "But I really have better insight now. And there's this old guy in our class. He's auditing one of my courses. He was demolition in the Middle East when he was stationed there." Her brown eyes sparkled with delight, making her look very pretty. "He's teaching us how to use ordinary household chemicals to make weapons!"

"He'll be expelled," her grandfather began.

"He does it before the professor walks in," she said with wicked glee. "I can make a flamethrower already!"

"Remind me to walk wide past your front door," Hollister chuckled.

"I wouldn't blow you up," she promised. "Just bad guys."

"And how do you know I'm not a bad guy?" he asked with an indulgent smile.

"You were watering your plants," she explained reasonably. "Bad people don't take care of plants."

Harris and Hollister exchanged amused glances.

"She's right, you know," Harris replied. "People who care for plants and gardens are nurturing people."

Hollister made a face. "Not always," he replied. "I knew a guy overseas who had this orchid plant that he carried everywhere he went. Another guy came in drunk and crushed it under his boot. Guy killed him, right there on the spot, without hesitation."

Amelia looked at her grandfather. "If we go by his house," she pointed to Hollister, "let's make sure we walk wide around the potted plants!"

Hollister chuckled with pure delight. He glanced at Harris. "Do you play chess, by any chance?"

"He's our local champ," Amelia said proudly. "He won a big competition a few years ago. We have the trophy on our mantel."

"Nice," Hollister said. "So, when you're free, how about a game?"

"I'd enjoy that," Harris replied. "Name a day."

"Friday night?"

"Perfect timing. I have to leave Saturday night on an assignment."

"My house or yours?" Harris asked. He added, "If we play here, you can have chocolate cake. Amelia's an amazing cook."

"Chocolate is my favorite," he replied, and smiled at Amelia, who blushed with unexpected delight.

"Then Friday it is. About seven?"

Hollister nodded and smiled. "Seven, it is."

The Friday night chess sessions were as exciting for Amelia as they were for her grandfather and Hollister. She made a point of cooking special desserts, things that Hollister would enjoy eating. In the meantime, she went to classes and learned more about chemistry than she'd ever dreamed she would. It was a hard subject, but she took to it like a duck to water.

Hollister wasn't a chemist, but he was an expert in some other areas, especially weapons.

One day in the autumn, he took her out to the target range at Eb Scott's school to teach her how to handle a gun. He had a .38 special that he let her borrow.

He was amazed that she put the first few shots within the smallest bull's-eye.

"You've been playing me," Hollister accused with mock anger. "You already knew how to shoot."

"Not a handgun," she said as she reloaded the automatic he'd loaned her. "I used to target shoot with a .22 rifle with some friends in high school."

"Well, you're pretty much a natural."

She grinned. "Thanks."

"Ever thought about going into police work?" he asked.

She shrugged. "I'm too squeamish. Shooting targets is one thing. Shooting people…" She glanced up at him. "I don't think I could."

"When bullets start flying in your direction, you'd be surprised how fast you could shoot people," he replied, and the smile he gave her was faint.

She wanted to ask if he'd shot people, but it wasn't something she felt comfortable talking to a relative stranger about.

"Now," he added. "Stance." He proceeded to instruct her about the three stances that law enforcement people, notably the FBI, used.

"It gives you a centered balance," he said. "Doesn't do much good if you shoot straight and then fall over your own feet."

"Good point," she nodded. "I'm good at that, though. Falling over my own feet, I mean," she chuckled.

"Your grandfather plays a great game of chess," he said.

"He's smart. He did black ops when he was in the military. I've never been able to get him to tell me what sort. He's very secretive."

"Most people in covert ops are," he replied. "It's how we stay alive. One of the more formidable mobsters of the last century said that three people could keep a secret if two of them were dead."

She laughed. "That makes sense."

"It does. Now, another thing. Trigger pull," he said. "It's an art. If you can master it, you'll never miss a target. Although you seem to have that down pat already. As I said, you're a natural."

"I like guns," she said simply. "Even though I'd rather blow stuff up."

"Why?"

"I don't know, really," she confessed. "I'm not keen on noise and I've never wanted to overthrow a country. But there's just something short of magical about mixing various substances and having them utterly destroy objectives."

He shook his head. "You and Cord Romero," he murmured.

"Romero?"

"He teaches tactics at Eb's place, when he's not on assignment. He's FBI."

"Wow." She glanced up at him. "They say getting into the FBI is like trying to join the CIA. You apply and then they take months checking you out, everything from grammar school up and all in between."

"They're elite organizations," he said. "It pays to be cautious."

"Does Eb Scott do that? I mean, check out potential students?"

"Of course he does," he replied. "Especially foreign ones. There are some devious people in the world, and our country has enemies."

"I guess so."

"We'll go a few more rounds, then I have to go to San Antonio."

"Okay."

She wondered why he was going but she never pried. It seemed to be a character trait that he appreciated.

In fact, it was. He watched her covertly while she fired the pistol. She was a conundrum. Brilliant, but reserved and careful. She never asked prying questions or droned on about the latest reality television show or online talent competitions or even fashion shows. He knew a socialite in San Antonio—Edie Prince, one whom he dated infrequently—who bored him silly with such information. He couldn't have cared less. He watched the news and occasionally a movie. Nothing else.

"Do you watch television?" he asked absently.

"Not really," she confessed. "I'm taking algebra and Japanese along with chemistry. I don't have the free time."

"Japanese?" he exclaimed.

"I've always loved the culture," she explained. "I pig out on old Toshiro Mifune movies on the weekends. Granddad has several of them on DVD."

"Good Lord." He fired several shots dead center into the target without even aiming carefully. "I thought I was the only samurai fanatic in town."

She laughed, delighted to have something in common with him. "Not really. Granddaddy loves them, too."

"I grew up watching them. They were my dad's favorite films. It was samurai or Westerns all the time when he was off duty."

It was odd, the way he sounded when he spoke of his father. She couldn't quite place the tone. It wasn't one of remembered affection.

He saw her puzzled expression and noted that she didn't reply. He reloaded. "That's one thing about you that I really like."

"What is?" she asked, glancing toward him.

"You don't pry."

She smiled. "I don't like people who do. I've always been a private person. I could never go on a social media site and pour out all my problems to a group of total strangers. Although it seems to be the new national pastime," she added with a laugh.

"Social media has been the ruin of our civilization," he said darkly. "That, and the internet. People don't talk anymore. They go out to eat and spend the whole time staring at their cell phones."

"I've noticed that. It's sad."

"If I had a family—and don't hold your breath—there would be an ironclad rule that nobody was allowed to bring cell phones to the table at mealtimes."

"We already have that rule," she said, grinning at him. "My grandfather said I needed to know how to talk to real people."

"I like your granddad," he said. "He's got more common sense than most people I know. Most brainy folks don't have enough to come in out of a rainstorm."

"His grandparents were Mennonites," she said.

His eyebrows arched over twinkling brown eyes. "Really?"

"Yes. His grandfather founded a Mennonite church over in Comanche Wells, down the road from Jacobsville. By the time Granddaddy grew up, it had become a Methodist church, but it had that beginning."

"That must be a story and a half," he mused.

"It really is. There's still a Mennonite community in Jacobs County, but it's way out in the sticks now. They have a small church and stores that sell all sorts of lovely things like home-made butter and sausages and eggs." She looked up at him. "I shop there every week. I don't like grocery stores much."

"Neither do I, but it beats snake and rabbit," he said under his breath.

"Excuse me?" She was all eyes.

"When we're on a mission, sometimes we're so far back in woods or jungle that we run out of protein bars. Snake is pretty good. Rabbit's better."

She made a horrible face.

He laughed. "Staying alive is the thing, you know. When you're starving, you'll eat anything that won't eat you."

"I guess so," she agreed, but she shivered.

He glanced at his watch. "I'd better get you home. I'll be late."

"Thanks for the instruction," she said.

"Anytime. It never hurts to know how to handle a gun." He made a face. "Scares me to death when somebody comes into a gun shop and buys a gun for protection when they've never shot one in their lives. It isn't that easy to use one, especially in a desperate situation. There have been any number of innocent family members who were shot coming into their own homes unannounced."

"That would be awkward."

They climbed into his big SUV and put on their seat belts. "Of course, some of those accidental shootings aren't really accidental," he added as he cranked the truck and pulled out into the highway.

"They aren't?"

"Like the irate wife who accidentally shot her husband twenty-four times." He glanced at her with twinkling dark eyes. "She had to reload in between."

She burst out laughing. "That's not really funny, but it is," she said. "Did she go to jail?"

He nodded. "And for a very long time. The reloading is what got her. She wanted to make sure he was dead."

"I don't understand people. Why didn't she just divorce him?" she asked.

"It was revenge. He was running around with her best friend," he explained.

"Oh. Well, in that case..."

"Don't kill people if they don't want to stay with you," he interrupted. "It's that simple."

"Oh, I'd never do that," she agreed. "I just hope I never have to pull the trigger on anything except a deadly snake or a rabid animal."

"I hope that for you," he replied, and he was momentarily somber.

She looked out the window. "We need rain," she said. "Everything's parched. Our few little tomato plants are wilting."

"Shade," he suggested.

"I've got them in the shade," she replied, "but ninety-degree weather wilts most everything, including me!"

He glanced at her and chuckled. She was wearing a tank top

with jeans and sneakers, and her long blond hair was up in a bun. He wondered idly how long it was when she let it down. She was good company, and he liked having her around. Of course, she was just a kid. So it wasn't a good idea to toss covert glances at those pert, firm little breasts under her top. He cleared his throat and looked back out the windshield, and he kept his eyes there the rest of the way home.

Amelia loved being with Cal. She knew that he didn't see her as anything except a young friend, but her heart sang when he came for the weekly chess match with her grandfather. She always had a special dessert for him. And while he and her grandfather were focused on their game, she could sneak glances at him. He was so handsome. She wondered that he was able to stay single. He must get hunted by women, even gorgeous women.

He was seeing somebody in San Antonio, her grandfather said. Cal hadn't told him, but it was gossip. The woman was wealthy, a socialite with a biting tongue who seemed hell-bent on landing Cal. So far, they were just friends, to her irritation.

Amelia knew that Cal was a grown man, and subject to male appetites. She'd never really felt desire, so she didn't understand it, but other women had said that most men couldn't go a long time without a woman.

It was painful to think that Cal would never belong to her. She thought of him constantly, loved being near him, ached to have him hold her, kiss her. But she had to hide those hopeless longings. If Cal ever knew about them, she'd never see him again. She knew that without being told.

She did wonder about his woman friend in San Antonio. But she never asked. One day when Cal was out of town, doing some job for Eb Scott, Amelia watched a luxury car park in Cal's driveway. A tall, willowy woman got out at the steps.

She was brunette. Very pretty even at a distance, with short hair and a knockout figure. She was wearing silk slacks and a silk shirt, and she looked rich. Very rich.

She spotted Amelia watering her tomato plants and walked over.

"Hi," she said lazily. "Have you seen Cal?"

"Hi," Amelia replied, and forced a smile. "No. We don't know where he is. Sorry."

The woman's eyes narrowed, and she studied Amelia closely. "You must be Amelia."

She laughed. "That's me."

"He said you like to blow things up?" she added warily.

Amelia grinned. "Only bad things. Honest. I'm a chemistry major."

"In high school, right?" she asked.

"Well, no, I graduated this year. I'm going to our community college now."

"Then you'd be, what, eighteen or so?"

"Eighteen and three months and ten days and," Amelia looked at her watch, "twenty minutes." She grinned brightly.

The woman laughed in spite of herself. "I'm Edie Prince," she introduced herself. "Cal and I go out together."

"Oh." Amelia just nodded. She didn't ask questions.

Edie gave her a going-over with her pale blue eyes. Eighteen. And she'd been afraid of the competition. She laughed at her own folly. Cal talked about this girl a lot, and she'd been jealous. But the girl was a kid, barely out of high school. Definitely not Cal Hollister's sort. He liked experience.

She relaxed. "Well, I'm sorry I missed him. Will you tell him I was here, please?"

"Of course," Amelia said. "Nice to meet you."

Edie nodded. "Same."

She sauntered back to her car, got in and sped away. Amelia let out the breath she'd been holding. So that was the sort of woman Cal liked? She wasn't impressed. Too much perfume, too much makeup, too much…everything. And the woman had to be the wrong side of thirty. Makeup only covered up so much.

She finished watering the plants and went back inside.

Cal was home two days later. It was Friday and he came over for the chess match.

"Want some chocolate cake?" Amelia asked him as he and her grandfather sat down.

"Yes," her grandfather said. "And coffee. Black. Strong!"

"Double that," Cal chuckled.

"Coming right up," she assured them.

"Oh, and you had a visitor," her grandfather told Cal. "Some woman in a black luxury car. She spoke to Amelia."

Cal's dark eyes flashed. "Edie."

"I don't know," Harris replied. "I didn't speak to her."

"She's an acquaintance," Cal said, and didn't add anything to that. But it irritated the hell out of him that the woman had come down here to nose around the town where he lived. She was possessive already. He didn't like it.

Amelia didn't say anything, but she saw that irritation in his expression before he concealed it. He must like the woman, or he wouldn't spend time with her. But it was obvious that he also didn't like having people pry into his life.

She fixed coffee, poured it into two mugs, sliced cake and presented it all to the men.

"You should learn to play chess," her grandfather commented.

"Never," Amelia said. "I've been slaughtered too many times on that board by you," she added darkly.

Her grandfather chuckled. "It's because you don't stop to think about your moves. You rush in and attack."

"So did Pancho Villa!"

His eyes widened. "He played chess?"

"He fought in the Mexican Revolution," she corrected. "And he only knew one method of fighting. Attack!"

"Well, that's definitely you, sugar," her grandfather chuckled.

"One day I might beat you," she retorted.

"Fat chance."

"Chess can be taught, just like shooting a gun," Cal interjected.

"I like shooting guns. I hate chess."

"Excuses, excuses," Cal teased.

"You two can have chess. I'll take mahjong."

"That's just memorization," Cal pointed out.

"Yes, well, I remember things better than I think them out," she replied. "Besides, mahjong is fun!"

"So is chess," Cal told her. "It's a magnificent relic of the past. They used to call it the game of kings, because they studied the use of tactics playing it."

"I hate tactics, too. But I like cake." She grinned and took her cake and coffee into the kitchen, to enjoy while she made rolls for tomorrow's meals. Meanwhile, she was able to angle the occasional unconscious glance toward gorgeous Cal, while he and her grandfather battled across the chess board.

Cal was going out the door with Amelia when he turned suddenly on the porch.

"Did Edie say why she came down here?" he asked abruptly.

"Not really," she replied with a hopefully disinterested smile. "She just said she was looking for you, and to tell you she'd been here."

"I see."

His hands were shoved deep in his pockets and the dark eyes she couldn't quite see were narrow and angry.

"She's really pretty," Amelia said.

He glanced down at her and seemed to relax a little. He studied her face. It wasn't beautiful, but it had character—like its owner. He smiled. "So are you, Amelia," he replied quietly. "It's not what's outside that matters. It's what's inside."

Before she colored too rapidly and gave herself away, she grinned and said, in mock horror, "You mean, my guts?"

He thought about that for a minute, threw back his head and roared with laughter. "Good grief," he muttered. He flapped a hand at her. "I'm going to bed." He was still shaking his head as he walked down the driveway.

Amelia was grinning when she went back inside. Her grand-father, who'd been eavesdropping, was also laughing.

"Your guts," Jacob Harris said, shaking his head. "Honestly!"

"He's somber a lot," she explained. "I like making him laugh."

"Well, Eb Scott said the guy has a reputation with his men, and it doesn't include laughter. In fact, he says he hardly ever smiled before he started coming over here. He was fishing," he added with some amusement, "about whether or not Cal had a case on you."

Her heart jumped into her throat.

"Of course not, I told him," he added without looking at her, which was a good thing. "After all, you're just eighteen, sugar. Hardly old enough to get mixed up with a professional soldier. You'd need to be street smart and a lot more sophisticated."

She nodded, averting her eyes. "Like that pretty lady who came to see him," she agreed.

"Exactly. She looked hard as nails, and she'd need to be!"

She raised both eyebrows in a silent question.

"Think about it, Amy," he said softly, using the nickname that only he had ever called her. "A man like that keeps his emotions under lock and key. It's a matter of survival, to be stoic and levelheaded. He's hard as nails—no sentiment in him. He'd never settle with a woman who wasn't his equal in tem-perament."

"In other words, he'd walk all over somebody less hardheaded."

"Exactly." He smiled at her. "Even if you were older, it would be a very bad mix." He shook his head. "You don't know what these men are really like until you've served beside them. Something you'll never know about," he added firmly.

"Absolutely not," she agreed at once. "I'm going to learn how to blow up stuff instead!"

"Amy…!"

"Controlled demolition," she interrupted with a grin. "It's how they take down buildings in big cities. It's fascinating! Just last week, we learned how to do timed charges…"

"Oh, no, not again!" he said in mock anguish.

"You know it fascinates you," she teased. "I could tell you all about it," she added.

"I'm really sleepy," he said with a mock yawn. "I have to go to sleep right now. So lock up, sugar, okay?"

"Retreat is like surrendering!" she called after him.

He threw up a hand and kept walking.

Chapter Three

"What were you doing in Jacobsville?" Cal asked Edie later in the week, while they had cocktails at her fancy apartment in downtown San Antonio.

"I was looking for you, of course," she replied in her softly accented voice. She threw down her cocktail and poured herself another. She drank more than he did, but he didn't pay it much attention. People in her social class drank more than most people.

"You met Amelia."

"Well, yes." She looked at him from under her lids. She was wearing a sketchy green outfit that left her midriff bare and outlined her pretty breasts. "I was curious."

He just stared at her.

"I thought she was competition," she purred. "But she's just a schoolgirl. I didn't know she was so young."

He sipped his own drink. "I don't like being checked up on," he said flatly.

"Oh, don't be mad, Cal," she chided softly, dropping down onto the arm of the chair he was sitting in. "I wasn't prying. I really did go down there just to see you," she lied. It wouldn't do to let him know how possessive she really was.

"Don't do it again," he cautioned, and the threat was in his dark eyes.

"I won't," she said at once. "I promise."

"I'm a free agent," he added. "And I have no plans to involve myself with anyone at the moment. I'm in a high-risk profession. I can't afford personal complications."

She sighed. "In other words, no sex?" she probed delicately.

"That's more blunt than I would have put it, but yes." He finished his drink. "The missions I'm on lately are intricate and involved. I don't want distractions."

"But that won't last forever, right?" she asked, toying with a thick strand of his pale blond hair.

"I don't know. I'm not sure what I want to do with the rest of my life."

"I could suggest some things," she said, about to move down into his lap.

He stood up. "Don't push," he cautioned quietly.

She made a face and filled another glass. "Well, it's hard not to," she said. "You're very attractive."

"So are you. But we're friends. That's all."

He was making a point. And she didn't want to lose him, so she agreed.

"I'm going out to the firing range. Want to come along?"

She made a horrible face. "Of course not! I hate guns!"

He raised an eyebrow and she flushed. She was feeling the alcohol and antsy because she needed something more than alcohol, needed it badly. She didn't dare let him see that.

"Sorry," she said at once. "I know they're important to your profession. I'm afraid of them, that's all."

"Okay. No problem."

"There's a fashion show at the civic center Saturday," she began.

"I'll be out of town."

"Ah, well, I'll go alone, then," she said.

"I don't do fashion shows," he chuckled. "We could go fishing when I get back…?"

She made a worse face. "Honestly, that's the most disgusting hobby of all. Nasty worms." She shuddered.

"You are not an outdoor person."

"Of course not," she replied. "I spent my youth in boarding schools, learning how to be graceful and fit into society."

Which emphasized the gulf between them. She was upper class, he was middle class. Besides that, he suspected that she was already in her midthirties, while he was just twenty-seven. He didn't think much about the age or social differences, however, because he had no intention of getting serious about her. She was just somebody to take around town when he was in the mood.

"How about Fernando's Friday night?" he asked as he got ready to leave.

"Oh, Cal, that's such a common place," she muttered.

"I'm a common man," he replied, and he wasn't smiling.

She went to him, smiling apologetically. "I didn't mean it like that. I just don't like Spanish music, or dancing, that's all. The symphony orchestra is performing next week, though. Debussy."

"I could stomach Debussy, I suppose," he said.

"It will do you good. Culture is important."

He made a face. "Culture."

"Yes. It's what makes us all civilized," she teased. "So. Go with me? I'll get tickets."

"When?"

"A week from Saturday night."

He thought about it. "I should be back by then. All right."

"You'll text me, yes?"

"I'll text you," he said easily.

She reached up to kiss him softly. She drew back at once, not wanting to push her luck. He'd been really irritated. "Have a safe trip home."

"Sure. Good night."

She watched him go. He never returned her caresses. But then, he was in a dangerous profession. He was also loaded. He hadn't told her, but she had friends who knew the sort of work he did and what it paid. She had social background, but she'd blown most of her inherited fortune gambling. She had an expensive habit, and although she'd tried to quit, it had become harder. She needed bankrolling.

Of course, Cal was also attractive, there was that. But it was as easy to care about a rich man as a poor one, and she was good at pretending. She finished the cocktail and went to her room to get what she needed to add a jolt to the liquor.

Cal, meanwhile, was still irritated at Edie's obvious possessive attitude toward him. He didn't want a woman hanging on him, trying to own him. He liked his own space.

He thought about how different Amelia was. She never pried or stalked him. She was funny and gentle, and she loved the outdoors. He wondered if she liked to fish. He'd have to remember to ask.

Fishing, Amelia thought, was one of the most relaxing sports there was. Especially when it was shared with a drop-dead gorgeous man who also loved it. They'd found a deep, wide stream, almost a river, under a bridge on a little-traveled dirt road that was known locally for bigmouth bass.

Amelia sighed. "This is great fun."

"Yeah, and the yellow flies just adore it," he muttered as he slapped another one.

"Your hair is yellow. They think you're a relative," she teased.

He chuckled. He laughed more with her than he'd ever laughed in his life. She made life seem uncomplicated. His had never been that, especially not now.

"They don't bite you, I notice," he pointed out.

"That's because I know simple, secret homemade solutions to keep them away."

"Such as?" he asked.

"I told you. They're secret ones."

"Might you share them with a friend who loaned you his spinning reel?"

She glowered at him. "A cane pole is just better for these things," she said with a sigh. She got up and handed him back the spinning reel. She then picked up her old cane pole with its hook, line and lead sinkers. She baited the hook and threw it in.

"Primitive," he pointed out.

She felt a tug on the line, but she let it run until the nice fish hooked himself. Then the battle began. She pulled and let the line slack, pulled again, slacked again, going up and down the bank.

"Wow, what a fighting fish!" she exclaimed happily.

"Can you tell what it is?"

"It's a fish. I told you…oh!" She drew back and jerked. The fish soared out of the water and landed at Cal's feet.

He picked it up with a finger through the gill. "A bigmouthed bass. About three pounds unless I miss my guess," he chuckled.

"Supper," she said, smacking her lips. She took the fish and put him in the bucket. Then she baited her hook again. "I'll catch one for you, too," she teased.

He sighed, looking at his spinning reel with disdain. "I think I'm losing my touch," he said.

"It's just that the fish in this creek are sort of primitive," she chuckled. "I don't think they like fancy equipment."

"So next time we come here, I'll bring a cane pole," he said with resignation.

"Might save that spinning reel for a trout stream," she said.

"Good idea. And where would we find one, in this heat?"

"Canada."

He glared at her. "I'm not going to Canada to catch a fish."

"Then get a cane pole and fish for… Oh, I've got another one!"

Cal let out a word that her grandfather often used if he hit his thumb with a hammer. Amelia burst out laughing. Cal just shook his head.

When they got back to her house, they had five big bass. Hers were four of them.

"I think I'll give up fishing and go in for surfing," Cal told her grandfather.

Harris laughed. "You can't ever compete with her at fishing, trust me," he told the other man. "It's an ego-smasher."

"I noticed."

"There, there, you were just fishing for trout instead of bass," Amelia said soothingly.

"Way too hot for trout fishing," her grandfather said. "Going to stay for fish? She makes homemade french fries."

"Wow," Cal said. He looked at Amelia. "Can I?"

"Sure," she chuckled. "There's plenty to go around. And I cooked some butterbeans with fatback last night, right out of the garden. I made fresh rolls, too."

Cal just sighed. "I really did the smartest thing in my life, moving across the street from you two."

"I'll bet you can cook," Amelia said cagily.

"I can," he replied. "Snake, turtle, crocodile…"

"I mean regular food," she laughed.

"I can if I have to," he conceded. "But no way can I make fresh rolls, and I love them."

"In that case, I'll make extra so you can take some home."

"If we only had real butter," he mused.

"But we do," she said, grinning. "I went to the Mennonite store early this week. We have real butter to go on them."

Cal sat down on the sofa near her grandfather's recliner. "I'll have to be dragged out," he threatened with a laugh.

"We won't do that," Amelia promised and went to work.

They walked him out to the steps after supper, which included an apple pie with homemade ice cream.

"I've never eaten better in my whole life," Cal told Amelia. "Thank you."

"Thanks for going fishing with me," she replied. "Granddaddy hates fishing."

"Yes, I know it sounds odd, but I really do. I used to hunt when I was younger, but I was never a fisherman."

"There's a good reason," Amelia volunteered.

Her grandfather looked sheepish. "I threw my line out too hard in a rowboat, capsized it and almost drowned my father. That was after I'd hooked his pants with another bad throw. He said that the only safe way to fish was to tie me to a chair and leave me at home. I took him at his word. I've never gone fishing since!"

They all laughed.

Amelia walked back inside with her grandfather. He was giving her strange looks.

"Something wrong?" she asked gently.

He went into the living room with her and sat down. So did she.

"There are men who are suited to small-town life," he said gently. "To picket fences and babies. That man across the street isn't one of them. He feeds on danger. He likes it. He won't settle, not for years. And quite frankly, if he does, it will be for somebody like that fancy woman who turned up at his house. She's the kind of woman who attracts such men."

She flushed. "I didn't realize it showed," she said sadly.

"It won't, to him. Only to somebody who knows you. But you can't afford to let him see it, not if you want him to keep coming here for friendship. If he sees it, he'll not come back, for pitying you."

She ground her teeth together. "I guess I knew that."

"It's harsh to say it, but always better to face an unpleasant fact than to ignore it. He's a handsome man, and he's got a way with him. But you're not his sort of woman, and there's that age difference. He's twenty-seven. You're eighteen. It wouldn't matter so much if you were in your twenties. But now it would."

She nodded. "I knew that."

"I'm sorry. I like him, too. But you have to keep those longings under control. He's at ease here. If you're careful, someday..."

She grinned. "Someday."

"Now go study those chemistry books," he said, waving her

away. "You have to learn to blow up stuff if there's ever a war down the road."

She laughed out loud. "Roll on the day. I'm dangerous!"

"Yes, you are. And my treasure," he added with a warm smile. "I'm so lucky to have you for company."

"I'm the lucky one," she replied. She kissed him on the head and went on to her room.

But she didn't study. She brooded. She was very attracted to Cal. She ached when she looked at him. Her grandfather was right, it would never do to let him see it. She would have to play a waiting game, be careful and secretive, and never let Cal see how much she cared for him. But could she?

Yes, she could, she thought doggedly. Because as hard as it was to pretend not to care, it would be harder to never see him again. Or, worse, to have him pity her for the feelings she couldn't help. That would smother her pride.

So she would keep her secret hidden and never let Cal know that she treasured him. Even if the fancy lady came calling again, and she might. She opened her chemistry book and turned to the page her lessons were on.

The summer went by slowly. Cal was home on and off, but mostly off on hush-hush assignments overseas for Eb. Autumn came, with colored leaves and harvest festivals and hayrides and turkey shoots.

One of the ongoing events in Jacobsville was a turkey shoot with frozen turkey prizes. The competition was stiff, but Amelia went every year. This year, a recently returned, and very surprised Cal, went with her.

"I can't believe that you shoot a shotgun," he said again as they stood waiting for their turns. "I've never known a woman who'd even pick up one."

She shrugged. "I've always loved weapons," she said.

"Yes, and she can shoot!" one of the other contestants added, glaring at her. "And much too well!"

"Sour grapes, Andy, you had the same chances I did," she replied with a grin.

The old man wrinkled his nose. "First, we had old man Turner, and he won every year. Then it was Rick Marquez, who's a detective in San Antonio. Now, it's you," he muttered. "A good man hasn't got a chance around here!"

"Yes, you do, Andy, you just have to outshoot me!" she replied. "And him," she added, jerking her thumb toward Cal, who grinned.

"Who's he?" he asked.

"He works for Eb Scott…"

"Oh, damn the luck!" Andy exclaimed and threw his hat on the ground.

"Eb sort of wins any shooting competition going, or his men do," she explained to Cal. "So most people know what's going to happen when one of them competes."

"Cheer up," Cal told the man brushing off his hat, "I do miss. Sometimes."

"Name the last time you missed," Amelia asked him.

He frowned. "Let's see, I was ten, and my uncle had taken me to a turkey shoot."

"And you missed?"

"I missed dead center in the bull's-eye," he explained. "It was just a hair off."

"I am never going to win a turkey," Andy muttered.

"The grocery store has lots of them," she pointed out. "And there's a contest downtown for six of them that are giveaways. It's a raffle."

"Got a better chance of being carried off by one of them UFOs than I have of winning a contest. And I hate buying turkeys!"

"Then send Blanche," she suggested.

Andy sighed. "Well, that's not a bad idea, I suppose." He grinned at her. "If I'd known you were coming this year, I'd have stayed home."

She laughed. "That's sweet."

"Nope. Just the truth. I'd wish you good luck, but the other people are going to need that," he said, nodding toward the assembly of hopefuls. "See you, honey."

"See you."

"Nice old guy," Cal said. "I hope he won't go hungry," he added suddenly.

"Andy drives a new Jaguar," she pointed out. "Every year," she added.

"Oh." He scowled. "Then why was he here?"

"Because he's cheap," she said, and grinned.

He chuckled. "Okay. I get the idea. I didn't want to think we were going to hustle some poor guy out of Thanksgiving dinner."

"That would never happen here. We have two charities that do nothing except feed the poor, especially at holidays. There are rumors that one of our local citizens pays to bus poor homeless people down here from San Antonio, so they get a good hot meal. We had several whole families last year," she added quietly, and her voice almost broke.

He patted her on the shoulder. "It's good that you care that much," he said, and he smiled at her. "I've become cynical about people. I'm always wary of being played."

"I'm hard to play," she replied, looking up. "And whole families, Cal," she added softly. "Just imagine how that must feel. You lose your job, your home, your car…" She ground her teeth together. "What a nightmare that would be, especially if you had children."

He just stared at her thoughtfully. It hadn't occurred to him. But then, she had no idea what his background really was, how he'd been brought up. He hoped she'd never know. It wasn't a pretty tale.

"Maybe I'm too cynical," he said after a minute.

She smiled. "It's the job you do," she said simply. "I know guys from high school who went to work for Eb. It changes you, changes the way you look at the world."

"I suppose it does." He glanced down at her. "Who do you know that works for Eb, besides me?" he asked suddenly, shocking himself and her, because it wasn't a question he had any right to ask. She was eighteen, for God's sake!

"Ty," she blurted out.

His eyebrows arched. "Ty Harding?"

She nodded.

He averted his gaze. "He's Native American. Different culture, language, religion, the works."

"I know. He and a girl I knew almost got engaged. Her people found out and actually came down here from the Northwest to talk him out of it. They even talked to his parents. They said that not only would it not work, but that he'd be an outcast in their family. There had never been a mixed marriage in the family, you see," she added.

"Not you?" he asked, frowning.

"Heavens, no," she laughed. "Ty and I are just friends."

"Oh."

It was hard to hide the joy welling up inside her, but she managed. Before Cal could notice the sudden glow, her name was called, and she stepped up to face the target.

She and Cal took home a turkey.

Cal was out of the country until the day before Thanksgiving. He came over for dinner the next day, having been invited by Amelia's grandfather. Amelia had been working nonstop in the kitchen for two days, which is what it took to bring all the food together, and she couldn't leave the stove. So Jacob Harris had to go over with the invitation.

He found a man who was worn to the bone and limping just a little.

"You're not in the easiest profession," he told the younger man.

Cal shrugged. "Sometimes we don't duck fast enough," he said with a forced grin.

Harris put a hand on his shoulder. "I'm an interfering old coot, and I should keep my mouth shut. But eventually, you're going to see something or be forced to do something that will shatter your life," he added quietly. "And when that happens, you'll have to live with the nightmares for the rest of the days you're on this earth."

Cal was quietly belligerent. "And you know this for a fact?"

"Didn't Amelia tell you? I was spec ops overseas," he added.

Cal felt his face tauten. He hadn't known that.

"And the nightmares," Harris concluded softly, "are horrendous." His eyes as he spoke were almost black with pain.

"I didn't know," he said.

"I lived and came home," he said. "But my poor granddaughter had to listen to me when I was bursting with the need to tell somebody, anybody, what I'd been through. I was almost crazy," he added. "They wanted to send me to a shrink at the VA, but I'd heard all about that from a buddy of mine." His expression was eloquent. "It was a guy who'd never shot a gun, never been in combat and knew nothing about war. He said it was all he could do not to deck the guy on his way out."

Cal drew in a breath. "You might get luckier than he did."

"I might not." He searched the other man's dark eyes. "I don't know what demons are driving you, but I suspect they're pretty formidable. It takes that to send a man into wet work."

Cal scowled.

"Yes, I know. Most of what you do is classified, and you aren't officially attached to any government. Plausible deniability. But the people who hire you don't have to live with what you do to accomplish a mission." He studied the other man's face. "For you to go into this," he added quietly, "you must have a pretty raw background to start with—something that you don't want to face, that you put yourself at risk so that you don't have to deal with it."

"You see too much," Cal bit off.

He sighed. "I've been where you are," he replied. "I don't talk about my past, either. Even my late wife, Doris, God rest her soul, wasn't told. I thought doing special assignments in the service would be exciting enough to put the bad things away, so that I didn't see them." He drew in a breath. "But what happened was that the exciting things were a hundred times worse than what I'd already had to live through. When I came home, I was a mental basket case."

"How did you cope?"

"I had a friend who'd been in combat for half his life, a mercenary. He talked me down. You remember that," he added. "If you don't want to go to a shrink, even though there are some really good ones, have somebody close who'll just listen and let you pour it all out. It might save you from trying to eat a bullet. In my case, it did just that."

"It's early days yet, but I don't think I'll run into anything I can't handle," Cal said quietly. "I'm not the type to commit suicide."

"Nobody thinks they are, until there's a good reason."

Cal was unconvinced, but he didn't say so. "Thanks for the pep talk," he said quietly.

"You're welcome. Now. How about a huge Thanksgiving dinner tomorrow that promises to throw your cholesterol so high that your doctor will feel it even before you get to his office?"

Cal chuckled. "I'd love it."

"Fine. You're invited. Oh, and it's informal. You can leave off the tuxedo," he joked.

Cal made a face. "Spoilsport."

Harris just laughed.

So Cal came for Thanksgiving dinner, and produced a perfectly cooked apple pie to go with all of Amelia's efforts.

"Nice pie," she commented, noting the way it was made with a fancy fluted crust all around. "Did you go all the way to San Antonio to find a bakery?"

Cal glared at her. "I made it myself, I'll have you know," he said with mock indignation. "Snake isn't the only thing I can cook!"

She burst out laughing. "Oh. Well, it's beautiful," she said, admiring it. "I can't even do a crust like that. It's elegant."

"I'll teach you how. It's not hard. That," he indicated the perfect homemade rolls she'd just taken out of the oven, "is hard!"

"It's not," she said. "Only a handful of ingredients, and the mixer does most of the kneading. It doesn't even take long."

"Fine. You can teach me to make rolls, and I'll share my pie decorating tips with you," he said with sparkling black eyes.

She chuckled. "It's a deal."

"But meanwhile, when do we eat?" he asked, admiring all the food she'd dished up on the big table that was used for cooking.

"In about ten minutes," she said.

"Can I help?" Jacob asked.

"Yes! If you'll start carrying things into the dining room," she told him, "I'll finish carving the turkey."

"You should let me do that," Cal protested. "I'm great with knives."

"You're hired," she said, handing him a sharp butcher's knife. "Go for it!"

He grinned. "Do you want boring flat slices of turkey, or something artistic, like leaves or unicorns?" he asked, deadpan.

The other two just shook their heads.

Chapter Four

Amelia noticed that Cal was unusually quiet while they ate. He wasn't a boisterous man by nature, but he seemed reserved.

"How did you do grade-wise this semester?" he asked her suddenly.

She grinned. "Straight As."

He shook his head. "I should have known. You're bright."

She laughed. "Not so much. I study hard, though."

"Chemistry, of all things," he remarked as he started on the apple pie, with a steaming cup of black coffee at his side. "I've never known a woman who studied chemistry."

"I love it," she said. "It's the most fascinating thing I've ever studied."

"You haven't blown up the lab yet?" he teased.

"They won't let us near the really dangerous stuff," she muttered.

"I hope they have good insurance," her grandfather mentioned dryly.

"I'm a very good student," she protested. "Even my professor says so. I will not blow up the lab."

"If you say so," he chuckled.

"Now, Fred Briggs, he did blow up the lab," she added. "All because Maria Simms walked by him in a low-cut dress and smiled at him. He mixed in the wrong chemical and the table blew up."

"My goodness," her grandfather said. "Was anybody hurt?"

"Fred got a little singed. But when Maria realized that he liked her that much, she started dating him. So I guess he blew up the lab for a good cause."

Cal chuckled. "Dangerous way to make an impression."

"Yes, and he almost made an impression right through the wall!" Amelia said with glee.

Cal shook his head. "And I thought I was in a dangerous profession," he said, chuckling.

"You really are, though," Amelia said, growing solemn. "Doesn't it bother you?"

He gave her a quiet appraisal. "Yes, from time to time. But then I think about what I'm doing, and why I'm doing it, and it doesn't bother me as much." He smiled. "We're protecting a group of people who are under the rule of a madman, who kills women and children of anyone who questions his authority."

"Oh, good grief!" she exclaimed, shocked. "Why doesn't the government do something to stop him?"

"Because he is the government," he replied. "He chased out the legitimately elected president and took his place. We contract with the legitimate president, who wants his country back."

She gave him a long look. "That's a noble cause," she said finally.

That comment, from her, touched something deep inside him. He felt a rush of affection that he quickly stifled. She wasn't fair game. She wouldn't be, for years, and he was a bad risk. He'd grown fond of her and her grandfather. He didn't want to do anything to jeopardize that friendship.

"Thanks," he said softly, and his eyes were quiet. "That means a lot."

"I feel the same way," Harris seconded. "It truly is a noble cause. But you can be killed even for doing something noble, if you're caught on the ground doing it in another country. I'm sure you realize that any authority would immediately disavow knowledge of your actions." He leaned forward. "And don't ever harbor a thought that our government doesn't know what you're up to. They may decide to turn a blind eye to it, if they agree with the purpose. Or they may not. In which case, you and your colleagues will be courting disaster."

Cal laughed. "We have backing from the people who count," he replied. "Eb has contacts high up in government."

"I hope they're people who wouldn't run to the exits if your exploits get exposed."

"Unlikely," Cal told him. "At least two of them would go down with us if we called a press conference to tell what we'd done, and why."

"A lot of people call press conferences, and nobody shows up except people with channels on the internet," Amelia interjected. "The legacy media is owned, and I mean owned, by corporations. They decide what you'll see and hear, and nobody stands up to them."

"All too true," Harris said sadly. "In my youth, journalism was held to a higher standard, and it wasn't controlled by any corporations. Not to mention that journalism in my parents' day was almost a sacred trust. In fact, my grandmother said that in her younger days, Walter Cronkite was known as the most trusted man in America. He was a newsman. She said he cried on live television when he announced the Kennedy assassination on the news." He paused. "She said everybody cried, regardless of their political parties, and that the whole nation was in utter shock."

"I guess so," Amelia said. "I remember Granny talking about it, too, things her father told her. There were conspiracy theories at the time, but a lot of new information is coming out all the time."

"I hope and pray that we'll never see another presidential assassination," Harris said solemnly.

"Well, not in this country," Cal remarked. "But in some countries, it's the only way to get rid of a vicious leader."

"Don't you get killed," Amelia said firmly, and she glared at him. "I mean it."

He laughed in spite of himself. She looked so fierce. "I promise you that I'll do my best to stay alive," he replied with a warm smile.

Her insides lit up at that smile, but she didn't let it show. She didn't want him to know how crazy about him she really was.

The conversation changed to local politics and charity dances.

"There's a dance for the animal shelter Friday night," Amelia told Cal at the beginning of the next week. "Granddad and I are going. I love animals."

"And yet you don't have any," he replied.

She smiled sadly. "Granddaddy's allergic to fur, which rules out cats and dogs, and I'm afraid of snakes. That just leaves frogs or lizards or fish, and they're all a lot of trouble. So I just pet other people's fuzzy companions."

"You should have a dog," he said. "Even a small one is good to warn you if there's an intruder. Come to think of it, geese are even better."

She blinked. "Excuse me?"

He grinned at her. "One of our guys lives on an island, and he has a flock of them. He swears that they're better even than dogs, because they start up at the first sound of footsteps. They're also dangerous. A goose is fairly large, and they can be very aggressive."

"I like geese."

He sighed. "Most men don't."

"Why?" she asked.

"Because if a goose comes after a man, it's with only one target in mind, if you get my drift."

She did and flushed.

He chuckled. "That's exactly why I don't have a goose."

"Good thinking."

He cocked his head. "If I'm here and I go to the animal rescue charity dance, are you going to dance with me?"

She had delicious chills up her spine. "I might," she said, hiding her delight in teasing.

"Can you dance?" he probed.

She shifted. "Sort of."

"Sort of?"

"Well, I know how to do a box step. It's just that my feet don't connect with my brain. So most people don't really want to dance with me," she confided.

"We'll work on that," he said, hating his own attraction. It was getting quickly out of hand. Fortunately, he had a mission the week after the dance. It would give him a breather, while he tried to get Amelia out of his mind. She was becoming essential to his happiness.

Amelia smiled. "Okay!" she said.

Meanwhile, Cal went up to San Antonio to talk to a man he knew at the police department. He'd been trying to persuade Cal to come back to the force and give up on merc work.

"You loved the job when you were a patrolman here," Jess reminded him. "You'd love it if you came back. We save the world, too, you know, just in a more legal sort of way and you're less likely to die in an explosion. Mostly."

Cal chuckled. "You're pretty persuasive."

"You're my pal," he replied easily. "Trust me, this is a really great opportunity. There's always plenty of room for advancement. The pay's still not bad. Not as good as you're making now, but the work is a little less traumatic."

And he'd know, Cal thought, because Jess himself had been spec ops in the military at one time.

"Do you ever miss the life?" he asked the other man.

Jess paused for a minute, thinking, and then one side of his mouth drew down. "Honestly, yes. But I'm married and I have two kids. What would happen to them if I got myself blown up in some country they couldn't even find on a map?"

"Good point. But I don't have that problem."

"I know. I was like you, once. But there's always the woman who'll make you settle down, even if you don't want to," he replied with a grin. "You'll see."

"It's unlikely. I don't want to get married. Ever."

The look on Cal's face when he said it made Jess change the subject.

"Well, anyway, think about what I told you," he said.

Cal smiled. "I will."

He went by Edie's apartment while he was in town. She opened the door, and he was surprised at the way she looked.

She was usually immaculately dressed, even at home, makeup on, hair combed. This woman was disheveled and looked as if she hadn't slept in weeks.

"What's the matter with you?" he asked worriedly.

"Just a few drinks too many," she replied with a hollow smile. "Come see me another time, okay?"

"Will you be all right?"

She waved a hand at him. "I'm okay, just hungover. I'll call you."

"All right. If you need me, I'll come," he said, genuinely concerned. He didn't have friends, but Edie was one. Sort of.

"Thanks," she replied softly. "Thanks a lot. See you."

She closed the door quickly.

He wondered how alcohol could leave a person looking like that. He knew she had no issues with street drugs, but maybe she was only saying that. She wasn't the sort of person to get hooked on drugs. Although alcohol was bad enough.

He knew about alcohol. He was the child of abusive alcoholics, both parents. His childhood had been a nightmare of yelling and pushing and sometimes beatings, if they were drunk enough. Of course, he could have called family services and he would have been taken out of that environment. But he knew foster care could be hit-or-miss, because three of his classmates were being fostered. None of them raved about it, and he was warned that as bad as things were at home, they could be worse. A lot worse.

So as he grew, Cal learned how to get around his parents. He became canny and insightful. He read books on alcoholism and learned about the reasons people drank. He also read about programs for detox. He actually tried to get at least his mother into one of the programs, but she backed out. And there was no hope with his father, who was mixed up with the local criminal crowd in Houston, just as he'd been in Cleveland, Ohio, before his father had moved the small family to Texas. Half the stuff in their home wouldn't pass a stolen item check by the police.

He thought that one day he'd be a policeman and clean up the neighborhood where he lived. But those thoughts were few and far between as he hovered between homework and horror. Eventually he graduated, and the first place he went was to the police department, to sign up. But not in Houston. A tragedy there, the death of both parents, had left him reeling. Even alcoholic parents were better than none, he thought sadly. It was a bleak time in his life. He needed a change. The army looked like a good fit at the time. Free college and all sorts of benefits. And his grandfather, the man he'd respected most of all in his young life, had been an army man. So he signed up.

When he got out of the service, after seeing some action overseas, he resettled in San Antonio and joined the police force there.

He went through the preliminary training, scored highest in his class on the firing range—because he spent half his time practicing—and then was placed on patrol duty.

It was the best two years of his life. He loved the work. But then he heard about Eb Scott and his group. They were advertising covertly for people to join, and Cal loved the idea of ad-venture. He was still young enough to long for foreign places and excitement, although he never drank or gambled. So he went to see Eb Scott. And he signed on. He felt bad leaving the department, but one superior officer was sympathetic, and told him there would always be a place for him. It was like a safety net. It gave him the confidence to go ahead with what he most wanted to do, at that stage of his life.

The move to a rental house in Jacobsville felt almost pre-meditated, because that was where Eb Scott had his base. Cal had worked out of San Antonio for several years, but when he signed on with Eb, living in Jacobsville made the commute a little easier.

Eb's group was into a hot situation right now in Africa, with the corrupt leader of a small nation there. The former president, a good man and a caring one, had been ousted by a lunatic with a ragtag army. The lunatic was destroying the communities under his control. The former president, backed secretly by several other nations, had contracted with Eb to oust the idiot in control. Eb had agreed at once.

They were getting organized right now to go in again, and this time they had the manpower to accomplish regime change.

But in the meanwhile, there was the dance at the community center, which Cal was looking forward to.

He hadn't told Edie about it when she called and asked if he wouldn't like to come up Saturday night and go out to dinner. He made an excuse and told her he'd see her the next day. She whined, but finally agreed that it would be fine. She'd probably be hungover, she added, but that was her problem.

He hung up, feeling guilty, as she meant him to. He knew alcoholics all too well. He hoped that he might be able to help Edie somehow get out of alcohol's grasp. He was optimistic that he could do it.

* * *

He almost didn't recognize Amelia when he moved through the throng of local citizens at the dance. He was wearing a gray suit, which highlighted his pale, thick blond hair and his nice tan. He was a striking man. Women eyed him as he moved around, looking for Amelia and her grandfather.

He'd passed over her twice while thinking privately what a glorious head of blond hair that woman had, shining and clean and hanging almost to her waist in back. He had a real weakness for blond hair.

And then, on the third pass, the woman turned around, and it was Amelia.

He stopped, laughing. "I didn't know you," he chuckled, moving closer. "You always wear your hair up in a bun." He admired it. "I didn't know it was so long."

She laughed, too. "It's a nuisance to wash, but I love long hair," she confessed.

"So do I," he said softly, and he reached out to touch its thick silkiness. "It's glorious."

"Thank you," she said shyly.

"Where's your grandfather?" he asked.

She shook her head, and nodded toward the back of the room where her grandfather and one of his friends were sitting on either side of a chess set.

"Chess, chess, chess," she moaned. "He never dances. He gets in the back with whichever chess fanatic friend of his who shows up, and they play chess until the last dance."

He laughed. "Well, whatever floats your boat," he mused.

"Exactly!"

"So why are you sitting here all alone?" he asked, indicating all the other people.

"Oh, I'm always on my own at these things," she said simply. "I don't mix well." She looked up at him. It was a long way, because she was wearing low-heeled shoes. "Most people aren't interested in how to blow up stuff," she whispered.

"I'm very interested," he replied, and slid his hand down to catch hers. "You can tell me all about it while we're dancing."

"I'll trip over my own feet and kill somebody," she objected as he led her to the dance floor. Her whole body tingled at the feel of that big, warm hand closed around her own.

"I'll save you," he promised, and drew her close.

It was the first time she'd ever been so close to a man, and it was shocking how much she liked it. She could feel the fabric of his suit jacket under her fingers and, deeper, his breathing. She could smell the spicy cologne he used and some sort of masculine soap, as well. He was always immaculate, even in regular clothing.

But it was the effect it had on her that caught her attention. She felt tight all over, as if every muscle in her body was tensing. She couldn't quite breathe normally.

And her heartbeat was doing a hula. It was very disconcerting, especially to a woman who spent most of her time with men in a lab at college, where she was just one of the guys. Now she felt like a woman felt with a man—at least, like the women in the historical novels she liked to read.

Cal was feeling something similar and fighting it. Why hadn't he realized that this was a very bad idea, and found a way to keep out of it? He hadn't thought past sitting with Amelia and Jacob Harris and having one of their usual conversations. He certainly hadn't thought about dancing.

It was sheer heaven, dancing with Amelia. Feeling her close in his arms, one hand at her waist, the other tangling gently in that glorious fall of thick, soft hair that smelled of roses.

"Your hair is incredible," he said in a hushed tone.

She smiled. It was nice, that he liked something about her. "Thanks. I wish it was the color of yours," she added.

"Why?"

"Because your hair shines like gold in the light," she replied. "Mine is dull."

"Not so. It's beautiful. I'm glad you wore it down, this once."

She laughed. "I wasn't going to, and then Granddad asked why I was hiding my light under a bushel. So I let it down."

"Good for him. I hope he wins his match," he added.

"You're kidding, right? He's playing with old man Ridgeway. He takes half an hour to make a single move. They'll be here till midnight, and when the cleaners get ready to lock up, Mr. Ridgeway will complain about being rushed out of a winning move."

He burst out laughing. "I never knew this town had so many interesting people," he said.

"Eccentrics," she corrected. "We're infested with them," she laughed. "But they're all nice people and we protect them from outsiders. Like Fred, who can find water with a forked stick, and Miss Betty, who can talk out fire and talk off warts, and old Bill, who can predict the weather without TV or radio."

"The things I missed growing up in the city," he said, shaking his head.

"San Antonio?"

His face tautened. "Cleveland, Ohio." He glanced down at her. "Now don't you say one word about my being from up north," he cautioned firmly. "Just because I'm not a native in Jacobsville doesn't mean I'm not a true Texan. I've lived here since I was six. That's more than enough time to be considered a native."

She burst out laughing. "That's the best defense I've heard yet."

"Ha! A likely story. You think we talk funny."

She was chuckling. "I think you talk just fine. And I hold no grudges. Honest."

"Fair enough, but it's our secret, got that?" he asked, looking around with mock unease. "And don't you tell a soul where I'm really from!"

"I won't tell," she promised under her breath. "I swear! I'll take your secret to my grave!"

He laughed, too, and suddenly pulled her close in an obvious hug, making her head spin with joy. "You light up all the dark places in me," he whispered. "I never laughed so much in my life as I do with you."

"I don't have dark places, but you light up my life, too. And Granddaddy's," she added quickly, so that she didn't sound too forward.

He perceived that. He was glad that she understood he wasn't hitting on her. He wanted to, of course. She made his heart skip. But she was far too young for a man of his experience. He liked sophistication. Besides that, she was innocent, and he still had some sense of honor, left over from his own grandfather. He barely remembered the old man, who was devastated when his only son decided to move to Texas. He'd been the babysitter for Cal all his life, and he said that it was like losing two sons instead of one. He said that a man had to be responsible for his actions and willing to accept the consequences of them. If it sounded like a soldier talking, it was because the old man had retired with the rank of lieutenant colonel in the army. He'd been in combat overseas, and he was military to his bones. He'd been Cal's hero. It had broken his young heart to leave the old man, who'd died not a year later. Cal's father hadn't even taken the family to the burial. He said he didn't want to lose his job with the city's sanitation department. But he really just plain didn't care. He had his father cremated and a friend buried the ashes beside his mother's grave, in the same church cemetery.

"You're really quiet tonight," Amelia said softly.

He looked down at her. "I was remembering my grandfather," he said simply. "He was a good man. We moved to Houston when I was six and left him behind. He died the very next year. He was in the army. A combat veteran." He smiled sadly. "He was my hero, when I was little."

That was odd. Shouldn't his dad have been his hero? But she never pried. She accepted what he decided to tell her and didn't ask for more. He thought it was because she didn't really care. But it was because she cared a lot and didn't want him to know it.

"When do you leave on your next assignment?" she asked.

"Monday, before daylight."

She looked up at him, dreamy with delight, smiling. "You come back, now. You hear?"

He chuckled because she'd drawled it like characters on a TV show. "I'll come back," he said, and hoped he could. He had a feeling about this trip, a bad one. He wasn't psychic or anything like that, but he had feelings, premonitions, intuitive insights. They'd already saved his life at least twice. He didn't talk about them.

"You dance beautifully," she remarked.

"And you haven't tripped once," he pointed out with a grin.

She shrugged. "I didn't want to tell you that I won a dance contest my last year of high school," she said, peering up at him with twinkling dark eyes. "I did the tango with one of my friends. He's from South America. He married my best friend." She grinned from ear to ear.

"You little devil," he said, and jerked her close to leave a playful bite on her earlobe. "That wasn't fair!"

She giggled with pure joy. "Yes, it was. It was so cute, listening to you persuade me to dance."

"I get even," he threatened.

"Oooh," she teased. "I can't wait!"

He laughed, shook his head and pulled her close for a minute. "I go to this place in San Antonio on Friday nights—Fernando's. They're famous for flamenco and the tango. We'll show the audience how the tango is done."

"Is that a promise?"

He drew back enough to see her face. She could feel his black eyes probing hers, feel his breath on her lips. "It's a promise," he said in a deep, husky tone, and he didn't smile.

It was a moment out of time, one of those moments when things are so sweet, so poignant, that it seems they can last forever. Of course, they don't. Ever.

He averted his gaze to someone he knew and waved, and then the music and the magic ended.

But she'd had her perfect evening. She held it to her like a security blanket, and every night, she relived it before she slept. And she worried. Because Cal was now overseas, not dancing, but fighting for his life most likely. She kept him in her prayers and lived for the day when he came home.

Cal, meanwhile, was on a flight to an airport in the middle of an African nation, Ngawa, that was being destroyed by two sides of a war for control. Along with his friends from Eb Scott's group, there were some older and more knowledgeable mercs on hand to help with strategy and tactics.

He'd heard of the three who turned up from nowhere. Laremos and a man called Archer, and one called Dutch. The three were legendary. The younger men stood in awe of them, despite their own well-honed skills.

Three of the older men found that adulation amusing.

Cy Parks was a marvel with Bowie knives. It was an education to watch him throw them. He never missed. He had black hair and green eyes and a mean attitude. He was the sort of man who could walk down a back alley with twenty-dollar bills hanging out of his pockets and he'd never be approached by a criminal.

Rodrigo Ramirez was a maverick. He worked for the federal government in drug interdiction from time to time, when he wasn't off with Eb Scott's group on missions. He spoke several languages, which made him invaluable in undercover work. He was also the wealthiest employee Eb had. He had the equivalent of the annual budget of a small nation in a bank somewhere in Denmark, where his father, a minor royal, had lived before his death. His mother was a titled Spanish noblewoman, and both parents had been wealthy beyond the dreams of avarice. There was a sister, as well. Ramirez spoke of her rarely, but with affection. They were the only two survivors of their family.

The third member of the small, tight group was Micah Steele. He'd trained to be a doctor, even had his medical license, but he'd taken exception to some of the rules he was expected to obey. And he'd jettisoned a potential career for merc work, which paid much better. He was blond and handsome, a ladies' man for real, and a deadly man with an automatic weapon. He had a father and a stepsister, but no other relatives. Rumor was that he hated the stepsister and made her life miserable.

Cal was fascinated by the men around him. He hadn't really lived long enough or worked in the field long enough to gain a reputation that anyone would take notice of. But he was going to change that. He was going to be as well known in merc circles as these men were one day.

He was intelligent enough to know how to listen and pay attention to details, which stood him in good stead with Cy Parks, who was the de facto leader of the bunch.

As they planned the incursion, and worked out the details, a demolition man, who was another legend, came on board. Cord Romero was the son and grandson of famous bullfighters in Spain. He'd been orphaned at a young age, but adopted by a kindhearted Texas woman, who raised him and a little girl who was his foster sister by adoption. After a brief career in the FBI and, rumor said, a wife who died by suicide, he'd gone into merc work more or less full-time.

Watching him work, Cal was forcibly reminded of Amelia and her capability with deadly chemicals. He mentioned it to Cord, as he put together small IEDs for use in the incursion.

"Does she want to do merc work?" Cord asked with twinkling dark eyes.

Cal sighed. "I hope not."

He was shocked at what he'd let slip. It was none of his business what Amelia did, but the thought of her in a camp like this, overseas, in constant danger, made his blood run cold. And that hit him in the gut like a fist.

Chapter Five

Cord Romero gave Cal a pointed smile. "You don't want her to do this sort of thing?"

"She's only nineteen," Cal said, pushing back his own feelings. "Her grandfather would be outraged."

"Then why does she study chemistry?" he persisted.

Cal scowled. "I don't know. I should have asked."

"Plenty of time," the other man said lazily. "If she's that young, she's got years to decide on a profession. She might teach." He chuckled as he said it.

"What's funny?"

"I tried that. Teaching," he added. He shook his head. "It's not for everyone."

"What was your field of study?"

"Chemistry," Cord said. His eyes twinkled. "I taught high school chemistry for a year fresh out of college. Even then, I was drawn to demolition. It got me into trouble with the principal and the school board."

"Why?"

"They objected to my slight deviations from the curriculum," he replied.

"He was teaching the children how to blow things up," Cy Parks interjected with a chuckle.

"Only little things," Cord argued. "My God, it was just one little desk, not a building. I even offered to replace the desk!"

"So your principal was ordered to replace you," Micah Steele added with a grin.

"And that was our good fortune, because this man is a genius with explosives," Ramirez said with a dramatic sigh. "There should be a prize for such things."

"There is. I think it's called prison," Cal told them.

"Ex-cop," Cy Parks said, jerking a thumb at him. "Ignore him. It might be contagious."

"Ignore him," Ramirez said, indicating Cy. "I've been DEA on and off."

"The 'heat,'" Cord muttered, jerking a thumb at Ramirez. "You can't even escape it here!"

"You were never arrested," Steele chuckled. "And you're FBI when you're not here, so don't crow so loud."

Cord gave him an international symbol of distaste.

Steele gave him one right back.

"And just imagine, nobody here has a straitjacket," Cal said under his breath.

Somebody threw a towel at him.

There was a young local boy named Juba who'd become a sort of mascot to the small group. He knew the area, having been brought up there, and he was a walking library on plants and animals.

Cy Parks was particularly fond of him. He had a young son and loved to show off photos of him on his cell phone. Of course, the phone stayed on the plane when the group was ready to go into combat. There, only satellite phones were of any use in the jungle.

It never ceased to amaze Cal that huge modern cities could cohabit with small rural villages. And the strangest thing was that the people in the villages were always laughing, always happy, in what seemed like inescapable poverty. While in the cities, people walked past each other without even a nod, frowning, lost in their own worries.

"This is an amazing place," Cal mused while they were waiting for a local militia leader to give them a situation report.

"It is?" Laremos asked.

"Look," Cal said, indicating laughing children amusing laughing adults. "Do you see anybody scowling and muttering about how hard life is?"

Laremos grinned. "Just us."

Cal laughed. "I live in a small town in Texas," he mused. "It's sort of like this. A lot of people are poor, but they always seem to find reasons to smile. In cities, you just don't really see that much."

"True," Laremos agreed. "I live in Guatemala. It's largely rural, in my area. Palm trees, sand, drug dealers…" He laughed. He glanced at one of the younger men in the group. "Still, at least we have groundwater, Gomez," he called to the man.

"Rub it in," Gomez called back. "But we have ancient Mayan ruins, as well!"

"So do we," Laremos countered. "And lovely streams and waterfalls…"

"Quintana Roo is abundantly blessed with water, thank you. It's just underground!"

"What, there's no surface water in the Yucatan Peninsula?" Cal asked. "Like our rivers in Texas that only run at certain times of the year?"

"I mean there aren't any rivers," Laremos corrected. "None at all."

"Good Lord! Why?"

"There was an impact thousands of years ago, a meteor called Chicxulub. It hit in the Gulf of Mexico and destroyed pretty much the surrounding area. I think that's why. Everybody has a theory. That's mine."

"I couldn't live in a place with no running water," Cy Parks murmured. "My place in Wyoming has plenty of it."

"He has a ranch the size of New Jersey," Dutch commented.

"You should move next door," Cy chuckled. "It's a great place to raise kids."

"Kids!" Dutch shivered. "Never in a million years! I break out in hives just thinking about it!"

"Woman-hater," Laremos said in a mock whisper.

"It goes beyond hate," Dutch said, and he didn't smile. He finished what he was doing. "Okay, there's our second IED. God, I hope we don't have to use any of them here," he added, looking around at the villagers.

"That I can't promise," Cy replied. "But we'll do our best." He smiled at Juba, who came running with an AK-47, a weapon that was old but still serviceable. Many of the young fighters still carried them.

"I need bullets!" Juba said with his big toothy smile. "And a candy bar...?"

Cy chuckled and got one out of his pack. "You're bankrupting me," he murmured as he handed it over.

"You have many. You are a rich American," Juba laughed, pulling the wrapper open. "The United States must be such a rich country to have so many sweet and wonderful things! I would like to go there!"

"And so you might, one day," Cy said, rubbing the boy's thick hair. He'd become very fond of Juba, who had been orphaned by the turmoil going on around him. He had a cousin in a distant village, but the cousin had five sons and didn't want him. So Juba hung around the village with his American friends, and some other nice soldiers who had come from overseas to help win the fight for liberation of his country.

"This is so good of you," Juba said, suddenly serious. "To help us, I mean."

"It helps us, too," Cy replied solemnly. "When we help to fight an evil that affects many lives, it gives us a feeling of, well, of purpose. Of doing something worthwhile."

Juba nodded. "Yes. It is what I would like to do also. Perhaps when I grow up, I will be a politician like our poor president who is in exile."

"If you do, we'll have your back."

Juba frowned, his black eyes questioning.

"We'll help protect you," he clarified.

"Ah." He grinned. "Just so!"

"Juba, can you take this to the French army over there?" Laremos called, raising a hand at one of the foreign fighters he knew.

"Legion-etrangere!" came the mocking reply.

"French Foreign Legion!" Laremos yelled back.

The Frenchman put a finger to his lips and went "Shh! Say ex-Legion, or I can't go home!"

Everybody laughed.

Cy Parks watched Juba run to do the errand. "I'd love to take Juba home with me," he said quietly. "This is no place for a child of promise, in a perpetual combat zone."

"Could you do it?" Laremos asked.

He nodded. "I have contacts. I'll use them."

Cal, listening, nodded, too. He liked being part of this incursion. He liked it a lot.

The group stayed a week, long enough to get a better picture of what would be needed for the upcoming offensive, including more weapons, more ammunition, the works. They'd worked out a battle plan with the other insurgents, all of them hoping to end this miserable standoff and get the country back to normal.

They flew home, just for a couple of weeks. Then it would be back into the fires of hell.

When Amelia saw Cal pull into his driveway, her heart flew. She had to grit her teeth to stop herself from running across the street and throwing herself into his arms. But that way lay disaster. He didn't know how she felt about him, and she didn't dare let it show. He'd already put up caution signs. No followers. He was free and he liked it that way.

He might change his mind one day. If he did, Amelia was going to be right there, waiting.

She cooked a huge dinner that night, anticipating that Cal would come over to visit. And he did.

She walked to the kitchen door as her grandfather let him in. "The prodigal returns!" she said dramatically.

He made a face at her and grinned. "Something smells nice."

"I saw your car pull in, so I made extra. You're welcome," she added pertly, and grinned before she went back to the stove.

At least, she saw no bullet holes or bandages, so he must not have been in any heavy fighting. Not yet, anyway. She sent up a mental thanks.

Supper was riotous. Cal had a dozen stories about his companions. Without giving anything tactical away, he described his friends.

"They're all pretty much misfits," he mused, "even though some of them came to merc work from law enforcement."

"Spec ops takes a different mindset," Harris commented. "It's a known fact that no man who can pass a standard psych profile is spec ops material." He chuckled.

"Is that true for you?" Cal asked.

He nodded. "I can't talk about it. Most of our missions were classified." He looked up. "But, believe me, I know the life. I'd be willing to bet that most of your crew is confirmed bachelors."

Cal nodded. "Only one has a family. That I know of. They don't talk about personal things much."

"I was the odd one out in my group, as well. It doesn't mix with family life." He glanced covertly at his granddaughter as he spoke, noting her lowered head, although he was certain she was hanging on every word.

"Still," Cal sighed, "it feels good to come home, even just

for a couple of weeks. That reminds me. How about Fernando's Friday night?" he asked Amelia with a grin.

She looked up, her face flushing prettily. "Fernando's?" She was still hanging on what he'd said about most of the men being confirmed bachelors.

"The tango?" he reminded her. "Flan? Flamenco dancers…?"

"Oh!" She laughed self-consciously. "Yes. I'd like that."

"Me, too. I don't do much dancing in Africa," he added, tongue-in-cheek.

"Do you have to do martial arts, too?" she wanted to know. "Besides, you know, blowing up stuff?"

"Definitely," he replied. "Eb Scott has experts in every field. He's going to have the finest counterterrorism school on the planet before he's done. It will put Jacobsville on the map— even if it's just a small map." He finished his cake. "That was delicious," he told her with a smile.

She grinned. "Thanks. It's just basic chemistry," she added with a wicked grin.

They all laughed.

"How about coming out to the school with me tomorrow?" he asked Amelia. "Do you have early morning classes at college?"

She nodded. "One at eight that's two hours, and one at ten that's an hour. I'm not taking a full courseload this semester."

"So, how about one o'clock tomorrow? We'll go out to Eb's place and I'll teach you some basic self-defense."

Her eyes lit up. "That would be great! But won't you be too tired? I mean, you've just got home after a really long trip…"

He drew in a breath and laughed. "You're always one step ahead of me. Yes, I am tired, and I have to see a man in San Antonio in the morning. Maybe day after tomorrow? What's your class schedule?"

"It's the same, every Tuesday and Thursday."

"Day after tomorrow, then."

"Does Eb go with you on these missions?" she wondered.

He shook his head. "He's got too much responsibility here right now. He used to, though," he added, smiling.

"Probably too many injuries to be an asset on a fast-moving mission," Amelia's grandfather added with twinkling eyes. "That was why I had to give it up."

"Well, you got married, too," she pointed out.

He grimaced. "Your grandmother wasn't too enthusiastic about seeing me lining up to be a battle casualty," he confessed. "And I was too crazy about her to make a fuss. By and large," he added, finishing his coffee, "the decision I made was the right one."

"Not one I'll have to make," Cal said with a weary smile. "I've got enough excitement in my life without adding complications."

"Wise man," Amelia said, smiling at him. And she was lying through her teeth, but Cal didn't realize it.

He shoved back his chair and got up. "Thank you both for the lovely supper," he nodded at Amelia, "and the conversation. But I'm ready for bed." He stifled a yawn. "It's a long ride home from where we were."

"Get some rest," Harris said as they walked him to the door.

"Planning to," he replied. He smiled at Amelia. "Day after tomorrow. At one. Okay?"

"Okay!" She was beaming.

He threw up his hand and went home.

Amelia's grandfather closed and locked the door.

"You're setting yourself up for some heartache, you know," he said very gently. "He's not a settling sort of man."

"Neither were you," she pointed out.

"I agree. There's always the woman who can turn a man's priorities on their head. But you're very young and our friend across the street is savvy in a sophisticated way."

"You mean he knows his way around women, and I'm stuck in double dating," she translated, but with a grin.

"Exactly my point. So you watch your step. He's the sort of man who can enjoy a day and walk away from it with no regrets. That's not you, sugar. You're a forever sort of girl."

She felt the heaviness of sorrow as she listened. "You're right," she agreed. "But hope is the last thing we lose." Her eyes met his. "He's…the whole world," she faltered, and flushed.

He put his arms around her and hugged her tight. "I know that. It's why I warned you. I can't live your life for you but have a care. I know a train wreck when I see one."

"Maybe it will be just a small train wreck with no casualties."

"Sugar," he sighed, "all wrecks have casualties. Just…be careful."

She nodded against his shoulder. "I will. I promise."

Cal woke to the ringing of his cell phone playing the theme from a popular action film. He reached for it, knocked it off the table and almost fell out of bed retrieving it.

"Damn," he muttered as he fumbled it open. "Hello!" he said belligerently.

"Well," Edie's voice came over the phone. "If that isn't a happy welcome!"

"Sorry. I dropped the damned thing," he muttered. "What time is it?"

"Eleven o'clock. Where are you? Weren't we supposed to have lunch today?"

"Lunch." He scowled. Now he remembered. He'd almost stood her up by offering to take Amelia to Eb Scott's place today, until she'd remarked that he must need rest. Something Edie was never concerned about. She didn't like illness or hospitals and avoided both.

"Yes, lunch! How soon can you be here?" she wanted to know.

He blinked his eyes. Food had no place in his thoughts at the moment. "About an hour, I guess."

"I made the reservations for eleven thirty," she said tersely.

"It will be an inconvenience if I have to cancel them and sweet-talk the maître d' into holding our table."

"I don't frankly give a damn," he shot back. "Eat it your-self!" He hung up.

Edie was adversarial when she wanted something, and she made his life miserable if he didn't fall in with her wishes. He was getting tired of it. He didn't like having a woman try to lead him around by the nose.

He showered and shaved. The phone had been ringing con-stantly. He finally answered it.

"I'm sorry," Edie said in a wheedling tone. "I'm really sorry. I didn't mean to sound so horrible, and when you're only just back in the States."

He relented, a little. "One more time, and you can find an-other friend to take you out," he said coldly. "Understand?"

Her indrawn breath was audible. He could almost hear her teeth grinding.

"Okay," she choked. "I get it."

"Fine. I'll be there in thirty minutes. We can get a ham-burger someplace."

"I changed the reservation. Half an hour will be fine. Really."

"All right."

He hung up. She was becoming a liability. He felt sorry for her, because she didn't mix well, and she had a drinking prob-lem. But pity only carried a man so far. He preferred Amelia, who was gentle and kindhearted and fun to be around. She wasn't as sophisticated as Edie, or as pretty, but she was a far better companion, despite her age. Not that he had any serious thoughts about Amelia. She, like Edie, had to be just a friend. He had plans, and they didn't involve white picket fences.

"I really am sorry that I was so brash," Edie told him while they ate their way through late lunch at one of San Antonio's finest restaurants.

"We all have bad days," he remarked.

"I have lots of those," she said with a sigh. She was picking at a salmon salad without much enthusiasm.

"Why do you spend so much time alone?" he asked her. "Don't you have friends besides me?"

"Loads of them. Rich people with connections," she said, laughing. "The best kind."

He frowned. "Money doesn't buy character."

She made a gesture with her fork. "It pays bills, though, and gets you where you want to be in life. I wouldn't be poor for anything!"

He was remembering Juba in the Ngawan village, a kid who had nothing but who was always smiling.

Edie, never observant, still noted his changed expression. "What did I say?" she wanted to know.

He shrugged. "There's this kid. Juba," he added with a nostalgic smile. "His parents were killed in one of the incursions, and he has nobody of his own except a distant cousin. One of our group is thinking about bringing him over here…"

"Good God, what for?" she exploded, wide-eyed. "As if we don't already have so many parasitic poor people pouring in here!"

The waiter, who'd just stopped by to ask about dessert, had a closed and locked expression.

"Nada mas, gracias," Cal told him. He added in a low tone, *"Lo siento. Mi amiga sabe nada sobre el gente quien tiene nada sin que El Dios. Entiende?"*

The waiter smiled at him. He nodded. *"Mil gracias."*

"La comida es muy sabroso," he added, smiling. *"Pero no nos gusta tener los pasteles. Pues, mas café, por favor?"*

"At once," the waiter said in perfect English and went away.

"You speak that awful language?" Edie asked curtly. She was fidgeting in her chair, nervous and getting more unsettled by the minute. "People who work in this country should speak English!"

"The waiter is from the Yucatan," Cal said icily. "His first language is Mayan. His second language is Spanish. His third language is English."

She blinked. It wasn't registering. She had beads of sweat on her forehead. "Why is it so hot in here?" she muttered. "They need to fix the air-conditioning."

"It's cool," he said, puzzled. She was wearing a short-sleeved dress. There was no reason that she should be complaining about the heat.

She wiped her forehead. "Easy for you to say," she muttered.

The waiter was back with the coffee. He served it, took Cal's credit card back to pay the bill and returned promptly, leaving the ticket in its little book on the table with a smile at Cal and ignoring Edie entirely.

"No manners," she grumbled as the waiter left. "He didn't even wish me a good afternoon."

"You're the one with no manners," Cal snapped as he finished his coffee. "And this is very likely our last lunch together."

He got up, leaving her to follow.

Once they were outside, he was almost vibrating with anger. She'd shamed him with her behavior. It wasn't something he'd seen in her before. He didn't like it.

"I'm sorry," she mumbled as she joined him on the sidewalk. "I don't feel well. I need to go home."

He took a long breath. He led her to the car, drove her home, saw her to her door and started to leave.

"Don't you want to come in?" she asked. "And have a drink?"

He turned and looked at her with an expression that could have started fires. "I do not," he said coldly. "Goodbye."

"Cal, I'm sorry," she wailed. "I'm really sorry!"

"You're always sorry," he said icily. "But you never change."

She shifted restlessly. "I have problems."

"Everybody has damned problems," he shot back curtly. "But most people just endure and get on with their lives. You make everybody around you miserable because you can't live with yourself!"

She glared at him. "I'm going in now."

"Then go."

He went back to his car and drove away. He didn't even spin gravel getting onto the road.

Edie picked up a vase on a table beside the door and slammed it into the carpet, shattering it. She hated Cal. She hated people who weren't in her social class. She hated the world.

She poured herself a large whiskey and sat down to drink it. She hated herself, she thought miserably. But drinking helped. It helped a lot. When she drank enough, she could forget her problems.

Cal would come back, she told herself. He always did, no matter how mad she made him. He was just tired. Sure. That was it. She had another swallow of her drink. She was already feeling much better.

Cal picked up Amelia at her house the next day. She was wearing sweats, neat gray ones.

He chuckled. "You dressed the part, I see," he teased.

"Well, I don't have a karate kit or anything," she replied, smiling. "This was the next best thing. Will it be okay, you think?"

He sighed. "It will be fine," he assured her, mentally comparing her behavior with Edie's. They were polar opposites.

"Is it karate or tae kwon do or tai chi that we'll do?" she asked. "I've been reading up," she added with a grin.

He chuckled. "Eb teaches all three. But mostly it's tae kwon do." He glanced at her. "What we learn for combat is pretty different."

"Different how?" she wanted to know.

"What Eb teaches at the school is defensive martial arts. In the military, or in merc work, you learn killing techniques."

"Oh."

"Don't tell me, you're squeamish," he teased.

She shrugged. "I can't even kill a mouse," she confessed sheepishly. "I caught one in the kitchen once, in a mason jar. Granddaddy said to kill it. I just couldn't. When he went to take his nap, I took it out to the back garden and let it go."

"It probably made its way right back into the house," he pointed out.

She laughed. "There were all sorts of delicious vegetables in the garden that year," she recalled. "Plus, I kept sneaking crackers and guinea pig pellets out to him."

"Amelia, you're hopeless," he groaned.

She chuckled. "I like animals. What can I say? I'd have loved a cat or a dog. I wish Granddaddy wasn't allergic. But I'd rather have him than a dozen pets."

"He's a sweet man," he agreed.

She sighed. "I wish his sister was," she groaned. "There aren't enough bad words to describe her."

"Where does she live?"

"Victoria, thank goodness, but she's coming to visit next week for a few days. She'll complain about her room and the food and the temperature in the house and then she'll mention all the things I need to correct about my looks and my behavior…"

"What's wrong with your looks?" he asked curtly, glancing at her. "And your behavior is great."

She flushed. "Wow. Thanks."

He shrugged. "You're not like a lot of women, who think they should have every wish granted, every complaint seen to at once."

"That sounds as if you know one," she fished.

"I do. She embarrassed the hell out of me at a restaurant, making nasty remarks about immigrants."

Her face softened as she looked at him. "We have this couple down the street, the Gomezes. They have three kids. They're some of the nicest people you'd ever want to know. Mrs. Gomez has been teaching me Spanish. I babysit her kids when she has to take her husband to the doctor. He's diabetic and he won't eat right, so he goes into comas periodically."

His heart melted. He compared that behavior with Edie's and just shook his head. "We have some Hispanic operatives in our group. Fine men." His face tautened. "That friend of mine remarked about how everyone living here should speak our language. I talked to our waiter, who was Mayan. He spoke three languages."

"That's impressive," she said softly. "People who put them down just don't know them, Cal," she added quietly. "A lot of the problem is they only learn about immigrants from what they hear on the so-called news."

He chuckled. "So-called news?"

"Try getting any real news out of them," she grumbled. "They're so busy not offending anyone that they're scared to tell the real news. They're an entertainment, not a source of information. Granddaddy says that reporters he used to know would refuse to work for any of the TV news stations, because they had integrity, and the TV news has none."

"I have to confess that I feel exactly that way." He pulled into a huge compound near a towering Victorian house, surrounded by quonset huts. "And we're here," he said, as a tall, rangy man in boots and jeans and a Stetson noted their arrival and started toward them as they got out of the car.

"Hi, Eb," Cal greeted him, shaking hands. "Remember Amelia?" he asked wickedly. He leaned forward. "She knows how to blow up stuff!"

Chapter Six

Eb Scott's green eyes laughed as he grinned at Amelia. "Oh, yes, I remember you. I've never seen anybody hit a bull's-eye dead center the way you do. Except him." He jerked his thumb at Cal. "Never misses." He just shook his head.

"I'd rather blow up stuff, though," she replied, laughing.

"If you get good at blowing up stuff, you may be asked to hire on one day soon," he told her.

She laughed, too. "I'd be delighted!" she said, and meant it. "But first I have to learn some more deadly recipes."

"You go to college?" Eb asked.

She nodded. "I'm a sophomore. Well, I'm in a degree program that I graduate from at the end of the year. Then I have to decide if I want to go the whole way to a BS in science or settle for an AS."

"Big decision," Eb agreed. "But you're young."

"Not so much," she laughed.

"Young," Cal said firmly and grinned at her.

"Come along and I'll give you the grand tour," Eb said as he led the way into the compound. "I've just added defensive driving for chauffeurs. Our courses are growing by leaps and bounds. So is our student population. I'd like to be with you guys in Africa," Eb added with a glance at Cal. "Maybe in a couple of weeks, if I can settle things here and get a competent manager on the place."

"You'd be welcome," Cal replied. "The more, the merrier, in this case."

"In any case," the older man replied somberly.

He took them through all the classes, although he didn't interrupt the instructors. Some of his teachers had been in elite forces. There was even a retired SAS guy teaching sniper tactics.

"We draw from all over the planet," Eb said as they continued over to the huge martial arts complex. "A good deal of ex-military can't settle. So teaching keeps them close to the action without risking the success of an incursion by adding them to it. You slow down as you age and collect battle wounds." He grimaced. "I'm carrying a few extra grams in my carcass from bullets the surgeons couldn't remove."

That was something Amelia hadn't considered—that modern men got shot and the bullets had to stay in them.

"They say that Doc Holliday had a lot of them in him that they didn't take out, back in the late 1800s," she remarked.

"Absolutely true," Eb agreed. "They had no antibiotics back in the day. Any surgeon probing for a bullet could cause a fatal infection. Bullets ricochet on bone. Sometimes they travel in unpredicted ways, depending on the caliber of the gun, the velocity of the bullet and the distance from the victim."

Amelia was hanging on every word. "Wow," she said.

Eb chuckled. "I should give you a place in my operation. You just soak up knowledge. And you know a lot already," he pointed out.

"She's going to finish college and teach other people how to blow up stuff," Cal said firmly. "Ask her granddad."

Amelia made a face. "I guess so," she agreed. "He'd never approve of me going off to war, no matter how much I'd like to."

Eb stopped and turned to look down at her. "War is hell, Sherman said, and he's right. Until you've been in a battle where you lose favorite comrades and have bullets flying right at you, you have no idea what war actually is." His eyes were dull and sad. "Every man has to learn that the hard way."

Cal hadn't, yet. His stint overseas in the military had been mostly mop-up operations, not front-line stuff. He just smiled. "I'm sure we all cope in different ways," he said.

"Oh, we cope." Eb sighed. "To a point. Let's find you a free mat."

Amelia learned to fall. She groaned and glared at Cal after the tenth back breakfall.

"When am I going to learn tae kwon do?" she asked with a little heat. "All I'm learning is how to fall down!"

"Falling down the right way is what will spare you many injuries," Cal told her with a smile. "This is always taught first."

She groaned again. "Okay," she said. "Maybe if a guy comes at me with a gun, I can just fall on him and win the fight."

"You'd need to gain a lot of weight first," he chuckled. "Okay. Side breakfalls…"

She sighed and followed his instructions.

From side breakfalls, on both sides, they progressed to front breakfalls. But she couldn't do it. She just stared down at the mat and then at Cal with misery written all over her flushed features, her blond hair wisping around her sweaty face as it threatened to escape the tight bun high on her head.

"It's too far down," she wailed. "I'll break my nose!"

"And it's such a pretty nose, too," he teased, tapping it with his finger. "That's why you do this," and he demonstrated falling to land squarely on his forearms, slapping the mat just before the impact.

"I'll break my nose," she repeated.

"No. You won't. Come on. Give it a try."

She hesitated. She glanced around her at the other students in various stages of training. Several of them were also doing breakfalls.

She took a deep breath, leaned forward and fell. She slapped the mat and landed on her forearms, her nose inches from the mat. She burst out laughing. "Hey, that's not hard at all!" she said breathlessly as Cal reached down and pulled her up in front of him.

"Nice fall," he said softly, pushing back the wisps of hair from her face. His dark eyes were quiet and curious as he studied her. She was game. She complained, but never meant it. She was fun to be around. She made him laugh. He hardly ever had, until she came into his life.

"Thanks," she whispered huskily, lost in his eyes, trembling inside with raging emotions that she could only barely control.

He came back to himself almost immediately and stepped back. "Okay, now that you know how," he said, and grinned, "back to it!"

She made a face at him, but she obliged.

Before they left the camp, Eb took them out to the shooting range.

He handed Amelia a .45 Ruger Vaquero double-action revolver, loaded, but with the cylinder pushed out. "Do your worst," he invited, indicating a man-shaped target in front of them on the range.

"Wow," she whispered. "I love this thing! It's like being in the last century, fighting outlaws!" She glanced at Cal. "I know, you prefer your .38, and I like shooting it. But I've never shot one of these!"

"Pretend the target is a highwayman and give him hell," Cal told her.

She laughed. She slapped the cylinder back in, aimed and sent six shots right dead center into the target without hesitation.

"Damn!" Eb exploded. "That pistol is heavy, too!"

"Double damn!" Cal seconded. "How did you do that?"

"I really don't know," she said simply. "It seems so easy to me, even with unfamiliar guns." She grinned at her companions. "This one is super!" she added, admiring it.

"If you ever want a job," Eb said, "you've got one here. I'd hire you in a minute to teach or to go on missions…"

"Never," Cal said firmly, and glared at her, because she was already caught up in the excitement and eager. "It's no life for a woman. And I'd bet real money that you've never had a woman on the place, as far as instruction goes."

"That's true," Eb admitted. "But then, I've never seen anybody do what Amelia just did," he continued. "Or what she did last time she was here, on this same range with the .32. Except you," he added, as he glanced at Cal. "Well, maybe you slipped once. But, almost never."

"What does he mean?" she asked Cal.

"I shoot a hundred times, I hit the bull's-eye a hundred times," Cal said simply. "Except this one time when, for God knows what reason, a bee landed on my nose when I fired."

"True story," Eb seconded. "Damnedest thing, I didn't know we had a bee on the place. Turns out, there was a whole hive of them in the wall of one of my outbuildings. We got a beekeeper to come over with a smoker and a hive. He found the queen, put her in the hive, all the workers followed, and he took the hive home with him." He laughed. "The fringe benefit is that I get a jar of honey whenever I want one. I love honey."

"I do, too, but I'm not a fan of bees on the shooting range," Cal replied.

"No kidding?" Eb just chuckled.

"I would love to work for Eb Scott," Amelia said on the way home. "That place of his is out of this world!"

"When you get through school, go talk to him," he counseled. "But your granddad will probably have something to say about it."

She sighed. "I think I can bring him around," she said. "I had fun!"

"I did, too," he replied with a warm smile. "You're good company, Amelia," he added quietly.

"Thanks. So are you," she replied softly.

He checked his watch. He'd agreed to take Edie to a concert she wanted to see in San Antonio.

"I'm keeping you from something," she said in an apologetic tone.

"Just a concert," he said. "But I've got plenty of time to get there."

"Okay, then." She smiled, but inside she was feeling abandoned. She'd have bet that his concert was being attended by another woman also. Probably that fancy city woman who'd been loitering around his yard sometime back. But she had no strings on Cal, who was determined to retain his freedom. She brightened a little. If he felt like that, then his fancy woman wouldn't have strings on him, either. It made her feel better. And, after all, she was young. She could wait for any happiness that might come her way.

Cal felt a strange surge of relief that she wasn't jealous. She must suspect that he had a date. But on the heels of that sensation came one of vague disappointment. It disturbed him that she wasn't bothered. He sighed inwardly. He was overthinking this. They were friends. He'd told her already that he had no plans to involve himself in a relationship. If she'd taken him at his word, and she seemed to, then she had no need to be jealous. He felt vindicated. He smiled to himself. Of course she wasn't jealous.

He glanced at her and smiled. She smiled back. Then she knew she'd done the right thing, by not reacting. She didn't dare let him know how she really felt. It would drive him away. That was the last thing she wanted.

He left her at her door.

"Thanks," she said, grinning up at him from a face surrounded by disheveled hair. "It was great fun!"

He chuckled, trying to imagine Edie in her place. The woman was always immaculate when they went out together. Involving herself in martial arts was the last thing Edie would have done. But Amelia loved it.

"Martial arts and blowing up things and guns." He shook his head. "I'd never have believed it when I first met you."

"I look like a wimp?" she asked with mock horror.

He laughed. "No. But you seemed so sedate and unflappable," he explained. "I didn't think you had a wild streak."

"Oh, is that what it's called?" she asked, amused.

"There's probably a better name for it," he replied. He brushed back strands of her golden hair. "You're pretty good on the mat."

She was trembling inside at the proximity and doing her best not to let it show. "Good at falling?" she asked, and rolled her eyes. "When I tell Granddaddy that I've spent the day falling on my face, he'll laugh himself to death!"

"No, he won't," he promised. "Don't forget. Fernando's tomorrow night." He gave her a long look. "Wear a dress," he added.

Her eyebrows shot up.

"So I'm sexist," he replied with a long sigh. "I just love the way women look in dresses, especially when we dance something as elegant as the tango."

"I'll find something appropriate, then," she teased.

He smiled. "Okay. I'll pick you up about six. We'll have dinner first."

"That sounds nice."

"They have great food. But the dancing's not bad, either. See you later."

"Okay. Thanks again."

"My pleasure," he said, and meant it. She was unique. He'd never known anyone quite like her.

She went inside. Her grandfather looked up from his news program. "Good Lord," he said. "Have you been caught in a car wash?"

She glared at him. "I've been falling. Just falling. I did nothing but fall for two hours!"

"Breakfalls," he said, nodding.

"Front breakfalls," she added.

He chuckled. "I tried to get your grandmother to do one of those. She ran out the back door and hid until I promised to stop hounding her about it."

She grinned. "Smart woman. Oh, and when I got through falling, Cal took me out to Mr. Scott's firing range and Mr. Scott handed me a .45 Ruger Vaquero!"

"Wow," he said softly. "That's one fine pistol."

"Yes, it is."

"Did you shoot well?"

"Six shots, all dead center," she replied.

He sighed and smiled. "You always were a natural with a gun. Well, with a pistol," he added. "But a .45 is a lot heavier than that .38 Cal carries."

"It didn't feel much different," she said. She smiled. "I wish I had one," she sighed.

"I offered to let you use my .12 gauge. It's heavy."

She glared at him. "It weighs more than I do, and it kicks like a mule. I'll shoot my .28 gauge, thanks very much."

"The .12 gauge is better. But you won't touch it."

She shifted. "I could shoot it if I wanted to," she protested.

"If you could learn how to pull the trigger on it," he retorted. "The stock is specially padded to cushion the recoil. But even with that .28 gauge, I never could get you to actually hit the damned skeet targets."

"I did try," she apologized. "Several times. It's hard for normal people to hit something going sixty miles an hour," she added. "Skeet targets are too fast."

"Well, we all have things we can't do. Speaking of which, I couldn't talk Valeria out of coming next week," he added miserably. "But she'll only be here for two days."

"Only two days. Gosh. I wish I had an appointment out of town," she muttered.

"It won't be so bad," he tried to encourage her.

"She'll start complaining when she walks in the door," she replied. "The temperature will be too cold. Her bed won't be made right. The food will be too greasy or too sweet or too something. And then she'll complain that the carpet isn't clean enough."

"I'm truly sorry that I couldn't head her off," he said gently.

"Maybe if she'd ever married, she'd have mellowed," she grumbled. "Honestly, though, I can't imagine a man brave enough to put a ring on her finger. Of course, she'd be putting one through his nose at the same time…!"

"Now, Amelia, she is your only surviving great-aunt," he reminded her.

"And your only sibling," she said, nodding. "I'm sorry. It's just…"

He smiled. "She's a pain in the butt. Yes. I know. But she's family, so we'll both grit our teeth and pretend we're glad to see her."

"If I can pull that off, I'll be ready to sign up for theater at school," she sighed.

"I know," he teased. "You're no good at getting up in front of people."

"True. I'd rather blow things up." Her eyes gleamed and she grinned. "I'm going to have a quick shower, then I'll start supper. How about a burger with homemade fries?"

"Delicious!"

"Coming right up, after I've cleaned up," she said.

"Might invite Cal to help us eat it," he suggested.

She shook her head. "He's got a date," she said, and smiled to let him know she didn't mind. "I'll be down in a jiffy!"

He watched her go with quiet, loving eyes, and when she was out of sight, he grimaced. She was smitten with their neighbor, who was far too worldly for a girl of her years—a green girl, at that. He hoped she wouldn't get her heart broken, but he had no control over that. All he could do was stand and watch and pick up the pieces, if her crush ended badly.

He knew men like Cal. They didn't settle down and raise kids. They were the sort of people who hacked a living out of the wilderness or sailed wooden ships across the sea to fight in wars, or founded settlements in dangerous places. They were adventurers, explorers, warriors.

Amelia wouldn't understand that, because she was a homebody. Despite her interests, she had no idea what such a life would actually be like. And she was too soft to adapt to it. So Cal would go on with his lifestyle and Amelia would end in tears, because there was no way she could cope with loving a man like that, a man who would live for adventure and immerse himself in it, regardless of the danger.

Edie was dressed like a debutante. She was wearing a sexy black cocktail dress with lacy inserts, spiky high heels and a shimmering wrap that accentuated her pretty complexion and short, dark hair. She looked good. Really good.

"Thanks for offering to take me," she said as they got into his car. "I've been looking forward to this for weeks!"

"What's playing tonight?" he asked.

"It's Mozart." She looked at herself in the mirror. "It was Debussy, but they changed it."

He managed not to react. He was fond of Debussy and Respighi and Dvorak. He hated Mozart with a passion. But he smiled at her. "That sounds good," he lied.

"How was Africa?" she asked idly.

"Ngawa. Dangerous," he replied.

"You're making a lot of money, though."

"Tons," he said easily. "Most of it, I've invested. Even in a low market, my investment counselor is making me money."

She sighed. "I've lost most of mine because I trusted a business manager who ran off with it. More fool, me."

"Sorry about that."

"I've still got some assets from what my father left me," she replied. Actually, she didn't, but she didn't want Cal to think she was stalking him for the fortune he'd already made signing on to fight in a foreign war. But that was what she was doing. Oh, he was handsome, and personable. That was dressing on top. His value was in his holdings. She was going broke, and she couldn't support her habit. If she could land him, she'd be on easy street. No more money worries.

"How's your little friend?" she asked suddenly. "The one who blows up stuff."

"Amelia?" He laughed. "I had her doing breakfalls all afternoon."

"Breakfalls!" She made a mock shiver.

"Then I took her out to the pistol range. She hit the bull's-eye six times in a row. With a .45 wheel gun."

"I hate guns," she muttered.

"They're my stock in trade," he reminded her.

"Nasty things. They make too much noise." She dismissed them. "The conductor is a friend of mine," she changed the subject. "He's friends with the mayor, so he got me an introduction. I know lots of important people in the city now," she purred.

He didn't know a single one, and he wasn't impressed. Why was she such a social climber? he wondered. But he didn't question her, because he really didn't care. She started talking about the program and he just listened.

They sat through the program with Cal growing more restless by the minute. When it finally ended, he was out of his seat with visible haste, escorting Edie out of the auditorium.

"Honestly, do we have to hurry so much?" she complained. "The president of the city's biggest bank was in the row behind us. I wanted to talk to him."

"You have money there?" he asked idly.

"No, but it's a good idea to speak to important people."

He stopped and looked down at her. "Why?" he asked with honest curiosity.

She gaped at him. "Because it's how you move up in elite society," she said, exasperated. "It gets you privileges."

"Why do you need them?" he persisted.

She drew in a loud sigh. "Honestly, Cal, you're such a dolt sometimes!"

He just grinned and led her to the car.

She hesitated at her front door and went close to him. "Don't you want to come in for a while and have a few drinks?" she purred.

"Not really, thanks," he said. "I'm tired, and I have to be up early tomorrow for a conference."

"You always have an excuse," she muttered as she moved away.

He just stared at her. "It's my life. I don't answer to anyone. Ever."

It was pleasantly spoken, but firm.

She grimaced. "Okay. I get it. Nothing interferes with the mission."

"Exactly," he returned.

"I'll see you again before you go back?" she asked.

"Certainly," he replied.

She smiled. "All right, then. Take care."

"You, too."

He walked to the car and drove away. He didn't look back. Not once.

Edie saw that and cursed and cursed. She picked up a vase and started to throw it when she realized its value. She put it back down, gingerly. No sense in costing herself money over a man who refused to get serious.

But he liked her, and he kept coming around. So she wasn't giving up. She had plenty of time.

* * *

When the big day came, Amelia was all thumbs getting ready for her night on the town with Cal. She'd only been on dates a handful of times, and never with a man she was crazy about. She had on her best dress. It wasn't really fancy, just a white off-the-shoulder Mexican-style dress, but when she paired it with white high heels and a lacy white mantilla and her mother's pearls, she looked elegant enough. Especially with her hair down, clean and gleaming pale gold in the halo of the overhead lights.

"Will I do?" she asked her grandfather.

He looked up from his paper and his eyes grew misty. He smiled. "You're the image of your grandmother. I swear you look just like her."

She smiled. "Thanks. I was worried that I wouldn't look elegant enough."

"You'll do," he said. "It's not a gala affair. You're going to Fernando's. Yes, it's high-class, but most people who turn up there on Friday nights wear jeans and boots," he chuckled.

She grinned at him. "I was going to, but Cal said you just can't dance a tango in jeans."

"He's probably right. You have a good time."

"I hope so," she said.

Cal was right on time. He wasn't overdressed, either, although he had on beige slacks with a yellow polo shirt and a stylish jacket. He looked handsome.

"Nice," he said, eyeing Amelia.

"She looks like her grandmother," Harris chuckled. "I used to take her dancing, but that was back in the dark ages."

"Can you do a tango?" Cal asked him.

"Not to save my own life," came the dry reply. "So you two go up to San Antonio and wow the crowds. I'll stay here with the dragon drama."

"The new season doesn't start tonight, does it?" Cal asked, because he was a fan, too.

"Last season. I bought it on Amazon," he said with twinkling eyes. "The whole season, so I can watch it whenever I like."

"That's one way to do it. I love the show."

"Me, too. You two have fun."

"We will," Amelia promised him.

"So will I. Joy before grief," he groaned.

"What was that about?" Cal asked her when they were on the highway.

"Great-Aunt Valeria," she muttered. "She's descending on her broomstick next week to visit for two horrible days. We'll go mad!"

"Is she that bad?"

"Worse," she glowered.

"Only two days, though," he said sympathetically.

"When she leaves, I'll be running through town howling like a wolf with sheer glee. And Granddaddy will probably set off fireworks."

"The things I miss, not having relatives." He shook his head.

"Nobody at all?" she asked gently.

He didn't reply. He was remembering things. Terrible things.

"They have flan at Fernando's," she interrupted his thoughts with a lilt in her voice, to distract him. "Right?"

"What? Oh. Yes, they do. The best flan in town."

"I didn't eat lunch," she said. "So I'd have room for it!"

He laughed. "Well!"

"I can make a flan," she added. "But I'm not good enough to compete with the kitchen staff at Fernando's. Their food is just out of this world."

"I think so, too. I used to hang out there every Friday night when I was on the police force."

"You were a policeman?" she exclaimed.

He laughed. "Yes, I was. For three years. Then I heard about the group Eb was forming. I'd grown restless. I wanted a change, a chance to make money, an adventure." He smiled. "It's been that, all right."

"Adventure is dangerous."

"Which makes it enticing," he replied, and wiggled his eyebrows.

She laughed at the twinkle in his eyes. "Is that it?" she teased.

"You like blowing up things. I like going to foreign places and helping change the world."

"Now I feel like a slacker," she said with a grin.

"Not you," he replied easily. He sighed. "I relax when I'm with you. It's a new feeling. I like it."

She wondered if it was a compliment. You relaxed with people who were familiar, who didn't excite you or challenge you.

"Thanks. I think?"

He chuckled. "It's a compliment. I'm not good with people," he added solemnly. "I don't...fit."

She sighed. "Me, neither."

He glanced at her and smiled. "Well, you stick with me, kid. We'll hold off the world."

"That's a deal!"

Chapter Seven

Fernando's was packed. They had to wait for ten minutes even though Cal had made a reservation.

"So sorry you had to wait," the waitress apologized as she led them to a booth near the pretty fountain in the center of the huge room.

"The food here is worth waiting for," Cal assured her with a smile.

She smiled back. "Your waiter will be right with you," she promised, and left.

Amelia was looking around. The restaurant was in a converted theater. It had a live band, exquisite woodwork, velvet curtains, red tables and chairs with real linen tablecloths and napkins and the staff dressed in red. The fountain in the center of the room dominated. It contained live Chinese goldfish and pretty floating lights.

"This place is awesome," she said, fascinated.

He smiled at her. "Everybody thinks so. I know it impressed me, the first time I saw it." He looked around. "He spent a fortune remodeling it, but he made back every penny. He's still making a profit, too. Amazing eye for detail."

"Who is he?"

"Fernando Reyes," he told her. "He was a former governor of some province down in Mexico. He came to this country a few years ago with a bankroll and decided to open a restaurant. The rest is history."

"He must be a fascinating person."

"Believe me, he is. He plays guitar and his wife dances the flamenco. It's the highlight of the evening. Before, and after, there's dancing. But first," he told her with twinkling black eyes, "there's food!" He indicated the approaching waiter.

"Good evening," the man said with a smile, handing them both menus. "What can I bring you to drink?"

"Sweetened iced tea," Amelia said at once.

"Piña colada," Cal said.

"Coming right up."

Cal laughed at her expression. "We'll be here for a while. If you eat while you drink alcohol, it doesn't have as much effect on you. I won't land you in jail."

"Well, okay. But if you do, you're coming along," she promised him.

He smiled affectionately. "Done. What would you like to eat?" he added, turning his eyes to his own menu.

She looked at hers. She was scanning it for the cheapest thing she could find, which was chicken.

He watched her. He had the measure of her by now, and he knew what she was doing. He pulled the menu down and met her shocked eyes. "Amelia, I could afford lobster every night if I wanted it, so stop looking at chicken dishes and order what you want."

She flushed. How had he read her so well?

"I was a cop," he reminded her. "We get good at reading people."

"Oh." She grimaced. "Well…"

"Besides, how many meals have you cooked for me?" he pointed out. "If you have to call it something, how about the repaying of a favor? And you're a great cook, by the way," he added with a gentle smile.

She let out a sigh. "I must wear signs," she murmured. "Okay. I love fish. And then there's flan…"

He chuckled. "Done. No wine?"

She shook her head. "It upsets my stomach. Or should I admit that?" she added.

"Figures," he said, smiling. "You aren't like any woman I've ever known. Not that you're…"

"If you say I'm not a woman, I'll hit you," she promised, because at nineteen, she certainly was a woman.

"I was going to say that you're not odd," he countered, grinning. "But you truly are unique."

She cleared her throat. "Thanks." She managed a nervous smile.

"And will you relax?" he chided. "It's the same thing as sitting at your table at home, except the surroundings are different. We're the same people in both places."

She let out a breath and laughed self-consciously. "Sorry. It's just that I haven't been on many dates. Even with friends," she added.

He toyed with his napkin. "I don't date that much myself." He didn't add that he'd been out with Edie and her behavior had embarrassed and irritated him. It hadn't encouraged him to escort other women.

Amelia, however, was the exception to the rule. She was polite and friendly to the waiter, grateful for the most minor services like coffee refills, and generally pleasant company.

They were finishing the flans when he stopped eating and just looked at her.

She lifted her eyes to his with her fork in midair and raised her eyebrows.

"Manners," he said.

She put down the fork. "Excuse me?"

"You have exquisite manners."

She laughed. "My mother was a stickler for them," she said softly, remembering. "Always say please and thank you, always be polite to people, even people you dislike. Never be sarcastic or abusive in your language. Never, never discuss politics or religion in public. And always treat people the way you'd like to be treated. That was Mama."

He sipped the last of his piña colada. "My grandfather was very much the same."

Her eyes fell to her plate. He never spoke of his parents; only his grandfather. There must have been a solid reason for that. Usually people were left out of conversations because they weren't liked.

"You never ask questions," he remarked.

She just smiled. "I hate that. I mean, I hate having people ask me questions about things that make me uncomfortable. So I don't do it myself."

He turned his glass on the table idly. "Such as?"

Her eyebrows arched again.

He chuckled. "What makes you uncomfortable?"

"Other women who think I'm backward because I don't do bedroom tours with strange men," she said curtly.

Now his eyebrows arched.

"My mother said a man will treat a woman the way she asks to be treated. These days, it's…it's…like Rome in its last days! They had orgies…!"

The waiter had just stopped at their table. Amelia's eyes widened in horror and her face turned beet red. And Cal, darn him, sat there laughing until tears came into his eyes.

"I meant, I was only talking about, I mean…" She reddened even more.

The waiter, a very hip-looking young man with his hair in a ponytail and wicked eyes, leaned down. "Ma'am, your secret is safe with me! Those nasty old Romans!"

Now she was laughing, too. So was Cal.

"Nice. You'll be able to retire on the tip," Cal told him, grinning.

The waiter grinned back. "Can I get you anything else?" he asked.

"Coffee?" he asked Amelia, who nodded enthusiastically. "Make that two," he told the waiter.

The waiter clicked his heels and bowed. *"Statim domine,"* was the crisp reply.

Cal inclined his head. *"Mille gratias!"* he replied.

The other man, blindsided, picked up Amelia's white napkin, with an apology, and waved it in surrender. "I'm a fraud," he said. "That's the only Latin I know!" he chuckled.

Amelia was gaping at both of them.

"I can read a little of it. My grandmother taught languages at university," he added with a smile. "She spoke several. Latin was one."

"Brainy people." The waiter put down the napkin. "I envy you, sir," he added. He smiled. "Back in a jiffy." He paused. "I, uh, can't say that in Latin, though." He wiggled his eyebrows and went toward the kitchen.

Amelia and Cal chuckled together.

"What are the odds?" she asked. "Honestly, I didn't know you spoke any other languages than English!"

"You speak Spanish," he pointed out, having experienced her almost flawless accent when she used it.

"Oh, so do you, and much better than I do," she replied gently. "But Latin! Gosh!"

"Only a few phrases, mostly famous sayings," he said. "My grandmother tried to get me interested, but I wouldn't listen. At least, not until my grandfather taught me that last phrase—a thousand thanks." He smiled sadly. "He was brilliant. I read a lot about him when I grew up. He's in one or two books on military theory. He could speak several languages, like his wife, my grandmother, and play piano. I took it up when I was grown."

"You can play?" she asked.

He shrugged. His eyes went to the band. "Matter of debate," he mused. He drifted away, his face locked and cold.

She leaned forward. "The waiter is loopy," she whispered. "I like him!"

It brought him out of the past, laughing. "Me, too. I wasn't kidding about the tip, either. Waiters don't make much. Tips are how they pay the bills when they get their checks."

"Think he's a student?" she asked.

His eyes were on the waiter, approaching with a coffeepot. "Let's find out."

"Almost instant refills. Sorry, we're busy tonight!" the waiter apologized.

"Not a problem." Cal fixed him with black eyes. "Okay, come clean. We've got a bet going. Are you a student?"

The waiter's eyes bulged. "How in the world…!"

"Latin," Cal said. "Latin. How many people do you run across in the course of a year who can speak even one word of it?"

"I can count them on one finger," the waiter chuckled. "Yes, I'm at university, majoring in Norwegian."

They both gaped at him.

He cleared his throat. "Listen, it's not nuts. Norwegian is a great language. Especially if you're marrying someone whose whole family speaks it!"

"Ah, the light breaks," Cal chuckled. "Are you planning to live in Norway?"

He nodded and smiled as he refilled their coffee cups with a flourish. "I'm a senior this year. So is she. But she's majoring in history, and I help her study for exams. This past month she had essays written by some of the classic authors. In Latin," he added with a chuckle.

"Congratulations," Cal said. Amelia seconded him.

"Thanks. We started going together as freshmen. I never thought I'd find anyone so kind." He saw their expressions.

"Kindness and a gentle heart are far more important than wealth or beauty or power. Kindness lasts."

"You should have majored in philosophy," Cal said with a warm smile. "You'd be a natural."

"Thanks. Can I get you anything else?" he asked.

"Not now. We're just going to wait until dinner settles, then we're going to shock the establishment with a tango," Amelia said mischievously. "He'll be dancing magnificently, while I fall over my feet into someone's table and create a tragic scene. There will be ambulances and rubberneckers."

The waiter leaned closer. "I'll keep a mop handy, so do your worst," he chuckled.

After the waiter left, Cal sipped coffee and studied Amelia with soft eyes. "You are one of the nicest people I've ever known, Amelia," he said quietly.

"Awwww," she said, treating it as a joke.

"I mean it," he corrected. "I've watched you when we're around other people. You're natural and open, and you genuinely like people. It's such a refreshing attitude."

She wondered if he was comparing her with his lady friend. If he was, she felt flattered. "I do like people, mostly," she said. "Not everybody. Some few members of the human race are just mean!"

"Yes, and you can find them in chat rooms under every single YouTube video and gaming forum," he agreed at once.

"I know!" She rolled her eyes. "Keyboard warriors! They're the same people who slink around and never look you in the eye in person." Her eyes narrowed. "Backstabbers."

"Nice analogy."

"You'd know about those, I'll bet, from your days on the force."

"I would, indeed. There was this one time," he recalled, "when we got called to a café where a victim of social media had tracked down the man who said hateful and very threatening things to him on his mother's funeral website."

"You're kidding!" she exclaimed. "Nobody could be that heartless...!"

"Somebody could, and was. He learned a valuable lesson about hate speech, litigation and possible arrest, all at the same time. His parents, who were contacted subsequently, were shocked, to say the least. They thought he was a quiet, studious boy who just liked being by himself. That was before they found the guns and pipe bombs in his closet, however," he added.

Her lips fell apart.

"Yes, people can be that mean, also. He hated one of his teachers and two or three classmates. He even had a battle plan and a camera shoulder mount. He was going to film it all."

"Mental issues?" she asked softly.

He was stunned.

"Well, normal people don't really do those things, do they?" she wondered aloud. "And if his parents didn't know what he was doing online, did they pay him much attention?"

"As little as possible. They had very responsible jobs. They told the prosecutor and the judge that, many times during the course of the trial. The boy was sixteen, which meant that he got sent to juvie. But he did get a psych evaluation. And medicine to treat a condition that his parents also didn't know that he had." He grimaced. "There are so many kids in homes where they're either neglected or abused. Too many."

She knew without being told that Cal had been one of those.

And when he looked up, he saw that knowledge in her odd, intent look. "Are you reading my mind?"

She didn't speak. It was the strangest sensation. Like falling a great distance. Like a firm, solid connection at the same time. "Most policemen are cops for a reason," she said quietly. "My friend Bobby was one. He had terrible scars. His father used a quirt on him. He never told anybody. His grandmother accidentally saw the wounds, called the police herself and had her own son arrested. He went to jail. He's still there."

"And Bobby...?"

She smiled sadly. "Joined the police force in town the day he graduated high school. They say he's going to be a great addition. He talks to grammar school classes about drugs."

"That's a nice success story. Many aren't."

"Life is hard."

"Very." He put down his cup. "So. Nice and full and comfy? Ready to shame those people who think they can dance?" His head jerked toward the dance floor, which was filling up fast.

She grinned. "Oh yes."

He laughed and led her to the dance floor.

The music was slow and dreamy when they started. Cal's arm contracted around her waist, and she shivered inside with feelings she'd never had with anyone else. It was always like this when she was close to him. Like bubbles coming up out of her body, like joy dancing in colored lights in her bloodstream. Like...being in love.

She bit down hard on that last sensation. She couldn't afford to give way to such thoughts. Cal wanted a friend, not a life partner, and she'd better remember it or there wouldn't be any more friendly dates. He would avoid her, to keep from hurting her, if he knew. He was basically a kind man.

But she didn't want that. So she laughed instead, disguising her unsteady nerves. "This is fun," she said.

His cheek brushed hers. "Fun," he agreed. His voice was deeper, softer than it usually was, and the hand on her back was idly caressing. The hand holding hers had it pressed to his chest against his shirt. Under it she felt muscle and thick hair. It was very sensuous, to dance like this.

He could feel her heart beating faster, hear her breath rustle under his chin. This was a very bad idea, but he loved the feel of Amelia in his arms. She made him feel different. Younger. More alive. Joyful.

"You're tangling me up," he murmured aloud, when he hadn't meant to.

"Oh. Sorry," she said, misunderstanding. "My big feet…"

He laughed, relieved. "No, that's not what I meant. You dance very well."

She forced a smile. "Thanks. So do you."

He started to speak just as the music ended, and then began again. The tango. A couple nearby groaned and left the floor. Two more followed. Only Cal and Amelia and two couples were left.

"And a one, and a two," he teased in her ear.

He drew her into the rhythm, delighted at the way her small feet followed his big ones perfectly as they drew together, moved apart, drew together again, all with a series of slow sliding steps and quick darting ones.

"This is awesome," she whispered, caught up in the excitement.

"Awesome." He could barely get the words out. He felt her firm breasts pressing hard into his chest, felt them harden at the tips. He felt her heart like a wild thing, beating into his. He smelled the faint floral perfume she wore and the fresh womanly smell of her.

His hand tightened at her back, bringing her even closer. Now his breath was also coming quickly, like his heartbeat. This was dangerous. He should stop. He should take her back to their table and drink something heavy enough to calm his nerves.

Except that it felt so damned good to be this close to her. He was trapped in the sheer sensuality of the tango, bound to her by more than a dance, more than a shared pleasure of movement.

She almost groaned aloud. His body was muscular without it being obvious, and his strength was as apparent even in dance as it was on the gym floor doing martial arts.

If only the dance would never end, she thought recklessly as she forced her gaze to remain at his collar. She couldn't look up. He mustn't see what she felt. It would be as plain as a whisper in her eyes.

They moved as one person, smoothly, seductively, interpreting the music with such grace that the two other couples attempting the tango actually moved to the sidelines just to watch.

The two people themselves were oblivious to their spectators. They were lost in the music and each other, caught in a web of growing hunger, need, exquisite pleasure.

His hand contracted around hers. "This is a bad idea," he ground out, feeling the passion rise abruptly.

"Very bad," she choked.

He thought that if the music lasted one minute longer, the dinner crowd was going to be shocked…

And just as he thought it, the music cooed to an end. And sudden applause from the sidelines saved Cal from an embarrassing interlude.

He laughed. So did Amelia. They made bows and went quickly back to their table, avoiding any more stares.

Cal was happy to sit down with his feet under the table and be only visible from the waist up. It had been a near thing. He didn't like his loss of control. It was disturbing. Amelia was far too young for any sudden approaches on his part. And he didn't want attachments. He couldn't afford them.

"Don't look now, but I think we won," she said in a stage whisper.

He chuckled. "Apparently."

She let out a breath and sipped quickly cooling coffee to help still her nerves. Thank goodness her hands didn't shake!

"I'm out of breath," she exclaimed, stating the obvious. "I don't get in much practice."

"Neither do I. I love tango," he added as his own pulse slowed.

"I do, too, but I haven't had anybody to practice with since Ty left town."

Ty Harding, she meant, and he felt his neck hairs stand on end. He wasn't jealous, of course. That would be absurd. He took another sip of coffee. He wanted to leave, but he didn't know how to put it across without sounding as if he was tired of her company. He wasn't. He was trying to avoid complications. Big ones.

She whistled softly. "I'm sorry, but do you think we could go home?" she asked, surprising him. "I have a big test coming up Monday and there's all the housework to get done, as well. Weekends are busy," she added, hoping that she wasn't making him feel that she hated his company.

"I was just thinking that I have to see some people tomorrow," he laughed, relieved. "Yes, I need to go, too."

She smiled her relief.

He left her at her front door. He looked down at her quietly. His whole being was in turmoil. She wasn't absurdly pretty. Her figure, while nice, wasn't extraordinary. She was young and sweet and not at all sensuous. Except that she stirred him up more than any woman in recent years. It was unwelcome. He wasn't ready to become obsessed over a woman.

She looked up at him, perceptive to his emotions. That tango had done something to both of them. Best not to allude to it, she thought.

"I had a great time," she said, grinning. "Thanks. For supper and the dancing."

"I had a good time myself," he said.

"Well…"

His head jerked to one side. "Well."

She drew in a breath. "You go back overseas soon, don't you?"

He nodded. "You may not see me for a few days. I have things to do before I leave."

She nodded, too. She understood what he was saying. He

was going to keep his distance because that dance had moved him as it moved her.

"Don't get killed," she said firmly.

He shrugged.

"Okay, don't get shot," she emphasized.

He smiled involuntarily. "Worried about me?"

"That would make me sound proprietary," she said with a smile back. "And we both know you can't be appropriated."

He pursed his lips and chuckled. "Nice perception."

She held out a hand, palm up, and frowned. "There isn't any perception. It's too dry!"

He burst out laughing and suddenly gathered her close and hugged the breath out of her. "Damn, you're fun to be with, Amelia," he said at her ear. He drew in a breath, which brought them even closer. "But I'm going to back off, and you know why."

"Of course I know why," she said softly. "I won't sulk."

"I know that, too." He didn't add that it hurt him to do it, because he had a pretty good idea that she was hiding more than she realized.

"Just come home."

He drew back and kissed her hair. "I will." He let her go and forced a smile. "Tell your granddad that when I get back, we'll have that chess match he's been promising me."

"I'll tell him," she said, and grinned. Her face was going to freeze in that position, but it sure beat bawling.

"Okay, then. See you," he added.

"See you, Cal."

She turned and went inside quickly, before he could see that she was acting for all she was worth.

Cal went home and had a full glass of whiskey with one ice cube. And he slept until almost noon.

Amelia groaned when she saw her great-aunt Valeria pull up at the front of the house in her ancient Mercedes. She could have afforded ten new ones, but this one suited her and she refused to give it up.

She was tall and willowy at sixty-six, dark-haired and dark-eyed and always looked as if she was sucking on a lemon. She was wearing a black dress that came to just under her knees with a sweater. It was in the eighties, but she wore a sweater when it was ten degrees warmer. She always felt cold. Amelia had wondered sometimes, wickedly, if the woman had ice where her heart should have been.

"Hello, Amelia," she said curtly, eyeing her great-niece with a disapproving glance. "Still going around in those horrible dungarees and T-shirts. Can't you dress more appropriately?"

"This is appropriately for a college student, Aunt Val," Amelia replied.

"Aunt Valeria," she corrected coldly. "I detest abbreviated names."

"Sorry," she replied, and didn't mean it.

Just as Valeria opened her mouth to speak, Amelia's grandfather came out on the porch.

"Valeria," he greeted his sister. "It's nice to have you here for a few days."

"Two days," he was corrected, and she tolerated a hug from him. "My luggage is in the trunk. I hope you don't have car thieves around here," she added.

"We aren't San Antonio," Amelia said without thinking, because in some areas of the city, that had been a problem. "Or even Victoria," she added mischievously.

"San Antonio has a symphony orchestra and a ballet company. Even an opera company," she informed Amelia haughtily. "And there are no common thieves where I live in Victoria!"

"Excuse me," Amelia apologized. But she didn't mean it.

"Stop being such a sourpuss," Harris chided.

She glared at her brother. "I know about these small towns. You're overrun with immigrants and criminals!"

Amelia started to speak, and it wouldn't have been happy words.

Her grandfather cut her off. "Let me show you to your room," he said quickly.

"You only have one guest room, and I know where it is," she snapped.

She went down the hall. Amelia and her grandfather exchanged resigned glances. Well, it was only for a couple of days. Surely, they could survive it!

Two days later, Amelia was praying for aliens to come down and kidnap the older woman and take her anywhere except here.

When she mentioned it to her grandfather, he had to stifle laughter. Both of them tiptoed around Valeria, who was the most demanding house guest anyone had ever had to put up with.

With pure mischief, Amelia introduced her great-aunt to an episode of *Fawlty Towers*, an old British situation comedy that featured a woman who was the living fictional image of Valeria Harris.

Her grandfather gave her such a glare that she felt scorched. She gave him an angelic smile. And pushed Play.

To her surprise, Valeria roared with laughter as the elderly woman on the screen refused to turn on her hearing aid to save the batteries, so that anyone trying to communicate with her had to shout.

Amelia and her grandfather exchanged amused and surprised glances.

When the show ended, Valeria was fanning herself. "What an amazing program! Where can I find it on TV?" she asked.

"It's rather old," Amelia replied. "And you have to get it on disc. Or on one of the streaming channels."

"Disc? Streaming channels?" Valeria was all at sea.

"I'll explain," Amelia said softly, and she did.

Valeria just let out a sigh. "I don't watch television, as a rule.

Most of it is so outrageous! I only watch old movies on the classics channel, when people had to act with all their clothes on. I'm sure it was much harder then," she added with a snarky smile.

She glanced at them. "I think I might stay another few days," she said, glancing around. "But you will have to cook with less grease, Amelia. I simply can't tolerate it!"

Amelia swallowed. "Yes, Aunt Valeria." A few more days. A few more days! Hell must feel like this…

"And some tea would be nice now, don't you think?" Valeria added.

Chapter Eight

A few more days. A few more days! Amelia was frozen in place in absolute horror.

Valeria didn't notice. She was leaning back with her eyes closed. "And Jasmine tea, none of that silly modern concoction. With one packet—only one—of that sweetener I like." She sighed.

Amelia almost choked. "Yes. I'll just…go make it." She walked away stiff-legged, thinking hell must feel like this.

Her grandfather, reading her very well, sat with twinkling eyes, watching his sister. "It's nice of you to extend your visit, especially considering the circumstances," he said pleasantly.

Her eyes flew open. "Circumstances? What circumstances?"

"Our neighbor, the one who takes Amelia dancing, just came down with a nasty fever. And he was just over here the day before you came. Did you notice how flushed Amelia looks?" He frowned. "She was exposed. She might even have it…"

Valeria rocketed out of her chair. "How dare you both expose me to something infectious! You know how fragile I am! The very nerve…and that man is a hired killer. What is Amelia thinking? You let her go places with such a person? Think of the scandal if it ever gets out that my great-niece is dating a…a…hit man!"

"Valeria, he's a soldier…"

"A hired killer!" she persisted. "The stain on our family name would never come off. People, common people, would gossip about us! The shame of it. Jacob, how could you?"

Amelia poked her head out of the kitchen door. "What's going on?"

Valeria wheeled, her face red with rage. "You're dating a hired killer. You'll put the family name in the toilet, Amelia. You'll shame us all over south Texas! And besides that, you've exposed me to a disease! How could you! How could both of you do this to me...? I am leaving!"

Valeria stomped down the hall to her room, still muttering.

Amelia looked at her grandfather with wide eyes.

He grinned and put his forefinger to his lips. She just nodded and smiled.

Fifteen minutes later, Valeria was headed back to Victoria.

"Brilliant," Amelia applauded him. "Just brilliant." She laughed. "I thought I'd go nuts. Sorry, Granddaddy, I know she's your only living relative besides me. But she's such a pain!"

"She's always been a pain. She erupts," he added. "She has rages. She lashes out. She pushed a waiter over a table one time and broke his arm. Her late husband had to pay damages in a civil suit, and she was lucky they didn't prosecute it as attempted homicide." He shook his head. "She's always sorry later, but that doesn't help much. She's capable of anything in those moods."

"I know. That's why I bit my tongue." She sighed. "She has issues."

"Many." He chuckled. "But she's gone."

"I'll throw confetti. And I'm not giving up my lovely olive oil, whatever she says. Grease!" She threw up her hands. "It's the best cooking oil in the world!"

"And tastes great," he added.

"Thank you for braving the dragon," she said. "If I had a medal, I'd give you one."

"Thank you."

"That was a nasty remark she made about Cal," she muttered. "She's very…" She waved her hand.

"Straitlaced?" He nodded. "Yes, she is. She has an overworked sense of family honor. The family name must never be besmirched!" He shook his head and laughed. "I wrote something naughty on the side of the principal's car our senior year in high school. She pushed me down that sheer wall behind the school building. I broke my arm."

"What?"

"She was very sorry afterward," he said. "I've always thought she had some undiscovered mental issues, to be honest," he told Amelia.

"What did your parents say?" she asked.

"They had a long talk with her about controlling her temper, but she was crying and apologizing and swearing she'd never do anything like it again. They just accepted that it was bad temper."

"It doesn't sound like bad temper," she pointed out.

"I know." He sighed. "They didn't believe in mental health issues, you see. Back when they were growing up, it was a taboo subject in a small, rural town like Jacobsville."

"She could have killed you!" Amelia pointed out.

"I did mention that."

"And?"

"She cried harder and hugged me half to death."

She sighed. "Still, they should have taken her to the nearest mental health clinic."

"Bite your tongue, girl," he teased. "And besmirch the family name by accusing her of being nuts?"

"It isn't nuts if you have behavioral problems."

"You're preaching to the choir. But not to Valeria. She was horrified that anyone would think she wasn't mentally sound!"

"At least she doesn't have to worry about it now, right? She was married…"

"She kept the family name and didn't take her husband's, have you forgotten?"

She pursed her lips and whistled.

"She said it was too much work to change all those documents, so she kept her family name. Her husband was an only child, and his father and mother were already dead. He was sort of a wimp," he added, chuckling.

She smiled. "I barely remember him. He was funny."

"Yes, he was, but Valeria told him how to do everything. He left her a fortune. Which I'm often reminded that she plans to leave to her dog, or her favorite charity of the week."

"We do very well without a lot of money," she pointed out.

"I saved when I was young and invested wisely," he agreed. "So now the dividends keep us in grocery money and incidentals."

"I could get a part-time job," she began.

"What for? You've seen a fur coat you want to buy?" he teased.

She hugged him. "I feel like I'm not carrying my weight," she said. "And besides, there's college…"

"College is a public one, so no exorbitant fees," she was reminded. "Books are the only real expense."

"I only have two, and I got used ones," she said. "And I get my degree next month."

"So you do," he said, smiling. "Then, on to school in San Antonio."

She hesitated. "I don't know," she said. She was thinking of the expense. She couldn't afford a car and there was barely enough money to manage as it was.

"Valeria values education," he reminded her. "She'd probably be happy to pay for your expenses."

"I think she might draw the line at helping fund me in learning how to blow up stuff," she pointed out.

"We wouldn't tell her that part," he teased.

She laughed. "I've been looking into scholarships. My grades are good. It's the transportation part of it," she added on a sigh. "And I don't want to live on campus. You don't get to pick your roommate and I'm not living with some strange boy!"

He ground his teeth together. "Valeria would never go for that, modern times or not."

"Exactly."

"We might arrange for you to ride with someone," he said.

She sighed. "There aren't that many people who work in San Antonio and live here," she said.

"Well, we'll worry about it after you graduate. Did you invite our neighbor?" he added.

She smiled. "Cal's going off on a mission in a couple of weeks. He won't be here, so I didn't ask."

He cocked his head and studied her. "And…?"

He knew her too well. She shrugged. "Things got a little… complicated…while we were doing the tango at Fernando's. So he said we needed a cooling-off period. Like he's not coming around for a while, until we both forget it."

He grew solemn. He nodded. "Considering his line of work, that was a wise decision. And I applaud his consideration for you."

"Me, too, but…"

"He's not ready to settle down," he interrupted. "Don't push. If you're patient, things will work out."

"Do you think so?" she asked.

He drew in a breath. "He was a policeman, which means he's seen some pretty awful things. But combat is another thing altogether. Most men who survive it never want to go back."

"But he was in the military," she pointed out.

"He was in the unit that more or less cleared away the debris, not the one that did the hard fighting. I don't think he's yet seen the madness that overcomes men in killing situations."

"You mean, he might give it up voluntarily one day?"

He nodded. "Time will tell."

"I hope you're right," she said on a sigh. She forced a smile. "Meanwhile, I'm going to graduate and start working on scholarships and transportation."

"That's the spirit!"

She missed Cal. It was amazing that she missed him so much. She graduated, with her grandfather in the audience, cheering when she received her diploma and turned her tassel. She worked hard on scholarship requests.

"I'm so tired of filling out forms," she wailed as they finished supper one night.

"It will be worth it," he promised. He grimaced. "Sugar, will you get me a couple of those acid reflux tablets?"

"Heartburn again?" she asked, fetching the bottle. "You need to talk to your doctor. He might have a preventative that would help."

"I go next month," he reminded her. "Meanwhile, these work. Sort of," he added as he chewed the tablets and swallowed them. The pain was pretty bad. He took deep breaths. Odd, how nauseated he felt. He was sweating. Of course, it was late summer. Even with air-conditioning, the house was hot.

"We haven't talked about the house," he said after the pain passed.

Her eyebrows arched.

"I haven't been quite honest with you. I guess I need to be."

"What do you mean?"

"You know those reverse mortgages you hear about on television? Well, I did that. I mean, I do have some investments, but they wouldn't keep us for a week." He shrugged. "It seemed the best thing to do, so that we didn't have to worry about money, you know?"

Her sense of security took a nosedive. "They aren't going to repossess the house or anything?"

"Of course not," he said, and patted her hand where it lay on the tablecloth. "But when I kick the bucket, they'll take possession, is what I mean."

"You're not doing that until I'm old, too," she said firmly.

He chuckled. "Well, I'm not planning to go, you know," he told her. "I'm just mentioning it. You'll get the stocks and bonds. They aren't worth much, I'm afraid."

"I'd rather have you than any of it," she said, and she smiled.

He smiled back. "You've been a joy to live with, sugar," he said. "I'm sorry you lost your parents, but I'm happy that I still have you."

"I've loved living here," she said. "And you're not leaving. Got that?" she asked firmly.

He chuckled. "Yes. I've got it."

It worried her, that her grandfather was sharing financial stuff with her. He'd never done that before. And he was eating that acid reflux medicine like candy. It couldn't be good for him. At least he did have an appointment to see his doctor. Maybe there was a stronger medicine. Meanwhile, she cooked nothing that was spicy.

Cal had stopped by just long enough to say goodbye, on his way overseas, a few days before she'd graduated. He wouldn't tell them where he was going, but he said it wouldn't be a lengthy stay.

"Take care of my friend, here," he told Jacob, shaking hands as he nodded toward Amelia. "Keep her out of mischief."

"Not to worry, she doesn't have anything explosive around here," her grandfather assured him.

He grinned. "See that you behave," he told her firmly, and hugged her just for a few seconds. "I'll be back before you know it."

She nodded, choking back tears with a big smile. "You be careful."

"I'm always careful," he drawled. He stared at her for just a few seconds longer than he should have and then dragged his eyes away. "I'll see you both."

They waved him off. Amelia swiped at a tear that escaped.

"He's fighting it, but he feels something," her grandfather said softly. "It shows."

"Really?" She turned to him, her eyes brimming with hope and anguish.

He nodded. He smiled. "Patience."

She swallowed. "Patience," she agreed.

"And day after tomorrow is graduation," he pointed out with a grin. "Got everything laid out?"

"Oh, yes. I forgot to tell Cal," she added with a grimace. "Well, he was leaving anyway, so he couldn't have come."

"He realized that. He left you something."

"What?" she asked excitedly.

"After graduation, he said, and that's when you'll get it," he replied with a smug look.

"Granddaddy!"

"Threats and intimidation won't work. You'll have to wait."

She sighed. "I know. Patience."

He grinned from ear to ear. "Exactly!"

Cal got off the plane with the rest of his small group. Eb was with them on this mission, because it was the most important one of all. This battle would decide the future of the small country they were trying to save.

Cy Parks was bending over a radiant Juba, handing him a Bowie knife in a beautiful, beaded rawhide sheath dripping fringe.

"That's some knife," Cal remarked to Eb Scott.

He chuckled. "Nobody knows more about knives than Cy."

"I noticed. He's deadly."

"One of my oldest friends," Eb added. He glanced at Micah Steele, who was broody. "Micah's having some family issues," he said. "I hope he'll keep his mind on what we're doing."

"He usually does. Or seems to," Cal added, because he still didn't know the group that well. "There's Eduardo," he said, waving to a big, smiling man with long black hair unbound. "I met him a few years ago. He likes to go to Fernando's in San Antonio and watch the dancers."

"He's a good man."

"One of the best. But those," he indicated Laremos, Archer and Dutch, "are the real legends."

"Headed for retirement after this," Eb confided. "They have other interests now." He studied the other man. "Are you sure this is the kind of life you want to live?" he asked abruptly.

Cal frowned. "Well, yes..."

"You were a cop. That's conventional. This," he said, indicating their surroundings, "isn't." His eyes bored into Cal's. "So far, you've seen logistics. You've never seen war the way it's waged here."

Cal just smiled. "You see a lot in police work. And I was in the military."

"You weren't a front-line soldier, were you?" he asked wisely.

Cal grimaced. "Well, no."

"You don't see this kind of warfare other places," Eb replied. "It's not too late to turn back."

Cal's eyebrows arched.

Eb knew a lost cause when he saw one. He laughed shortly. "Okay. I'm convinced. Just keep close to us when the shooting starts, all right? It's easy to lose track of where your comrades are. Ngawa isn't like other places, other wars."

Cal nodded. "I've read about that."

Yes, read about it, not experienced it, Eb was thinking. This kind of warfare had left many a man either drowning the memories in alcohol or, sometimes, eating bullets. Cal had a soft heart, and that could be a liability. He'd do what he could to shield him. But it might not be enough.

"And here we are again," Rodrigo Ramirez said with a grin as he joined them.

"How can the DEA spare you?" Eb teased, shaking hands.

"Because they don't know I'm here, compadre," he whispered loudly. "Surveillance is a misery I try to avoid. Six days in a parked car, trying to look unobtrusive," he groaned.

"At least I hope the cars were changed daily."

"Twice daily, and it did not help," Ramirez muttered.

"Well, this will make you long for it."

"You think?" Ramirez flashed him a grin and went to speak to the others.

Cal had seen horrible things. He thought they were horrible. In retrospect, after he returned to the States much later, he realized that those things in the past were only minor disturbances.

Juba, the Ngawan child the group of Americans had adopted as part of their contingent, ran toward a nearby building for cover, just as the worst of the firefight began. A ragged soldier behind a machine gun had just thrown a small pack into the doorway. He aimed and shot it the instant Juba jumped over it. Cy Parks had yelled and yelled, but Juba hadn't stopped. Not until the explosion. Not until Juba screamed and the world went up in a rain of straw and pieces of lumber and pieces of Juba.

"Oh, God," Cy groaned when they managed to get to what was left of the little boy. The band of AK ammo around his thin body was lying in pieces around him. He was missing an arm and a leg and there was a huge gash in his small belly from which matter exuded.

They knew there was no power on earth that would save him.

They used pain medication from their packs to stop the screaming. Then Cy sat with the agonized child in his arms, held close, wrapped in the woven blanket Juba wore, talking softly to him in a broken voice, until he, mercifully, died. While the soldiers who had set the trap lounged in a nearby machine-gun nest that held the whole unit at bay, catcalling that the kid was a waste of skin and soon they'd do the same thing to his so-called friends.

Nobody spoke. Cy gently laid the little boy down, closed his eyes. When he looked up, his green eyes were like emerald flames. The fury inside him was visible. He got up, his .45 cocked and ready, his attention fixed on the machine-gun nest from which the explosives had been thrown. From where the catcalls were still coming.

"Cy, no!" Eb Scott yelled above the gunfire.

But they were pinned down. There was almost no cover. They lay flat in the dirt of the small village, bullets hitting around them like hail.

Cy didn't hear, didn't answer. His furious gaze was fixed on the machine gunner who'd made, and set, the explosive that had killed Juba. The man had been bragging loudly about his talent while Juba died in Cy's arms.

Cy plowed right toward the nest, cursing every step of the way, ignoring the shouts of his comrades.

The gunner laughed as he turned the machine gun on the man approaching. Cy walked right into the gunfire, oblivious to the bullets that, amazingly, mostly missed, until he reached the gunner and emptied the .45 into him at point-blank range.

"Look out!" Cal yelled as two men started toward him from behind.

Cy reacted immediately, whirling. Two knives flew from under the loose sleeves of his jacket, burying themselves up to the hilt in the approaching insurgents. Cal had never seen anything like it.

Cy whirled, bleeding, and started toward the rest of the men firing at them from cover where the dead machine gunner lay.

"Bring him down!" Eb yelled over the gunfire.

Laremos and Dutch and Archer tackled him, and it took all three of them to stop him. They managed it just as three other insurgents opened fire directly at their grieving, furious comrade.

Cal was firing for all he was worth. He was usually one of the most accurate shooters. But all around him, men were screaming in pain. Insurgents on both sides were bleeding from wounds, everything from lost limbs to fatal hits in the body. It was a nightmare of sounds and smells. He was shaking. He hadn't realized it. He was firing, firing, and the gun was empty, but he couldn't stop. Despite his service on the police force, his time in the military, this was a type of gore he'd never experienced in his life.

Eb was yelling at him, but he was deaf to his comrade's voice. All he could hear were the screams. All he could see was blood, blood, more blood…!

"Fall back!" Eb yelled again.

Eduardo grabbed him by his pant leg and dragged him backward with the retreating group. At the edge of his vision, he saw what was left of Juba. The little boy had been laughing with them, begging chocolate as they massed for the attack, carrying an AK that weighed almost as much as he did. The bullets were still flying as both sides tried to gain ground. But Cal was so disoriented that he wasn't sure where his lines even were, and still Eduardo dragged him backward, flat on the ground, with dust filling his mouth, his vision, with bullets hitting all around them.

And even as reinforcements arrived, he was still lost in the horror of it.

Cal realized what Eb Scott had tried to spare him. This was unlike police work. Commando war was down and dirty, bloody, full of mangled, bleeding bodies, of people screaming from wounds that left them without arms or legs or both. It was a war where children carrying AKs and pistols and rocket launchers, hyped up on drugs, came at them in droves and were cut down. Children the age of Juba, who had known nothing except war.

They'd reloaded their weapons during a lull, and they were waiting for the signal to attack again. As they moved forward, Cal spotted one of the child combatants lying on the ground with his leg half off, screaming. Cal turned toward him, despite the fact that the child was with the enemy forces. He needed help.

Eb was yelling at him, yelling for all he was worth. Cal couldn't make out the words buried in gunfire.

As he approached the child, the boy's hand went to a .45 automatic that had been lying under him. He laughed as he shot at Cal, just one shot, before the loss of blood led him to unconsciousness and then death.

Cal felt the blow against his upper thigh, as if someone had beaten it with a fist. He was suddenly weak, and he couldn't get up. How odd, he thought. Nothing was wrong with him. Why couldn't he get to his feet?

Eb was standing over him, calling for medical supplies, his eyes wild.

He tried to ask why Eb looked so worried. He felt wetness under him. He looked down. He was bleeding. He was bleeding badly. Had he been shot? He was only trying to help the boy.

His eyes went to the child who'd shot him. The pistol was lying beside him. His eyes were open. His leg was in a pool of blood.

"The…child…" Cal could barely speak. How odd.

"Dead," Eb said coldly.

"Still…bleeding," he added. The boy couldn't be dead because blood was still pumping out of him.

"You can't save someone with a wound like that," Eb said calmly as he started to apply bandages. "He's dead. His body hasn't realized it yet. He only has a minute or two left."

Micah Steele was beside him now with a hypodermic needle. He shot it right into the vein at the crook of Cal's elbow.

"What...?" he started to ask. Then the pain hit him. All at once. Fire. Blood. Anguish. He'd never felt anything so horrible. He wasn't going to start yelling. Men didn't do that. Except they did. He groaned aloud.

"Peace, compadre," his friend Eduardo said from somewhere close by. "Be still. Let the medicine work."

There was another shot. The pain began to recede, bit by bit. He was staring around at all the bodies. There were so many. Some were children, boys of grammar school age who would never grow up to be doctors or lawyers or even soldiers. Boys. Little boys. Torn to pieces by bullets, by bombs, by people, well-meaning people, who only wanted to save their government so that they could grow up in a safe place, with hope for the future. Bright ideals. Swimming in blood. So much blood...

"They're bringing Cal home today," Amelia's grandfather told her when he came home from the post office.

She brightened. Until she chewed on the words he'd chosen. Not Cal's coming home. Somebody was bringing him home. Whole other connotation.

"Bringing him...?" Her heart stopped in her chest.

He sat down at the table, dropping the few pieces of mail onto the tablecloth. "He was badly wounded," he told her. "It's going to be a long recuperation."

"Oh, no!" She sat down, heavily. "But, he's alive?" she added quickly.

He nodded. "Alive. Eb and his men, some of them, got back last night." His face was hard. "I think it was a battle that none of them will ever forget. And some of them will never be the same. Cal, especially."

"That bad?" she asked in a husky tone.

He nodded. "That bad."

She drew in a long breath. "I can take care of him," she said.

"Let's wait and see if they send some of their own people," her grandfather told her.

"You're worried about gossip," she said.

He smiled. "Really?"

She grimaced. "Sorry. I knew better."

"Valeria, now, that's another story."

"What she doesn't know won't bother her," she reminded him with a grin.

"I suppose so," he conceded. He reached again for the bottle of acid reflux medicine.

"When is that doctor's appointment?" she asked.

"Three weeks," he said. "Not that long a wait."

"You could see somebody sooner, at one of those walk-in clinics," she suggested.

He shrugged. "I'd rather see my own doctor."

"You can't bully the people in the walk-in clinic," she translated.

He chuckled. "I'm okay. Just heartburn. Now stop worrying!"

She gave in. "Okay."

He patted her on the back on his way to get a Coke out of the fridge. "I'm glad you worry about me. Now stop doing it."

She laughed, as she was meant to.

Cal came home in an ambulance. Eb Scott drove up just as Amelia came running from across the street.

She was terrified and unable to hide it. She followed the men with the gurney, and Eb, into Cal's house and waited while they settled him on his bed.

"I'll see about a private duty nurse," Eb began.

"I don't need a nurse," Cal said through his teeth. "I'll be fine. I can walk!"

"No, actually, you can't," Eb said, aware of Amelia hovering.

"I'll take care of him," she said quietly. "What do I need to do?"

"Get a rope," Eb said curtly. "A strong one. We'll tie him to the bed!"

"I said, I can walk!" Cal tried to get up.

"Aaaaaaah!" Amelia said, using the tone her grandmother had always used with her when she tried to do something stupid. She put her hands against his broad chest where his shirt was parted in front and pushed gently until he was horizontal. His eyes were wild. She'd never seen such an expression. "You aren't going anywhere," she said shortly.

"Thank God," Eb said under his breath as Cal made one small effort to resist her and abruptly gave in and lay back down—not without a harsh glare.

"You have prescriptions," Eb said. "I'll go get them filled. You'll need groceries. I'll see if I can find somebody to cook for you…"

"I can cook," Amelia said. "I even know how to bribe him with his favorite food," she added.

Eb managed a short laugh. "Okay. Are you sure?" he added. "It's not a pretty wound and it will need to be watched for signs of infection."

"I can blow stuff up," she said, and wondered why both men looked so traumatized when she said that. "I'm not squeamish."

"All right, then," Eb said gently. "I'll go to the pharmacy and the grocery store."

"Petty cash is in a jar on the kitchen table," Cal said heavily.

"Not a problem." Eb went out behind the ambulance guys and closed the door.

Amelia looked down at him, thankful that he was still alive, even if he was wounded. But the way he looked was troubling. She'd never seen that expression on his face in all the time she'd known him.

"It was bad, wasn't it?" she asked.

His dark eyes were shimmery with pain. "You have no idea."

"Well, you're home and safe now," she said. "I'll take care of you," she added quietly. "It's all right."

He was fighting horrible memories. Hearing things, seeing things he could never share except with a comrade who'd been there. He looked at Amelia, but he didn't see her. He saw Juba, in pieces on the killing ground. It was a picture he was never going to get out of his mind.

His life was never going to be the same again. And this was just the beginning of the nightmare as he tried to adjust to life as it would be from now on. Eb had been right. He had no idea what he was letting himself in for. Now he had to try to live with it.

Chapter Nine

Amelia cooked for him and kept the house clean. Her grandfather came and sat by Cal's bedside sometimes. He and the younger man spoke with the door closed, shutting Amelia out. It was a conversation she wasn't allowed to participate in.

"You guys shut me out," she complained to her grandfather the week Cal came home, while she was fixing supper. She carried plates across to Cal for each meal, even breakfast.

"You're not ready to hear these kinds of stories, sugar," he said gently.

"I'm no wimp," she teased.

"No. But this isn't polite conversation, either," he said solemnly. "Cal needs to talk to somebody who's been where he is right now. Amelia," he added quietly, "this is going to be a long haul. He isn't ever going to be the man you knew again."

She finished frying chicken, took it up and moved the pan off the burner as she clicked it off.

"You're scaring me," she said.

"Cal was a policeman," he said. "You see terrible things when you do police work. But this kind of war that he's seen, it's not something he can share with you."

She sighed. "I want to help."

"Be his friend," he said simply. "You never push, which is just what he needs. I can listen to him and advise. But what you can do to help is just keep him fed and quiet, while he tries to get past it."

She grimaced. "Was it really bad?"

He nodded. "I did spec ops," he said. "But even I didn't see the kind of combat he was exposed to."

"Did they accomplish what they meant to do, at least?"

"Yes. They put the legitimate government back in power," he replied. "And it was a noble thing. They saved thousands of lives." He smiled. "There were people from all over Africa, all over the world, helping. Combatants and support people, all of whom volunteered and risked their lives to support the cause."

"It must be nice, to make a difference like that," she said.

"It is. But there's a terrible cost. Cal is paying it right now."

She grimaced. "He'll get over it, though, right?"

He hesitated. "He'll learn to live with it," he said. Which wasn't the same thing. Not at all.

She became Cal's unofficial home health unit. He didn't want her to see what was under the big bandage on his thigh, but he was running a fever by the fourth day, and she insisted.

His leg was in bad shape. There was a small hole in the front of his thigh, and a much bigger one in the back of it. The flesh around it was red and hot.

"I'm calling Eb," she said.

"It's just healing," he argued.

"It's just rotting off," she replied, and kept dialing.

Eb came over with a tall, husky blond man who looked more like a wrestler than a doctor. He probed and cleaned the wound and dressed it again.

"I'm changing the antibiotic," he told Cal. "And you need probiotics, as well." He looked up at a worried Amelia. "Do you…?"

"Yes," she said, nodding. "I have to cook for my grandfather and keep him healthy. I don't feed him or Cal anything fried except an occasional chicken, and I cook mostly veggies and fish dishes. With probiotics."

He smiled. "Good."

"How's Colby?" Cal asked, because during that two-day firefight, Micah Steele had been forced to amputate a fellow combatant's arm in the field.

"Not adjusting well at all," Micah replied. "I'm sending him to a psychologist I know in Houston. Good doctor. Keeps snakes." He shuddered.

"Nothing wrong with boa constrictors," Cal said. "I used to have one."

"I like big lizards," Amelia said.

They both stared at her.

She shrugged and grinned.

"Okay," Micah said as he got up. "Here." He handed Amelia a prescription. "Lucky for you I didn't quit medicine until after I got my license. I keep it. Comes in handy."

"He'll be okay?" Amelia asked as he stood up.

"If he does what he's told," the big blond man replied.

"I'll make sure he does," Amelia said. "Thanks."

He smiled. "If it doesn't improve in three or four days, have Eb call me. I live in Nassau, but I'm up this way pretty often on business."

"Okay."

"He's nice," Amelia told Cal.

He drew in a long breath. "The whole unit's like that. I think…" He picked up his cell phone from the bedside table. "Hello?"

There was a pause. He glanced at Amelia and away. "No, I've got all I need. Yes, I know how you feel about sick people. No problem. Sure. Bye."

He hung up. It was a woman, Amelia was certain of it. But she just smiled. "I'll go get your prescription filled."

"They've got my credit card on file," he said. "I'll call and have the medicine charged."

"Okay."

* * *

Amelia went out and he watched her with concern. She was too involved with him. He was going to have to work through this bad time, and he didn't know how he was going to cope with the trauma. Edie had phoned to tell him she was glad he was alive but, of course, she wasn't coming near him. She couldn't bear sickness. It was just a failing she couldn't help.

He thought about how nurturing Amelia was, and he felt guilty. He wanted her. It was a growing problem. He wasn't certain how to cope. He didn't want to get tangled up with a girl her age, and especially with an innocent. She was getting to him.

Combined with the problems he already had, Amelia was one he didn't want to have to tackle. He was going to have to step very carefully. He didn't want to hurt her.

Meanwhile, he was dealing with a trauma he'd never experienced. It had sounded like such a great line of work. Loads of money, excitement, adventure. Eb had tried to warn him. He hadn't listened. Now he was going to pay the price.

Of course he'd seen bad things while he was doing police work. Life on patrol was never boring, you worked wrecks, you worked domestic disturbances, gang warfare, escaping criminals, all sorts of things. But you didn't generally see people blown apart.

Like the rest of the unit, he'd become fond of Juba, the orphan they looked after when they were on the ground. He was just a kid, but already he could field strip the old AK-47 he'd been given by a comrade, and he knew how to clean it. It was his most prized possession.

Cy Parks had taken the loss harder than any of the rest. He had a young son back home in the States, and he had naturally gravitated toward the young boy. They became close. Cy was always bringing him presents, things he'd probably never seen, like Game Boys and drones.

Then, in a space of seconds, Juba had disobeyed a yelled

order to stop. He'd gone into a building and hadn't seen the explosive that Cy had spotted. Body parts rained down along with part of the building the bomb had been set in. Not too far away, a cheer was heard and then unrelenting taunts and catcalling. The men in the machine-gun nest who'd given the cheer would pay a hard price for it.

But that was to come later. In the meantime, Cy had cradled the boy in his arms—what was left of him. Amazing, that Juba was still conscious. They'd doped him as much as they dared, hoping the pain would recede just enough. Because he'd lost too much blood to live. Micah Steele had just shaken his head when the men watching asked about Juba's chances. The injuries were too great, the blood loss too much.

So Cy rocked him in his arms until he died. It was a memory that haunted all of them. But it wasn't the only one.

When Juba died, Cy went looking for the men who'd cheered when the building went up, the group that had bragged about setting the bomb.

Nobody had ever seen anything like it. Cy walked right into the bullets, firing as he went. The nest was in a pivotal area, and it had been stonewalling the foreign troops, making it impossible for them to relieve the company up ahead.

Cy changed all that. He took out three men in the space of a heartbeat. There was a fourth man who'd been sitting among the parts of an IED he was constructing. Cy dropped the automatic rifle and started throwing knives. There wasn't a lot left of the bomb maker when he was through.

Micah patched Cy up while he sat and smoldered, furious that the men who'd killed Juba had been granted such an easy death. He looked like death warmed up himself, but, God he was game! He got to his feet, patched wounds and all, refusing any pain meds, grabbed an automatic rifle and fell in with the company. Together, they marched into the thick of the battle.

The bomb that killed Juba wasn't the only one they encountered. There were others. Too many others. They were concealed in hidden spots, in cunning ways, the way you'd set a trap to catch a wild animal. Except that these devices didn't catch anything. They blew men to component parts.

They say you can get used to anything, Cal thought blandly, but it was a lie. You never got used to seeing things that he'd seen in combat. He would never forget it. Maybe it would dim, as a memory, as years went by. But despite the lure of big money and adventure, nothing would get him back into the field. Even police work would seem tame by comparison. He had every intention of going back to work for San Antonio PD when he was healed enough.

One of his comrades, Eduardo Perez, was the morale booster of the bunch. He had a bloodthirsty past, but something about the tone of this campaign had changed him. He became religious. He wasn't aggressive about it, but he did pray with any of the men who needed it, and because of his own ferocious past, the men respected him, even those who weren't religious. After the worst of the combat, when all the men were bandaging wounds and looking for extraction and trying to cope with even more horrible memories, Eduardo announced that he was going to study for the priesthood. In fact, another of their group, Jake Blair, was also questioning his own lifestyle. And Jake spooked even some of the worst men in the group. They called him "snake," because he could get into places most of them couldn't. The men with the best hearing couldn't detect even a footfall when he went out to scout for them. All he carried was a Bowie knife and a .45 auto. And he was never wounded. Not even once.

They'd started out with many sympathetic comrades. But they came back with only a handful. And most of them, oddly, ended up in Jacobsville. Because of Eb Scott's new anti-terrorism training camp, the town was becoming a name that people remembered. And the sting of battle memories was easier when shared.

Cal had wanted to talk over his experiences with the other

members of the group, but they were all coping in their own ways. It had been a godsend that Amelia's grandfather had been in special ops during the Mideast wars. He hadn't seen quite the things that Cal had. But his own experiences were not much less bloody, and they wore on his conscience. Cal looked to him more and more for guidance as he worked his way through the horror to some semblance of a normal life.

The fever was burning him alive. He felt sick to his stomach, as well. Amelia was taking such good care of him. She was so unlike Edie, who liked his company but wouldn't go near him while he was sick. He wondered why he even took the woman on dates. He felt no desire for her, none at all. That part of him that was sensual had gone into eclipse since Amelia came into his life. He thought about how innocent she was, how careful of her reputation here, in this very small rural community. She'd laughed when he mentioned it once. She said she didn't want to be that woman that everybody pointed out in stores. It sounded odd to him, who'd lived mostly in impersonal places, in cities. But as he spent more time in Jacobsville, he began to understand.

It wasn't really that people were judgmental. It was that they had certain standards that went back two centuries. They didn't apologize for them, or try to explain them. They were just part of the community. If you stepped outside the bounds of what was considered decent and right, you were looked at. No pressure. No censure. Just eyes, staring. Nonverbal restraint.

Before social media, that silent restraint had been responsible for keeping morality in check, for holding families together, for discouraging things that used divisions and tears. Here in Jacobsville, some people still felt that way, felt that tradition had a place at the table. People in very small towns were clannish. They were many generations of people who knew each other well, who thought and acted alike, who didn't easily accept radical viewpoints of any sort. And because Jacobsville hadn't really moved with the times, some transplanted city dwellers who'd tried to live here had moved right back into their former homes in cities. Not everybody could fit in. Not everybody wanted to.

Cal wanted to. He hoped he could. He loved Jacobsville. He loved the people, the customs, the feeling of belonging to a family. And it was. A family. A small community where most people shared relatives, who had a long history in this part of Texas. To Cal, who'd lived impersonally and anonymously for so long, it was a revelation.

And especially now, it felt very comfortable, while he tried to get back on his feet. Without Amelia and her grandfather, his recovery might not be as easy, and certainly not as nurturing. He'd never known any of his neighbors in apartments where he'd lived in the past. In Jacobsville, he quickly learned his surroundings, and the people who lived in them.

He moved restlessly in the bed. He didn't want to sleep. The nightmares came again and again. He hoped they might stop one day. He'd asked Amelia's grandfather about them. The older man had just said that they diminished. He didn't know if that meant in frequency or in vivid detail. He hoped it was both.

The front door opened. It had a familiar squeak, like in a haunted house movie. He loved the old place.

"I'm back," Amelia said, as she dropped her purse and jacket off on his sofa and made her way to the bedroom. "Two things," she said, holding up the bag. "A new antibiotic, and pain meds."

"I hate pain meds," he began.

She just sighed. "The pharmacist said that if you have to fight the pain along with the infection, you won't heal as fast," she said, and stared him down.

He made a face.

"That's what he said," she repeated. She cocked her head and smiled faintly. "Then he mentioned how you pill a cat, by rolling it up in a towel."

He sighed. "Okay. Pest," he added.

She grinned and went to get him something to drink with the pills.

He was too sick to eat supper. The medicine would work, she was sure, she was hopefully sure, but his fever was pretty high. Micah had said to give him Tylenol for the fever, which she did.

She took his temperature again. It was still high. "You need to be sponged down," she began.

"No." He said it very firmly for a sick man. He glowered at her. "I'm not having you bathe me in bed!"

"Oh, for God's sake, Cal," she began, throwing up her hands.

"When you've been married for a year, come back and we'll talk," he replied.

She made a face. "All right. But if the fever doesn't come down soon, I'm calling Eb Scott, and he can sponge you until the fever's down!"

He shifted. "Okay," he said after a minute.

"You are a prude," she accused as she started to leave.

"And you're bluffing," he said, with a knowing look that made her flush. "You know as much about men as I know about theoretical physics."

"Well, that may be, but I'm never going to learn it here."

He chuckled in spite of himself and groaned because any movement hurt his leg.

"The pain meds should kick in soon," she said encouragingly. "I wish you felt like eating. I made potato soup."

"My favorite," he sighed. His eyes closed. "Maybe later."

"Maybe later."

She pulled the covers over him. "I'll be in the living room reading if you need me…"

"You'll be at home taking care of your grandfather if I need you." He picked up his cell phone from the bedside table and showed it to her. "My phone has your number on speed dial. If I get into trouble, all I have to do is push one button."

She was reluctant, but he was in one of his stubborn moods,

so she knew it would do no good to argue. "Okay," she said on a sigh. "I'll leave. But I'll be back at suppertime."

"Bring soup," he said, and forced a smile. "Hopefully, my stomach will settle by then."

She beamed. "Optimism! I approve wholeheartedly!"

He smiled back. "And thank you, for all the kind care," he added.

She shrugged. "It's no more than you'd do for us, Cal," she replied with a smile. "See you later."

He reflected on that when she'd gone. Yes, he thought. If their situations were reversed, he'd be a fixture in their home. It was a revelation. He'd never been overly generous with his time in the past. But he was getting lessons in sacrifice both from Amelia and her grandfather. He hoped there would come a time when he could repay their kindness.

Amelia was back at suppertime, along with her grandfather. She carried in a bowl of potato soup, which Cal was now able to eat.

First, she checked his fever, and found that it was much reduced. "Thank goodness!" she said heartily.

"The meds are working," he replied. "I feel just a bit better."

"Bullet wounds take time to heal," Amelia's grandfather said as he dropped down into the easy chair they'd placed at Cal's bedside.

"You'd know," Amelia said. "Granny said you had more than one."

He chuckled. "I did, none of them drastic, thank God. And you got off lucky," he added to Cal. "An in-and-out wound without hitting bone. I won't go into how rare that is."

"Steele told me already," he chuckled as he ate. "Amelia, this is the best potato soup I've ever had, and I'm not exaggerating."

"I'm glad you like it."

"Now go home and let us talk," her grandfather said, but with a grin. "And yes, the soup was delicious. As usual. How about dessert, in about an hour?"

"Dessert?" Cal's eyebrows lifted.

"Chocolate cake with vanilla frosting," she said.

"My favorite," Cal sighed.

"Mine, too," the older man chuckled.

"I'll bring slices when I come back," she said. "Don't forget to take the antibiotic," she added to Cal. "It's three times a day, not two. And Tylenol for the fever in," she checked her watch, "two more hours."

Cal rolled his eyes. "Shades of Nurse Jane," he mused.

She laughed. "I'm better at blowing things up, but I can do nursing when needed," she said, and then wondered why he seemed paler. "You okay?" she asked quickly.

"I'm fine," he lied, and forced a smile.

"All right. Back in an hour," she said, and breezed out.

The older man waited until he heard the front door close before he spoke. "She doesn't know about IEDs, except how to make them," he pointed out. "And she'd never have said a word if she knew what you'd been through."

"I know that." He finished his soup and put the bowl down with a sigh. "I thought I was tough enough for any sort of military action," he said. "I was an MP when I was in the service, though, and I never got into any of the real fighting. When I came out, it was San Antonio PD. I thought I'd seen everything." His eyes closed. "Dear God, what human beings can do to one another!"

"Yes, I do understand," he replied. "It will take time for you to get past this, I won't lie to you. But eventually it will fade to just a bad memory."

"What about the nightmares?" Cal asked, tight-lipped.

The older man sighed and gave him a sad smile. "Well, that's the other thing. They don't stop. They just come less frequently."

"That's something, I guess," Cal replied.

"Take time to heal. Don't rush back into anything. You'll be laid up for a while. You'll be able to get around better, but you have to be careful about that wound and watch for any sign of infection. Like the one you've got right now."

"Amelia insisted on calling Eb because I had a fever," he said curtly, and didn't mention that she'd looked at the wound, because it was in a rather intimate place.

"She was right," he replied. "You don't want to wait until red lines appear and it starts to turn green," he added with pursed lips and twinkling eyes.

Cal managed a laugh. "No, I don't want that. It may be mangled but it's still a leg."

"It's not the only wound, I imagine?" the older man said slyly.

Cal drew in a breath. "No. I took two bullets in the chest. Fortunately, they were fired from a distance and barely penetrated the muscle. Micah patched me up while we were regrouping. I'd just gotten back to a comfortable level when we went back into offensive missions, and I was wounded again." He shook his head. "I didn't know I was so careless."

"Has nothing to do with it," the elderly man said. "I took three bullets in the chest when I was just walking from one tent to another. Laid me up for almost two months." He smiled. "I never told my wife, but she found out for herself when I came home." He burst out laughing. "I'll never forget what she said."

Cal's eyebrows lifted.

"She said she hoped all the meanness in me leaked out those bullet holes before they got plugged up!"

Cal laughed and grimaced when it hurt.

"She was a tiger, my wife," he said warmly. "I miss her every day. Amelia's so much like her. She's got guts. I haven't found anything yet that she's afraid of."

"I thought I hadn't, too. Life teaches hard lessons."

"Life is all about lessons," was the reply. "We don't know why we're put here, or what purpose we serve. But we all have our own ideas about that," he added. "The problem is that some people aren't satisfied until they force you to believe the way they do. And that's how wars start."

"I'm learning about that."

"Tell me about Juba," the older man began.

Cal's eyes were terrible to look into.

"I know. It's an open wound and I'm rubbing salt into it. But until you talk about it, it's just going to fester until it causes real damage. You have to get it out."

Cal closed his eyes. Then he sighed. He looked at the old man. "I've been hiding my head in the sand."

"Won't help. And I should know."

Cal smiled. "Okay."

So he told Amelia's grandfather what had happened. His voice broke a couple of times, because he'd been fond of the boy. But he got through it.

"I didn't have to see such things," the old man told him, "but I know men who did. Some of them turned to alcohol and drugs to forget. Two committed suicide. Those were the ones who couldn't, or wouldn't, face it and come to terms with it." He leaned forward intently. "I don't mean you to be one of those. That's why I was insistent."

Cal looked at him with new respect. "I see."

"Not just yet. But one day, you will. We're all terrified when we go into combat in the first place. One of the things we learn quickly is how to lean into the fear, instead of avoiding it, and use it to help us do desperate things when we have to. Any man who tells you he's never felt fear is either a liar or a serial killer," he added ruefully.

"That's a hard thing to admit," Cal replied.

"Of course. We're men. We're strong. We can face down armies with a knife between our teeth and an auto rifle. That works fine in video games, by the way, but it's a killer in real life. I was shaking all over when I went into my first incursion.

One of the older men in the group took me to one side and taught me how to deal with it. It worked. After that, I owned the fear, and I used it. I think it's one of the reasons why I came home, and many of my comrades didn't."

"I guess a lot of myths go up in smoke when we see combat for the first time."

"All of them do," he said.

Cal stared at him. "I'll never be able to thank you enough for this," he said. "I haven't been dealing with it well. In fact, I haven't been dealing with it at all."

"It's not easy. It helps to talk to other people who've been in your situation. Eb Scott would listen anytime you needed him to. He's a good man. I know several of his students. He's teaching them the right way, using experts in every field as instructors. He's going to put Jacobsville on the map."

"I'm glad he's doing well. I wish I'd asked more questions, done more research, before I threw my hat into the merc ring, however."

"Universal feeling. Me, too."

"To his credit, Eb did try to talk me out of it. I wanted in more for the feeling of purpose than quick cash, to know that I was doing a noble thing by helping the right people back into power." He sighed. "Nobility has a lot of definitions these days. Not all of them laudable ones."

"War is hell," came the reply. "Sherman said so and made it so. People in some states back east still use his name as a curse."

"So do some of the Plains tribes that he fought."

"Still, he was effective, in a burned-earth way."

"When you're hit, hit back hard."

"It usually works, too."

The front door opened. "I have cake!"

"Come right in," Cal called back, and both men laughed.

Cal was fed cake and given meds. Then a reluctant Amelia followed her grandfather out the front door.

"I feel mean, leaving him. He's a long way from well," she told her companion.

"Yes, but it's a very small town," he pointed out with a grin. "And do you want to be that woman who's always pointed to?"

"Now you sound like your sister," she chided, laughing.

"I do. She'd have a fit at what you've already done, if she knew." He paused when they were back in their own house. "What about that woman who came to see him?" he asked suddenly.

"Edie?" She shrugged. "She called him while I was there. Apparently, she can't abide being around anybody sick or wounded. Lovely woman." She rolled her eyes.

"I don't imagine it's her nursing skills that interested him in the first place, sugar," he said gently. "Just…don't let yourself get too involved. You know what I mean?"

She smiled. "Of course. He's my friend," she added, hiding the fact that her heart was already in jeopardy and that the thought of his leaving Jacobsville terrorized her at night. She knew he wasn't likely to continue with merc work, and that was a blessing. But he was surely going back to the city. There were rumors that he wanted to sign back on with San Antonio PD. She hadn't asked him yet. She didn't have the nerve. Plus, she didn't want it to be true.

Life without Cal would be no life at all. And she'd only just realized it since he'd been wounded.

She didn't know what to do. He wasn't a man who'd settle down to life in a small town, marriage and kids. He was too freedom-loving, too adventurous. Any woman who tried to trap him would regret it for the rest of her life.

Maybe Edie would do that and get kicked to the curb. That was the nicest thought Amelia had all night.

Chapter Ten

Amelia went every day to take meals to Cal and make sure he took his meds on time. He was getting better. The antibiotics worked fast. Too fast. He got up and tried to walk and the wound started suppurating. So Amelia called the doctor.

But Micah Steele was out of the country. So she called Eb, and was told to try a local doctor, Copper Coltrain. She thanked him, hung up and had a panic attack. Copper was known in Jacobsville. Very well known. For his temper and his attitude.

On the other hand, she had to do something. Cal refused to go to the emergency room, so it was call the doctor or trust to luck.

"Don't worry," her grandfather said when told about Cal's stubbornness. "I've got this." He picked up the phone and punched in numbers.

Amelia was amazed at how easy he was with the man on the other end of the line. Obviously, he wasn't scared of the redheaded doctor.

He hung up. "He'll swing by after he makes rounds at the hospital. About one," he added. He grinned. "I had to bribe him, though."

"I heard. Two slices of chocolate cake…?"

"Oh, I thought we might give him three. After all, you've got the ingredients to make more…?"

She just laughed.

* * *

She let her grandfather go over to Cal's when the doctor arrived, carrying several slices of cake in plastic wrap in a grocery bag. It wasn't that she was afraid, of course.

She chided herself for her cowardice. If she couldn't face down one doctor, how was she going to face down people in college in San Antonio when she started classes in two months? And how was she going to deal with the public if she got a job using her new skills?

That was in the future, she reminded herself. She'd worry about that problem when she had to. Being shy was a lifelong issue. It had kept her free of boyfriends—well, except for Ty Hardin, who'd been in her high school graduating class. He'd signed on with Eb Scott's group as a merc. She'd only seen him once since then. He had a crush on her that wasn't returned. He was a nice guy. Clean-cut, smart, a gentleman. But her heart was pointed in another direction, despite the hopelessness of it.

A few minutes later, her grandfather came up the steps. The doctor was just driving away.

"He said it's not anything to worry about unless it starts pumping out blood or…well, Cal's okay. He put on a temporary bandage, just while it's closing. He'll be fine."

"Thank goodness! I'd have driven him to the emergency room—assuming the truck would crank—but he refused to go. It's beyond my powers to forcibly dress a tall man and carry him bodily to our precarious method of transportation," she added with a grin.

He chuckled. "I see your point. You did the right thing. Although," he added slowly, "you might wait a couple of hours before you go over to check on Cal."

She stared at him. "Any particular reason?"

"Well, until he stops cussing would be one."

She pursed her lips. "Okay. I'll go make something edible."

"Good idea."

She went into the kitchen and didn't see her grandfather smothering laughter.

It was late when she went back to check on Cal. Her grandfather had been doubled over with acid reflux. He had medicine for it, but it wasn't working. Finally, he mixed up some baking soda in water and drank it, and he said it worked. But he looked bad. He was pale and his shirt was palpitating where his heart was.

"You need to go back to the doctor," she said firmly.

"It's just heartburn," he assured her. "I had a physical only last month. That's when he recommended these tablets for the reflux. You take them for ten days and they work. But not on the first day. You have to use the chewable tablets until they do work."

"Oh. Okay," she said, relieved.

He grinned. "I'm fine. A lot of people have this problem. It's why I can't eat spicy foods or drink alcohol. Maybe that's for the best."

"About the alcohol, sure, but give up spicy foods?" she moaned. "I can't live without the occasional taco or fajita or chimichanga!"

"I know. I miss them."

"I'm sorry. I'll try to enjoy mine enough for you, Granddaddy," she promised.

He just smiled.

Cal was sitting up in bed reading a book on his cell phone when she walked in. He gave her a glare that could have set fire to kindling.

"Now, now," she said before he could speak, "let's not jeopardize our potato soup and chocolate cake over a little matter of the doctor coming out to see you."

The glare didn't subside. "You didn't even come over while he was here, you chicken."

"I know his reputation," she said. "Nobody ever said I had to sacrifice myself for a friend. And I am keeping one nicely fed and medicated." She smiled.

He drew in a breath. "Honest to God, I thought I was back in grammar school. That man…!"

"He's a very good doctor. Everybody says so."

"His bedside manner would do a cobra proud!"

"I like cobras," she said. "They're really cool to look at."

"You wouldn't like to be bitten by one," he pointed out.

She looked around the floor. "I hope you aren't planning to drive that point home…?"

"I don't keep cobras!"

"Our deputy sheriff has an albino python," she said. "It weighs a hundred and ten pounds and it's absolutely gorgeous! It has yellow-and-white-patterned skin and red eyes!"

He rolled his eyes. "I never would have figured you for a woman who liked snakes."

"Well, I don't. I mean I don't like all of them. Especially rattlesnakes. I almost got bitten by them twice." She shivered. "But black snakes and king snakes are okay."

"Why?"

She made a face. "Because black snakes aren't dangerous and king snakes eat poisonous ones."

"How do you know all that?" he wondered.

"Ty Hardin. He was in my graduating class." She made another face. "He had this awful crush on me. I laid awake nights finding ways to avoid him. I mean, he's nice and all, but he just isn't my type."

He cocked his head. "What is your type?"

She sighed. "That gorgeous man who played in *Game of Thrones*," she said. "The blond one who lost his hand."

"He was a…!"

"Please." She stopped him. "There are ladies present."

"Oh, yeah? Where?"

Now she was glaring.

"Okay. Sorry." He sighed. "And I guess you were right about calling the doctor. He said it wasn't an emergency, but I needed to slow down trying to get back on my feet. Rome wasn't built in a day."

"It really wasn't," she pointed out. "The more you try to rush recovery, the more you'll set it back."

"Were you eavesdropping?" he asked, "because that's exactly what he said." He laid his head back on the pillow. "I guess you're both right. I just feel useless lying here. I've got a hundred books, and I don't want to read any of them."

She held out her hand for his phone. Her eyes popped. "What do you do with this thing, just call people and read books? There are no weather apps, no earthquake apps, no news apps, no mahjong, no solitaire… This is just pathetic!"

He was staring at her. "What?"

"Mahjong. It's my favorite game. And I love solitaire."

"I used to play that with a deck of cards."

"Now you can play it online."

He grimaced. "I guess a few apps wouldn't kill me," he said. "And I like games. Go ahead. Load it up."

"You mean it?"

"I mean it."

She grinned and pulled up the Apps app.

She'd created a monster. Now all he wanted to do was play solitaire. He played it between bites of supper and while he was supposed to be sleeping. He played mahjong, too, and loved it once he got the hang of it. He added other games, as well. It kept his mind occupied while his body was healing, and Amelia didn't have to fuss so much.

Meanwhile, Amelia's grandfather's heartburn seemed to be getting more frequent, despite the medicines he was taking for it. With a little coaxing, she convinced him to phone his doctor's office and make an appointment. There were plenty of medicines that worked for that condition. He just needed the right one.

Cal improved day by day once he was convinced that trying to rush his recovery was doing his body no favors.

The wounds healed enough that he could stand to wear sweatpants, which meant he could get around the house and out onto the porch. He mentioned driving and Amelia went through the roof.

"I'll check with the doctor first," he promised. And muttered, "Anything to keep peace," under his breath.

She grinned. "I'm a pest, I am."

He laughed. "You are. But a nice pest. And you really can cook!"

"Thanks. It's just basic chemistry, though." She didn't mention making bombs. Her grandfather, while giving away no secrets, had told her in confidence that certain things shouldn't be discussed around their neighbor.

A stranger came to see Cal one day, loaded him into the car and drove him away. He was gone until almost dark. When Amelia went over to take his supper, after his visitor left, he told her what was going on. Not all of it. Just what he was comfortable confiding. It was going to upset her, and he didn't want to do that. Not now.

"I'm thinking about going back into police work," he explained at the table while he ate the delicious spaghetti and garlic bread she'd carted over. "In San Antonio, where I worked before," he added.

She almost sighed aloud with relief. "You're not going to try to go back out with Eb's group?" she asked.

Her tone told him things she wouldn't. He smiled gently. "No. Other peoples' wars should be left to their citizens."

"Good for you." She smiled. It hadn't occurred to her that he might want to live where he worked, and he wasn't going to burst any bubbles. Not yet. When he was ready to leave the rented house and move into the apartment he'd already put down a deposit on—then, he'd tell her.

He was able to get around very well. Amelia was ready to sign up for her college classes and get on with her future. She was reluctant, of course, because it was going to take her right out of Cal's future. She had to work harder by the day to hide her growing love for him. He didn't want it. He'd even made vague references to not wanting to be tied down for a long time yet.

So, she told herself, she'd go along and hope that he'd keep in touch with her and her grandfather. It wasn't hopeless. There was always hope.

Life, at the moment, was going along at a nice, easy pace. Which meant, of course, that disaster was hiding around the corner.

One morning, two days before her grandfather's doctor appointment, he complained of heartburn at the breakfast table. While she was getting the baking soda he'd asked for, he keeled over out of his chair and hit the floor, stone dead.

It was amazing, she thought, how numb and cold you felt when a crisis happened to you. It was like going on autopilot. She phoned 911, thought about the process she'd need to go through—everything from the clothes she'd need to take to the funeral home, to arranging the funeral, to phoning her great-aunt, seeing a lawyer about probate, even checking the status of the house's equity. She thought about all that while she sat on the floor beside her still grandfather and talked to him, telling him how much she loved him, how much he'd meant to her, how she was going to miss him.

She choked up and the tears came about the time the ambulance arrived. They examined him, started CPR, tried the paddles. Then, after a long and futile effort, they loaded him up in the ambulance, and called in for orders. Amelia told them she'd follow them to the hospital. They just looked at her with pity. They all knew the end of this tragedy.

"I know," she told them, and managed a smile. "I'll call the funeral home."

The female EMT just nodded and smiled at her before the door closed.

Cal's car was gone. Now that he could drive again, he often took off just to look around. He said he needed to get his mind off things.

She managed to get the truck cranked and drove to the hospital. They told her, of course, what had happened. It was a massive heart attack. If her grandfather had been in a room in the hospital, they couldn't have saved him. She thanked the EMT for trying—because they were getting ready to go on another call when she passed them on the way in—and the EMT hugged her.

"I lost my dad last year," she told Amelia. "I know how it is."

"Thanks," she whispered, and managed a smile.

That night she'd already phoned the lawyer's office for an appointment and called her great-aunt with the news and been told that she'd be down the following afternoon to help. *Oh, joy,* she thought, *I'll never escape her.*

She'd be pressed to go home with her great-aunt, she knew that already. The house had been reverse-mortgaged, but unknown to her, her grandfather had sold it months ago to keep finances going. Worse, his bank accounts were almost empty. She cursed herself for not realizing how things were, and not getting a job after her graduation from community college.

She wouldn't be able to afford the rest of her education now, not unless she inherited a fortune—fat chance—or was lucky enough to have people at admissions overlook her dismal SAT scores. She knew the material, but tests shook her. She never did well on them.

So here she sat at the table, too sick at heart to cook, with no money, no home and, worst of all, no Granddaddy to tell her, "Sugar, it's going to be all right."

The thought just dissolved her in tears.

While she was crying her eyes out, she didn't hear the front door open. She felt a pair of strong arms pull her out of the chair and hold her close, rocking her while she cried.

"I only just heard. I'm sorry I wasn't here," he said tightly. "The one time you really needed me, and I let you down."

"It's all right," she said, swallowing grief. "I got everything done. I have to take Granddaddy's clothes over to the funeral home, but I'll do that tomorrow."

"Have you eaten anything?"

"I can't," she said in a whisper. She drew in a breath. "My great-aunt's coming down tomorrow from Victoria. I wish she was here now…!"

"You don't want to be alone."

"Isn't it silly? I don't believe in ghosts, and I know Granddaddy would never hurt me. It's just…"

"I know. It's that there might be ghosts."

She nodded and nuzzled her cheek against his warm strength.

"I'll stay with you tonight."

She looked up.

"Nobody will know," he teased. "The lights are still on in my house and they're on an automatic timer. My car's in the driveway. Unless you're expecting company at this hour, it will be our secret."

"Nobody's coming. They'll come tomorrow with food. The church always does that when somebody dies."

He scowled. "They bring food?"

"Yes. Everybody brings something, even if it's just biscuits or a vegetable dish or fruit or a roast." She smiled. "It's for the family, so everybody can eat without having to cook."

"What a nice custom."

"It is."

"How about digging me out a pair of your granddad's sweatpants for the night? We were the same build. And I know he wouldn't mind," he added gently.

She smiled. "No, he wouldn't. He was fond of you."

"I was fond of him. He got me through a rough patch of my own."

"He said it helped him, too." She pulled back reluctantly. "I'll find you something." She paused. "Thanks, Cal."

He shrugged. "Small town, big family," he said gently.

She smiled.

It was comforting, having Cal in Granddaddy's bedroom next door. She thought she'd sleep without any effort. She couldn't. She worried about the future. She cried silently at her loss. She tossed and turned, and still the tears came.

The door opened and closed. Cal eased into bed beside her and pulled her against his bare chest. "I thought it would be like this," he said quietly. "I couldn't sleep, the night after... well, before I got shot."

She pressed close, aware that her thin cotton gown was letting her feel far too much of his warm, hair-roughened muscular chest. It made her feel shivery all over, and it wasn't with fear. She caught her breath.

He heard that. He felt something, too—the sudden hardness of her nipples against him, even through the cloth. His big, warm hands spread on her back and became caressing.

He had to keep his head. He told himself that while he felt all of him go rigid with the most intense desire he'd ever felt in his life. She was innocent. She was a virgin. He'd come in to comfort her, not to seduce her.

But he'd wanted her for, oh, so long, and here she was, warm and tender and clinging, and he was only human.

She felt him turn her, felt his weight on her. She was going to protest until his mouth gently covered hers and explored it in a slow, expert manner that made her into a limp cloth. His hands smoothed away the gown, and it was wonderful, the feel of them on her bare skin. She caught her breath as they moved slowly from her silken back onto her rib cage, with just his thumbs smoothing over the underside of her breasts.

She'd never done anything intimate with a man. She had no experience at all that would help her save herself. The feelings were too new, too explosively passionate. She hadn't known that she was passionate until she felt his leg easing between both of hers, and his mouth deepening the kisses until they were invasive and hungry and overpowering.

It had been cool in her bedroom, but now it was hot. She moved under him, her leg sliding over his, her mouth answering the passion she felt in his. Her short nails dug into his back as his mouth shifted down onto her breasts and smoothed over them, causing sensations that arched her back and brought helpless moans out of her throat.

After that, it was impossible for him to stop. It had been a long time between women, and Amelia was the most delicious morsel he'd ever tasted. She was butter and cream, exquisite.

He ate her like candy, from head to foot and back again. By the time she finally felt his body against hers without the intrusion of fabric, she was his willing partner. She moved with him, lifted for him, clung and arched and held him even when the flash of pain stiffened her against him.

She recalled vaguely that he'd asked if she was okay, if she wanted him to stop, and she'd put her mouth on his and lifted again and again to the slow, hard thrust of him in a nonverbal answer.

It was a feast of passion. They went from one position to another, all over the bed, almost onto the floor, clinging to each other, drowning in kisses, feeling ecstasy build until it exploded in both of them, and they cried out together as the sweet, sweet anguish of fulfillment left them shuddering in each other's arms.

* * *

For lazy minutes they lay together, gently touching, without recriminations, without regrets. Until inevitably, he turned to her and kissed her again. And she turned into his body and welcomed him as if it was the first time, all over again. Until they, finally, slept.

She was under the covers, back in her gown, when the door opened, and Cal came in with a cup of coffee.

"I can only cook snake, at the moment," he said gently. He sat down beside her, putting the cup on the bedside table. He brushed the long, soft blond hair back from her face and just stared at her.

She stared back, robbed of words. It had been the sweetest experience of her life, although she was very uncomfortable in unmentionable places, and too shy to say so.

"I want you to promise me something," he said quietly.

"Okay."

"I want you to go to the pharmacy and get the morning-after pill," he said. "I was reckless, and I'm sorry. It's been a long time, and I wasn't prepared."

"I can do that," she said, trying to sound sophisticated.

He drew in a sigh as he looked at her. She was beautiful, he thought, without makeup, without artifice, and it wasn't purely physical beauty. She was unique in his whole life. He smiled gently.

"I'm not ready for undoable things," he began.

She reached up and put her fingers softly against his mouth. "I know all that. It's okay."

It wasn't, but she was a good actress.

He looked relieved. "All right, then. I'm going to go home and start getting things together…"

"Together?" She felt the shock all the way to her feet.

He grimaced. "I wasn't going to tell you yet. I'm sorry, it slipped out." He took a breath. "I'm signing back on with San Antonio PD. They have an opening. I put a deposit on an apartment there. I'm moving to the city. I'm sorry, Amelia. I wasn't trying to hide it. I just thought…"

She could see what he'd thought. It was all over his face. She had a crush on him, and he didn't want to hurt her. He still didn't. But he wasn't a forever-after man, and he wasn't ready to settle down.

"It's all right," she said. "You'll be okay. And San Antonio is a nice city."

He raised an eyebrow. "It's nice if you don't do police work there," he replied.

She shrugged.

He frowned. "I didn't mean for this to happen," he said, struggling for the right words. In fact, he was confused and uncertain, and trying to understand why. He felt guilt as well, because she'd been innocent, and he'd taken something that she'd most likely saved for marriage—if women even did that sort of thing these days.

"It takes two people to make mistakes like this one," she said simply and didn't notice the flicker in his eyes. "No worries. I'll take care of everything."

The words hurt. He wasn't sure why. He got to his feet. "If you ever need me," he began.

"Thanks," she said. "But I'm moving, too. The house was only Granddaddy's for his lifetime. It goes to a Realtor now. I'll probably stay with my great-aunt until I get signed up for college."

"That's right. Your major is going to be chemistry, right?"

"Yes." It was a lie. She couldn't afford college. There were grants, of course. She'd have to start late or wait until spring. But that wasn't his problem.

"Well, thank you for taking care of me, when I needed it." He drew in a breath. "I've got a big bankroll…"

"If you offer me money, I'll hit you," she said, and her dark eyes flashed.

"I wasn't going to. Not the way you mean. But if you need help with college…"

"That's nice of you. But I have scholarships," she lied, and smiled.

"Oh. Well." He drew in another breath. "You take care of yourself. I'll see you at the funeral."

"Okay."

He paused at the door, his back to her. "I had good intentions, Amelia. I really did."

"I know that."

He paused again, half turned. Then went out and closed the door. She waited until she heard the front door close before the tears fell.

Her great-aunt arrived in great glory the next afternoon. By then, Amelia had washed the bed linen and her gown. She wished it was as easy to wash away the shame. She'd meant to go to the pharmacy. In fact, she did go. Old Mrs. Smith was at the counter, and she just couldn't work up enough nerve to ask her grandmother's best friend for a morning-after pill.

So she went home and the truck wouldn't crank, so she couldn't drive to San Antonio to get one, either. She called the local shop and had them take it in, only to be told it would be a couple of days at least before they could even get to it, but the mechanic thought she'd blown up the engine—there was an oil leak that she hadn't discovered, and the oil pan was empty. He said gently that it would be cheaper to buy another vehicle than to fix it. She said she'd think about it.

Then her great-aunt walked in, and there was no more time to try and do anything about her reckless night. She'd worry about it when she had time, although she didn't think it was the right time for anything to happen. She hoped it wouldn't. Even if it did, she could never tell a man who didn't want her something like that. She had too much pride. She'd messed up her life royally, but it had been because she loved him so much that she couldn't help herself.

The funeral was well attended. The house was full of food, which she'd invited friends in to help them eat. Her great-aunt, not the most social of people, was touched by the kindness, and by the friendly people who found her interesting. She didn't dress rich, so they took her for a relative in bad financial shape, like Amelia. It made her beam, to find out that people could like her when they thought she was poor. It amused Amelia, who saw a whole new side of her rambunctious relative.

Cal did come to the funeral, but he had a woman with him. Amelia recognized her at once. It was the woman who didn't like sick people, who'd come looking for Cal that one time.

It made her sick to her stomach to see how quickly he'd tossed her aside for the city woman. But she put on a good show. She greeted them after the graveside service and introduced her great-aunt and her plans to move to Victoria. Edie, condescending until she saw the great-aunt's chauffeured limousine, was suddenly all smiles and charm when Amelia finished hugging friends and joined the older woman at the car.

"All the best, Amelia," Cal said, forcing a smile.

She forced one, too. "I wish the same for you...both," she said, including Edie. She avoided his eyes as she slid into the limousine just ahead of her great-aunt.

Cal was feeling more guilt than he'd expected. Amelia had been closer to him than anyone in his whole life. He'd seduced her and then ignored her, and now he'd paraded Edie in front of her. He didn't know why. He hadn't meant to hurt her so much, and at such a time. He knew she loved him. It was blatant.

He also knew that he was a bad risk. Maybe it was best to make her regret what they'd done during that long, sweet night, so that she could move on. He just hadn't known that it would hurt so much.

Chapter Eleven

Probate was a little easier because in his will, Amelia's grandfather had left what little there was to Amelia. It was a longstanding will, which he'd never changed. It was just as well, because there was very little that anyone could inherit. It did, however, give Amelia a break from having to deal with the legal aspects. Her great-aunt had her own fine attorney and he handled everything.

Amelia moved in with Valeria in Victoria, although it was a wrench to leave Jacobsville where she was born. She found a job as secretary to an attorney, through her great-aunt's attorney, which made life a little easier. It didn't pay a lot, but it allowed her to pay rent—which she insisted on doing—and buy a few new pieces of clothing.

She forced herself not to think about Cal. She didn't know anybody who had ties to him, and that helped a lot. Absence, she thought, might just do the trick. It was a lie. She thought about him all the time, missed him, relived that night over and over in her thoughts. She wasn't going to be able to stop loving him. But at least she wouldn't have Edie rubbed in her face over here with her great-aunt.

Life went on, in a dull, everyday way. Amelia went to work, came home, cooked, watched the news with Valeria and went to bed.

Valeria couldn't understand why her great-niece went to bed with the chickens, and said so.

"I'm just tired," Amelia replied with a smile. "I think it's aftereffects of losing Granddaddy."

Valeria sighed. "I know, child. I miss him, too. Except for you, he was the last family I had."

"What was he like, when he was young?"

She shook her head. "The black sheep of the family! Honestly, he embarrassed Mama so much that she threatened to give him away. You know, family names are handed down for generations. Black marks are handed down with them. So far, there's never been a blight on ours. It's quite an accomplishment, in this day and time." She shook her finger at Amelia. "You make sure you never disgrace us, either, young lady. That's an order."

Amelia just grinned and said, "Yes, ma'am."

But it grew harder and harder to do much of anything when she got off work, and she was feeling nauseous. Her clothes were growing too small, and it wasn't because she turned the dryer heat up too high. Her breasts and her waistline were expanding.

With something like panic, she bought a home pregnancy kit after she got off work the next Friday and took it home, sneaking it into the bathroom. She could tuck the used kit in the tote she carried to work and dispose of it someplace Valeria wouldn't see it.

But all her plans flew away when she actually used the kit. It was positive. She was pregnant.

She sat down on the commode lid and felt the shock all the way to her feet. She had no contact with Cal, who'd already said he didn't want ties. She had a job, but she lived in a small-ish city with a reputation-conscious elderly woman who would never adjust to a pregnant out-of-wedlock great-niece. So what did she do now?

Dazed, she dropped the kit into the trash can without thinking and went to her room and sat on the bed. Panic would surely set in soon. She had to figure out what to do next.

Not that she had any intention of getting rid of her child. She could move back east or west, someplace where Cal would never know she was still alive. He'd think she'd used the morning-after pill, so he had no need to check on her anyway. She could go away, invent a fictional husband...

She looked up to find her great-aunt in the doorway, holding the box and the used pregnancy test in her hands.

"You little slut!" she hissed.

Amelia got off the bed. "It's okay. I'm going to move out. Nobody will know. I can go back east..."

"Disgraceful! It was that mercenary who lived across the street, wasn't it? Oh, yes, my brother told me all about how close you were. He did this and just left you?"

"It's not like that," Amelia began.

"You tramp! You pack your things and get out of my house right now!" she almost screamed at the younger woman.

There were many replies that Amelia could have used, but none of them would have worked. "Okay," she said softly, because her volatile relative was about to lose control. "I'll just go downstairs and get my suitcase out of the closet," she added, and walked toward the staircase.

"Of all the evil, despicable things women do to themselves these days, they're no better than...!"

Amelia wasn't listening. She got to the staircase and the first step.

"How could you, Amelia?" Valeria wailed. "How could you do this!"

"Aunt Valeria," she began.

"You...traitor!"

In a fever of rage, Valeria reached out and pushed her, violently.

Her horrified face was the last thing Amelia saw. The last thing she heard was, "No! Oh, no, I didn't mean it!"

She came to in the hospital with a concussion and she'd lost the baby. The doctor, an older man, was apparently her great-aunt's physician.

"Valeria is very sorry," he said at her bedside. "She has these rages. You may not know that she's diabetic and she cheats on her diet with candy and sweets. It's landed her in the hospital twice. I know," he added gently, "it doesn't excuse what she's done to you. But it explains it."

"I won't go back there," Amelia said solemnly. "And I won't see her." She looked at the doctor with sad brown eyes. "I wanted my baby. I loved his father, so much."

The doctor winced. "I am truly sorry. Is there any way I can help?"

"If someone would go to my great-aunt's house and pack my things," she said, "I'd be much obliged. I had my cell phone in my pocket…"

He opened the drawer beside her bed, took it out and handed it to her. "Good thing you have a charging case," he added.

She turned the charge on. "It is. I'll call my employer and explain. Or sort of explain. God knows, I wouldn't want to embarrass my snow-white aunt for any reason," she added bitterly.

He didn't answer that. "I'll ask one of the aides to do that for you after she gets off work. She can bring your stuff in with her tomorrow."

"Thanks very much," she said.

"It's little enough to do. And I am sorry."

Her bags were packed and brought to her hospital room, along with her notebook computer.

Valeria, still in the heat of anger after having been up all night, and hearing from her physician that Amelia had lost the baby, remembered hearing that Cal had gone back to work for the police in San Antonio. It was his fault, all of this. Her great-niece would never speak to her again, all because of him. He'd ruined the girl, dirtied her reputation. Valeria had regrettably lost her temper and done something unforgiveable. The guilt about the baby ate at her until she realized that it was all Cal's fault. None of this would have happened if he hadn't seduced her innocent great-niece. Then he'd just walked away, with no consequences, leaving the girl to take care of herself. Well, he wasn't getting away with it, either! She tracked him down.

He answered the phone, puzzled because only a handful of people knew him well enough to call him.

"I'm Amelia's great-aunt, Valeria," she introduced herself with sugary sweetness.

"Amelia!" He groaned. "How is she? Is she okay? I was going to call her last night and check on her. I should have done it sooner, but things have been hectic around here…"

"That's why I phoned. To tell you how she is. I just wanted to tell you not to worry about the baby," she said in a tone dripping with sarcasm. "Amelia went to a clinic yesterday, and had the baby removed. So you're all set now, aren't you? You can go on your merry way with no consequences whatsoever and seduce someone else's innocent relative!"

And she hung up.

Cal just sat for a moment, shocked out of his mind. He'd assumed that Amelia had taken the morning-after pill, so he hadn't been concerned. He'd missed her terribly, but he'd been dealing with the aftermath of Ngawa, and his mind had been on much more horrible things than poor Amelia and how she'd managed after her grandfather died. It shamed him that he'd just walked away, without telling her how he really felt. Not that he'd realized how he felt, until very recent days. He'd known where Amelia was, and he had every intention of getting her back into his life. Until right now, when he knew how little emotion she felt for him. She hadn't bothered to tell him about their child. She didn't want it. The thought tortured him. He thought she loved him. It was the one certainty in his miserable life. Had she thought he wouldn't want the baby? That he'd cut her out of his life? Or had she just never loved him in the first place?

He still had Amelia's phone number. He tried to call her, but the call went to her voice mail. Since she'd never set it up, she never got it. She didn't recognize the number in her missed-call file and assumed it was a telemarketer and erased it.

That night a very drunk Cal showed up at Edie's apartment. She was feeling good, high as a kite, and delighted to see him—in any condition. "Why, come in! You look like something the dog brought in, darling," she laughed.

"She got rid of it."

"Excuse me?"

He sat down heavily, his head in his hands. "I lost my head. I swear to God I thought she got the damned morning-after pill, but she didn't. She was pregnant. She went to a damned clinic!"

"Well, sweetheart, if you wanted her to take the pill, why is getting rid of the child so shocking? It's the same thing."

"It's not." His dark eyes were blazing. "She should have told me. She should have given me a choice!"

"Her body, her choice," she replied.

"Fathers have no rights?" he asked belligerently.

"Boy, are you high," she murmured. "Listen, most women don't want kids. They ruin your figure and your life, and you never look the same. I never wanted any. I still don't."

He'd thought of nothing but Amelia for days. Missed her. Ached to see her. Guilt had kept him away. He'd just walked away from her, without a word of explanation. Now he was in a fog of misery. He'd meant to go after her, now that he'd finally reconciled himself with the anguish of Ngawa. In fact, he'd gone to a jewelry store and bought a set of rings. Amber diamonds, unique, like Amelia with her blond hair and dark, dark eyes. He'd been thinking about marriage. He knew she loved him. And he was only just discovering the anguish of a life that she wasn't part of. He'd had plans, to go and see her in Victoria. As he'd told her aunt, he'd meant to phone her that night and try to explain. And now, this. Proof that she wanted nothing more to do with him. If she'd loved him, she'd have wanted the child.

"She betrayed me," he said furiously. "She sold me down the river!"

"That's right," she agreed. "She truly did. So," she added, cocking her head, "why don't we pay her back? Let's get married. That will show her how little she means to you!"

"Married." He blinked. He was having trouble concentrating.

"Sure! Let's go get a marriage license!"

"I'm drunk."

"No problem. I have strong coffee. I'll fix you right up."

So three days later, he married Edie in the office of the justice of the peace. And immediately afterward, he sent Amelia a text message, having remembered belatedly that she hadn't ever set up voice mail on her phone. It was one of the things he'd promised to help her do.

But he tried calling again, and this time he got through.

"You miserable excuse for a human being!" he raged the minute he heard her voice. "You didn't want the baby, so you just got rid of it? I had no right to know, to be told what you planned to do?"

"Cal, please listen…"

"To what, more lies? Damn you! Damn you to hell! I thought you were different, that you valued life, that you cared about me, that you…" He broke off. He couldn't even say the word. "Well, great, you're free now, no need to disturb your perfect life with any complications, right?"

"It's not…!" she tried again, horrified at what he was thinking.

"I never wanted you for keeps in the first place," he said in an icy tone. "One night was more than enough. Edie and I just got married, by the way, so thanks for helping us out by making sure I wouldn't be hit with child support. And you have a terrific life, Amelia. Just don't ever get in touch with me again. I hope you burn in hell!"

He hung up, wishing he could have slammed the receiver down. He was still cursing ten minutes later, and he'd made inroads into a new bottle of rum he found in Edie's liquor cabinet. By the time she came back from her shopping trip, he was passed out on the sofa.

Amelia had answered her cell phone just as they were getting things ready to release her from the hospital. She just stared at her phone blindly. How had he known about the baby? Maybe one of the hospital staff knew him and had phoned him. He must be in and out of the hospital a lot in his line of work, talking to victims of violent crime. But this was Houston, not San Antonio, so how would he have known?

The furious tirade had broken her heart. She'd still loved him, despite everything. But his harsh condemnation ended that part of her life very neatly. Cal thought she'd deliberately gotten rid of the baby. He wanted nothing to do with her. He was married. He wished Amelia in hell. And her only crime had been to love him.

Now she had no ties, nothing to hold her to Texas or Jacobsville, even less to her great-aunt. With the small amount of money she had left, she hired a car to take her down to Jacobsville and wait for her while she spoke to Eb Scott. On the off chance, she had her belongings with her.

She could lie to the world, but not to Eb. She told him the whole miserable story, from the beginning to the painful end.

"He didn't seem like that kind of man," Eb said when she finished. "But then, we never really know people, do we?"

She smiled sadly. "I guess not." She cocked her head. "I have no place to go. I lost my job because I couldn't contact them for two days to tell them where I was—and I wouldn't have dared tell them why I was in the hospital, or my great-aunt would have murdered me. You said once that you'd give me a job if I asked. I'm asking."

He studied her. He'd never trained a female operative, but she was good material to work with. She was smart, and a dead shot—something he'd tease her about for years, that he trained her to shoot—and she could follow instructions.

"Okay," he said. "But you're on trial temporarily. That work? Either one of us isn't satisfied at the end of a month, we'll make decisions."

She smiled. "Okay. Thanks. And you won't mention any of this to Cal, if you ever see him? Promise me, please."

"Easy promise," he replied. "And his loss."

"He's married."

"What?" Eb asked, shocked.

"This fancy woman he knows in the city. I guess she was more his style than I was. He called me…" She didn't add what else he'd said.

"Did you answer him?"

"Blocked his number." She smiled sadly.

He chuckled. "Nice move. Okay." He got up from the table. "Let's get you settled."

She hadn't told him about the rest of the furious one-sided conversation, that Cal hated her guts and accused her of getting rid of her child. She still wondered how Cal knew.

There was one attempt by her great-aunt, in the years that followed, to contact her, to apologize.

She didn't answer the text. In fact, she blocked Great-Aunt Valeria's number. She could forgive an old woman who had a dangerous medical condition. But wanting to be around her was another thing altogether. It was too much a reminder of the anguish.

She could have gone back to college and studied chemistry, but learning the skills of demolition from a real-life expert—

Cord Romero—was so much better than sitting at a desk. She was a good student.

And not only in demolition. Time after time she won competitions on the firing range.

"I taught her everything she knows," Eb would lie glibly.

Everybody laughed. They knew better.

She learned all the dark skills of a mercenary, and learned them well. Within months, Eb was sending her on missions. He was careful to exclude her from anything especially dangerous, without her knowledge. He didn't want her death on his hands. But she made him proud.

There was only one slip, although it was a bad one. She set the time just a few seconds off on an explosive device, and a man died. She took the heat for it from his friends, one of whom later went to work briefly as a foreman for one of her clients. She never denied her part in the man's death. She went to his funeral and let his relatives get all the anguish out of their systems. She knew how they felt. Her lost baby was never far from her thoughts. But at the end of the funeral, she was forgiven, because that was how Texans lived their faith. Without forgiveness, faith was a poor thing.

Ty Harding showed up once in Wyoming when she was working as a bodyguard for Wolf Patterson's future wife. She was polite but cool to him. She wanted no more involvement with men. She listened to her comrades talk about women they'd been involved with, because they treated her as just one of the guys, and she learned how few of them ever really cared about a woman they took out. It was a painful lesson, but she learned it well.

She became, in her turn, a person of faith, because it was all she had to hold on to in some of the desperate situations her work took her to.

The men teased her about it, but they stopped using profanity and obscenity around her, and talking about their conquests. They saved that for bar crawling, something in which Amelia never indulged.

The years passed slowly. She heard about Cal from time to time from people who didn't know about her involvement with him. He was now a captain in the San Antonio Police Department. Someone mentioned that strings had to have been pulled because that was a meteoric rise. She knew better. Cal was just conscientious and careful, and compassionate. Well, he had compassion on the job. None for the mother of his lost child.

His wife had died, she heard. It didn't interest her. That was the past. She lived from day to day, mission to mission. Life had made her tough as nails.

Or so she thought.

Until one Friday evening she went into Fernando's in San Antonio when she was between missions to get takeout. And she walked right into Cal Hollister.

She gave him a look that would have fried bread and went straight out the front door and hailed a taxi. She didn't even look his way as the car pulled out into traffic.

A day later, she found him behind her as she exited her apartment and started down the street to the restaurant where she was to meet a clandestine contact for Eb.

She whirled and glared at him from eyes like hot flames. "What do you want?" she asked icily.

"I want to talk to you," he said shortly.

"What would you like to say that you didn't say six years ago just after your wedding?" she asked with venom.

He closed his eyes. "I was drunk when I married her."

"It takes three days to get a marriage license," she said sweetly. "Were you drunk for three days?"

His own dark eyes burned. "What if I was?"

"Not my problem," she said. "And I'm working, if you don't mind."

"Working? At what?"

She turned, pulling back her jacket to reveal the gun at her hip. He looked shocked. "You're in police work?"

"I work for Eb Scott," she said quietly. "I'm one of his top operatives."

She could have sworn he lost two shades of color from his tanned face. "Operative...and he hired you?"

"He trained me." She gave him a cold look. "When I got out of the hospital, I had nowhere to go. I couldn't stay with my great-aunt and I lost my job. I went to see Eb and he hired me."

"Wait, what do you mean, when you got out of the hospital? I thought it was a clinic."

"A clinic?"

He was really glaring now. "The clinic where you had the baby, removed, I believe your great-aunt said when she called me?"

She looked at him with horror. Great-Aunt Valeria had done that to her, lied to Cal? "She called you," she said, as if in a fog.

"Yes, she called me, to make sure I knew that I didn't have anything to worry about..." He was hesitating because of the look on her face. "Hospital?" He was still trying to make sense of it.

She drew in a long breath. So now she knew why Valeria had tried to apologize. It wasn't enough to push her down the staircase. She'd ruined any hope that Cal might care about her. Not that he had. He'd married that woman, hadn't he?

She looked up at him with sad eyes. "Some things are better just left in the past," she said. "I'm sorry about your wife. Someone told me, I don't even remember who, that she'd died."

He'd hated his wife. He stared at Amelia, idly wondering why she looked no older than she had when they were close. She hadn't aged. "What hospital?" he persisted.

She just smiled. "It was a long time ago. We're different people now. Strangers. And I'm working. Goodbye, Cal."

"Working on what?" he asked before she could turn away.

"Nothing that concerns you. A project of Eb's overseas."

His blood ran cold. "Overseas, where?" he asked curtly.

"Cal, this doesn't concern you. It's Eb's business. I'm not breaking any laws here. I even have a concealed-carry permit for the pistol, okay?"

He was still just staring at her. "You haven't aged," he said, almost in a daze.

She laughed shortly. "Thanks. But it's not true. Harding said just the other day that I was going gray."

"Harding? That guy who had the crush on you?" he asked.

She nodded. "He's working for Lassiter's detective agency again. He left it, but he went back. The money was too good. He works out of Houston, but he helps us out sometimes."

He hated the idea of Harding. He was still jealous of her, after all the long years in between, all the anguish.

"Why didn't you tell me?" he asked harshly.

She raised both eyebrows. "About what?"

"You know damned well about what!"

"When it would have mattered, you didn't want to know," she said simply. "I tried to get the pill, but my grandmother's best friend was at the pharmacy counter. I couldn't do it. Then the truck broke down so I couldn't get to San Antonio and then Great-Aunt Valeria came."

He saw the pattern, all too well. "You had my phone number."

"You walked away at my grandfather's funeral and never said another word to me."

Reminding him, subtly, that Edie had been with him. Another in a long line of mistakes he'd made along the way.

He shoved his hands into his pockets. "I was dealing with things I could barely face. My whole life was in flux. I made… bad decisions."

"You made the ones you needed to make," she said simply.

"Edie was gorgeous," she recalled with a sad smile. "I'm just ordinary, but she would have drawn eyes everywhere. Isn't that what men want? A wife that makes other men envious?"

He was shocked speechless. She thought he'd thrown her over for Edie because she wasn't pretty enough for him. It was an absolute lie, and it made him even more ashamed, that he'd given her that impression.

"It was a great gesture, though, bringing her to the funeral. Making sure I couldn't say anything that might embarrass you."

"That wasn't why," he said heavily.

She looked at her watch. "I'm really late. Just chalk the whole thing up to misplaced lust and don't worry about it... Cal!" she exclaimed, because he had her by the shoulders and he looked devastated. Anguished.

"It wasn't," he bit off.

She laughed. It had a hollow sound. She drew back from his hands, and he let go. "I work with men. They talk, all about their conquests, how they talk a woman into doing what they want and how they get rid of her afterward. I've been educated. I know all the tricks."

He winced. "It wasn't like that."

She just sighed. "It was exactly like that. You said it yourself. You'd gone for a long time without a woman, and I was very obviously besotted."

"I never said that about you," he said curtly.

"Really? Edie did. She said you laughed about it, that you were both very grateful that I, how did she put it, removed the problem baby from the equation." She even smiled.

Edie had called her. He hadn't known. What in the world had she said? On the other hand, Amelia had gone to a clinic. A clinic!

"Women are treacherous," he said coldly.

"And men are weasels," she shot back. "I'm going."

She turned and walked off toward the restaurant.

"Will you stop threatening to pull a gun on me and listen to me?" he yelled, losing his temper.

She had her hand on her pistol without thinking. "I am not trying to shoot you!" she raged.

He was suddenly aware that two of his own officers were standing by a patrol car, along with a very pregnant Clancey Banks and her husband, along with a tall, Italian-looking man who held a pretty brunette in his arms. They were all suppressing laughter. Cal was never flustered or out of control. The gossips would feed on this for weeks, he thought irritably.

He cleared his throat. This wasn't going to be easy to explain. And, worse, the object of his hunt had escaped. He didn't even see which way she went.

The rest of the day was taken up with Clancey giving birth to her first child. Banks, a Texas Ranger and the proud father, was absolutely strutting. The baby was precious. He hated wishing it was his. He'd almost had one. Thanks to Amelia, that had never happened.

He got through the rest of the day and went home, to the Santa Gertrudis ranch he'd bought years ago with some of the proceeds of his brief mercenary career. His wife had hated the place, preferring to drink herself to death at her apartment in San Antonio. All those years married, and he'd never touched her. She threw Amelia up to him all the time. He didn't care. He hated Amelia for what she'd done.

But he couldn't get out of his mind what she'd said, about being in the hospital. Why would they put her in the hospital after she'd gone to the clinic? Had there been complications?

And what sort of mission was Eb sending her overseas on? He thought of two possible areas of interest in the news and his blood went cold.

He made a pot of coffee, sat down with a cup of strong black Colombian and called Eb Scott.

Chapter Twelve

"Well!" Eb exclaimed. "It's been an age since I've heard from you. How've you been?"

"Better," Cal said heavily. "Listen, I know it's none of my business. But where are you sending Amelia?"

There was a brief pause. "That's not your concern," he said quietly.

Eb was like himself, there were limits to how far you could go with him, even in conversation.

"She won't talk to me," Cal said.

"I'm not surprised."

"Did she tell you what she did six years ago?" Cal asked, irritated at the other man's tone.

"Before or after she got out of the hospital?" Eb asked.

"Why would they take her to the hospital to get rid of a baby?" he asked, all at sea.

Now there was a pregnant pause. "She didn't tell you?"

"I…didn't give her much of a chance to speak. I was angry and hurt. I said a lot of things. She blocked my number so I couldn't call her again."

"Your wife did."

"I didn't know that, until Amelia told me, today. My wife and I didn't speak often. She was usually too high to notice whether I was around or not," he added bitterly.

"I see." Eb was stunned.

"Amelia said she'd been in the hospital. I thought there were clinics for that sort of thing."

"Her great-aunt pushed her down the staircase," Eb interrupted. "That was why she was in the hospital," Eb said. "That was what happened to the baby, too. Amelia isn't the sort of person who goes to a clinic. How can you say you know her, but you don't know that about her?" he added.

"Her great-aunt…what?"

"Pushed her down the staircase. She said Amelia had disgraced the family."

"Surely, that wouldn't have been enough to provoke such a response," Cal said, accustomed to such incidents from years of listening to tragedies in his job.

"It would if Amelia had refused to get rid of the child, Cal. I imagine that's why. And that's not all. She lost her job, her home, her baby. She had no money and no place to go. That's why she came to me."

Cal's eyes closed. He'd made assumptions. He'd been certain that Amelia didn't want his child. He hadn't checked on her after the passion they'd shared. He'd even taken Edie to the funeral as armor. He'd done every damned thing in the world to show Amelia how little he cared. And there she was, pregnant, her grandfather dead, no place to live except with her prejudiced great-aunt. Afterward, she lost the baby and Cal told her that he was married, that he blamed her, that she could go to hell…

Amelia, with the world shattered at her feet, so desperate that she signed on with a bunch of mercs and went to war because she had nothing left. Nothing. Nobody. Least of all, a man who cared about her. He felt the sting of moisture in his eyes.

"Then your wife called her, and she probably had a few things to say about how you felt, if you told her the story you thought was the truth." Eb added his own measure of salt to the wound.

"I didn't know that Edie had done that," he said on a heavy

breath. "Even when she was sober, she was the kind of person who enjoyed rubbing salt in open wounds," Cal added bitterly.

"So Amelia lost everything and she had nothing left to lose. So she came to me and asked for work. I didn't have the heart to refuse her."

Cal's heart was breaking. After what he'd done to Amelia, it was no wonder that she wouldn't speak to him. He'd accused her with no evidence except a snarky phone call from her great-aunt, and he knew Valeria was a fanatic about the family name. Why hadn't he tried harder to talk to Amelia? Why had he hesitated? Because, to his shame, he'd believed Valeria. He was never going to get over the pain of doing that. He'd have to live with it for the rest of his life, along with the nightmares that never ceased.

"Cal?"

"What? Oh. Sorry. I was just...thinking. Eb, if you can, please don't send her someplace where she's likely to be killed. I have no right to interfere with her life, but I can't..." He stopped, just before his voice broke with emotion. He collected himself. "It's my fault. All of it. What happened. I don't want her to run away from me and into something she can't handle."

"You could go and talk to her."

"I followed her all over San Antonio, trying to do that. She listened to me and smiled and just kept walking."

"She's very bitter about what happened. I think your wife has a lot to answer for. And Amelia's great-aunt, as well."

"They were accessories. I was the devil in the mix. It's so funny, how you can go looking for something your whole life, only to realize that you had it under your nose, and you threw it away."

"Life's like that."

"Life sucks."

Eb chuckled. "Yes. Sometimes. You should get married and have kids."

"No chance of that. Not anymore. Take care of my girl, will you?"

"I've always done that. Come out and see us sometime. The facility's expanded. We're teaching all sorts of new stuff, including computer hacking. In fact, I think we have a couple of card-carrying Feds here checking us out undercover."

"I might do that one day. Thanks for the information. I won't mention where I got it."

"Good thing. She can still outshoot me."

"Take care."

"Sure. You, too."

After a few minutes, during which he relived every bitter word he'd said to Amelia, every stupid thing he'd done to her, Cal got up from the table, poured out his coffee, grabbed a tea glass and filled it to the brim with rum. He opened the refrigerator to look for ice. His cell phone dropped but he didn't see it. He closed the door and opened the freezer unit on top. He opened the ice tray and added one ice cube to his drink. Then he sat back down at the table.

This was a stupid thing to do, his brain told him. Shut up, said his aching heart.

Two days later, one of his officers came looking for him. Lt. Rick Marquez was a favorite of the captain's. It was Rick who usually got sent to talk him down when he drowned his problems. It had only been a couple of times. The last one had been bad. The captain had happened upon a bank robbery and stepped out of his car with his pistol drawn right into the path of one of the robbers pointing a loaded shotgun at him. He fired and threw the shotgun up. The criminal died. The captain stayed drunk for days.

Clancey Banks, who was the closest thing to a relative he had—he'd more or less adopted her little brother and her years ago when she'd been his secretary—got him to the phone. But he was totally incoherent except to say that he was sick of life.

Which spooked her, and she called his office and told them they'd better get somebody out to Cal's ranch, pronto. She would have gone, but the new baby had a cold and she wasn't leaving him.

Word got around, just in the department, that the captain was on a bender. Nobody was brave enough to wander out to his ranch and try to talk him down this time until Marquez volunteered.

It became obvious very soon that intervention was going to become a job. The front door of Cal's ranch house was unlocked. When nobody answered several knocks, Rick walked in. The captain was lying facedown on the living room floor. Snoring. Yep, he thought. It was going to be a job. If not a career.

Rick got the captain as far as the sofa—he was a big guy and dead weight. He left the unconscious man long enough to find a blanket in the bedroom that he brought to cover his superior with. Then he went into the kitchen and made coffee.

"I don't want any more of this!" Cal raged, red eyes blazing as he finished the third cup that Rick had almost forced down his throat.

"I don't blame you. What the hell kind of coffee is this, anyway?" he added, sniffing it.

"Vanilla. I think. The wrong kind. I bought it and thought I'd take it back and exchange it for Colombian, but I never did." He made a face. "It tastes like a pastry."

"I think it's supposed to."

The captain drew in a long breath and sat back on the sofa. It all came rushing into his head, now that he was sober—halfway at least. Amelia. The staircase. The baby. The concussion. Edie. The rushed marriage. The nightmares. It all conglomerated in his head like Jell-O in a fridge.

He bent over, with his hands on his knees propping up his throbbing head. "I was happier drunk," he muttered.

"Everybody is happier drunk, but it would be a terrible scandal if they had to fire you for it, sir," Rick pointed out.

Cal sighed. "Yeah."

Rick had no idea what had set the captain off, but other officers had mentioned seeing the captain following a blond woman around town. The woman wouldn't listen to him. There had to be a history there, but it was obviously something personal and Rick didn't like to pry.

"Is there anything I can do?" he asked finally, his tone concerned.

Cal took a deep breath. "Yes. Get me a priest."

Rick gaped at him. "Sir, suicide is a very bad way to handle personal problems...!"

He glared at his subordinate. "I don't want to commit suicide! I want to talk to Father Eduardo Perez. He's at the Catedral de Santa Maria. I think his number's on my cell phone. If I can find my cell phone..." he mumbled, still not quite sober.

"I'll look for it," Rick said, and got to his feet. "When did you see it last?"

"I was pouring a drink and looking for an ice cube," the older man mumbled.

Rick finally found the missing phone after searching through every drawer in the room. After the conventional places, he looked in the unconventional ones. The phone was in the refrigerator. He took it out. Fortunately, it warmed up quickly and there was a dial tone. He just shook his head.

He carried it back into the living room. Cal still hadn't stirred. "It was, uh, in the fridge?"

Cal looked up, deadpan. "Don't you keep yours in the fridge, Lieutenant?" he asked blandly. "Does a hell of a job keeping them from overheating."

Rick smothered a laugh.

Cal didn't. He chuckled out loud as he took it from Rick. "I went to get an ice cube for my drink. I looked in the fridge for it." He looked up at Rick. "No comments," he said firmly.

"Sir, I swear, I never meant to say a word," Rick assured him. "Where you keep your phone is nobody's business."

"Yeah? Well, I'd better not hear any gossip about it when I'm back in the office tomorrow."

"You won't, sir. I can guarantee it," Rick said with a carefully placid expression.

"Good enough. Go home, Marquez. I'm all right now." He hesitated. "And...thanks."

"No problem, sir. Glad to help."

Cal waited until Rick's car started up. Then he dialed. A deep voice answered. "Can you come over for a few minutes?" he asked. "I think I really need to talk to somebody."

There was a deep chuckle. "Ten minutes."

Father Eduardo was something of a legend in San Antonio. He lived and worked in a section of San Antonio that had belonged to the Little Devil Wolves gang—mostly teenagers, responsible for some of the bloodiest murders in the history of the city. When Father Eduardo had first become rector of the parish, seven heavily armed members of the gang decided to get rid of him.

The guns weren't enough to save them. After calling an ambulance for the most injured two, the priest went with the rest of them to the hospital and waited patiently while they were treated. Two of them converted on the spot. The rest left him strictly alone—especially when they discovered that he was best friends with the leader of the rival, and more deadly, gang, Los Serpientes. Over a period of months, the Little Devil Wolves had been prosecuted into oblivion, and good riddance. The Serpientes, while still deadly, were kindness itself to children and the elderly. So was Father Eduardo.

Eduardo had been with Cal and Eb and the others in the African conflict. All of them were scarred from the experience. When Cal was really down and tormented by memories, Eduardo was the man he called for help.

"This time it isn't Ngawa, is it, compadre?" Eduardo asked over yet more cups of the detested vanilla coffee.

Cal shook his head. "I was infatuated with a girl I knew in Jacobsville when I got home from Ngawa. Things happened. She lost her grandfather and her home and had to move in with a great-aunt in Victoria." He took a deep breath. "She was pregnant. Her great-aunt pushed her down a staircase. She lost the baby."

"I am truly sorry," Eduardo said. He scowled. "She wanted it?"

He nodded. He drew in a breath. "I was told that she went to a clinic. Her great-aunt phoned me to say that. Then my late wife also called her to thank her for getting rid of an encumbrance." He looked up. "So helpful, both of them. I hated Amelia for what I thought she did. I called her and cussed her out, without giving her even a chance to explain. Then, a few days ago, Eb told me what really happened." He drew a breath and winced. "Amelia's great-aunt pushed her down the staircase. She lost the baby, got a concussion and was in the hospital. Lost her job. She'd already lost her grandfather." He shook his head. "And I just found out what Amelia has been doing for a living for the past few years. She's working for Eb Scott." He lowered his head and sipped coffee to hide the anguish he felt. "She won't even talk to me."

"I assume you said something to her all those years ago?" Eduardo probed.

He drew in a breath. "Some terrible things," he replied. "Plus, I got married at once, to show her how little I cared." He looked at Eduardo. "You know how that worked out. Living with Edie was hell on earth. Not that I didn't deserve that, and more, considering what I did to Amelia's life."

"So that is the past," Eduardo replied. "What about the future?"

He grimaced. "Eb's sending her on some mission overseas. He won't tell me what."

"I can only imagine where," Eduardo replied.

"Exactly." He looked up. "I can't live if she gets herself killed. She's all I've thought about for years. Even when I blamed her, when I thought she didn't want the baby, I couldn't stop caring." He looked away. "I detested my wife. I couldn't touch her."

Eduardo didn't reply. He'd once been married, before he took the collar, and lost his wife and child in a horrible way. He'd never thought of having women since then.

"I remember what she was like."

"I was very drunk when I married her." He looked up. "I don't drink, usually."

"I know that, too."

He finished his coffee. "I don't know what to do. She won't listen."

"You could pick her up for jaywalking."

Cal gave him a speaking look.

"Flowers? Candy? A mariachi band?"

"She'd throw away the flowers, stomp on the candy and probably shoot the mariachis," Cal said gloomily.

"Then take her dancing at Fernando's," Eduardo said gently, smiling.

"Optimist."

"I believe in miracles. I see them every day."

"That's your business. You deal in miracles. I deal in the lowest common denominator of humanity, crime."

"If you never expect miracles, you never see them," Eduardo continued gently. "First, you must believe."

He met the priest's warm dark eyes. There was such kindness there, such compassion. He felt his doubts slowly melt. He smiled. "Okay," he said. "I'll try."

"And that is the first step," Eduardo replied. "Now, I have a question."

"Of course. What is it?"

"Where in the world did you buy this truly detestable coffee?" Eduardo asked, making a face at the coffee cup.

Amelia was sitting all alone in her apartment, sipping black coffee and waiting for Eb to send over a man with details of her new assignment. Phones could be hacked. It was better to do it in person.

Her mind kept going back six years. She'd been young and in love for the first, and last, time. And life had tortured her. Everything that could possibly go wrong in her life, had. She missed her grandfather terribly. Valeria was the only relative she had left. Despite the woman's apologies, Amelia wanted nothing to do with her. The loss of her child was a torment. Cal had thrown her away like a used napkin. But she hadn't been able to stop loving him, even then. She'd wanted her baby.

She sipped coffee and thought of the lonely, bitter years in front of her. If she caught a bullet on this assignment, who cared?

The knock at the door startled her. Finally, she thought, the messenger.

She opened the door. "No," she bit off. "He wouldn't have sent you…!"

Cal edged his way inside, gently but firmly, and closed the door behind him. "We have to talk. You know that."

She glared at him. "There's no need. We're not the same people we were six years ago. I don't look back. Ever."

"That was me, six years ago," he said. His black eyes searched her pale ones. "I threw you aside and walked away. I need you to understand why."

"We won't see each other again," she emphasized. "I'm not coming back after this assignment. Not to Texas."

He looked worn. "I smell coffee."

She hesitated. "All right. But I'm expecting someone."

His heart fell. Another man. Why hadn't he expected that? She was young and she had an allure that had nothing to do with physical assets. She was a nurturing person. They were rare in Cal's life.

He followed her into the kitchen. "Father Eduardo and I had to drink vanilla coffee. I bought the wrong kind and didn't return it."

She glanced at him. "Vanilla?"

He made a face. "Yes."

"I'd rather drink muddy water," she said simply. She poured him a cup of hot black coffee and handed it to him as he sat down at her kitchen table.

She warmed her own cup and sat down with him. It was going to be an ordeal, but maybe he was right. Maybe they had to talk it out before he could let go of the past.

"Six years ago," he began, "you wouldn't have been able to understand what I'm going to tell you." He leaned back on her sofa with his coffee. "In fact, I wouldn't have told you six years ago. You were so incredibly innocent. About men. About life."

She frowned. She didn't understand.

He saw that. He laughed hollowly. "Ngawa was a nightmare, even for the more experienced mercs." He took a sip of coffee. "We had this kid that we sort of adopted in our unit. We had plans to bring him to the states after the mission was through." He drew in a long breath, hating the image that popped in 3D, in full color, into his mind. "His name was Juba. One day we moved into an enemy position. There was a house. In the doorway, an explosive. Juba ran ahead of us to check it out, with his AK-47 shouldered. They shot the explosive while he was taking cover." He shivered. "Have you ever seen a man blown up, Amelia?" he asked quietly.

She hesitated. Nodded. She swallowed down the nausea. "I set a charge a few minutes too soon. A man died." Her eyes closed. "I've had to live with it, and with the survivors who were his friends. None of us can forget it."

He was shocked. He hadn't yet connected her expertise in demolition with her actual job for Eb. "You do demolition work for Eb," he said suddenly, and fear carved a cold place in his heart.

"Yes," she replied. Her eyes were cold as they met his. "I'm good at it now."

He sipped coffee. He had to talk her out of going overseas. He didn't know how. "Cy Parks sat with Juba in his arms and rocked him until he died," he continued quietly. "It was just the beginning of the horror. I saw things, participated in things, that I wish I could forget. Sometimes the memories get really bad, and I drink." He sat up, putting his empty cup on the coffee table. "Marquez, who works in my office, just came over to talk me down. This is the first time I've been completely sober in several days."

"The memories…" she began.

"I didn't know your great-aunt pushed you down a damned staircase," he said, his black eyes flashing. "I didn't know that Edie had called you."

The information sat on her like a hundred bricks. She just looked at him, her eyes wide.

"I stayed away from you after that night because I knew I wouldn't be able to stop if we were together again," he bit off. "It was why I took Edie to your grandfather's funeral. I wanted you all the time." He looked up at her. "Besides that, I was trying to deal with the aftermath of what happened to us in Ngawa, and I wasn't able to cope with it. I couldn't tell you about it because you wouldn't have understood. Not like you can now," he added.

She took a breath. "I've had my own feet in the fire," she said quietly. "I know what it's like. Well, sort of. Eb always has me behind the lines doing demo work."

God bless Eb, he thought fervently.

"So you understand some of what I was going through. I was an emotional train wreck," he continued. "I had to deal with the memories, get back into the world. That meant going back to police work and moving to San Antonio. Edie was always around. I didn't encourage her. My mind was on you most of the time, but guilt and mental anguish kept me away. I had no idea about the baby…" He bit off the rest and his eyes were on the carpet.

She felt his misery. It was a devastating blow, to realize that what she'd been hating him for was the result of outside interference from two hateful women.

"I thought that, because you stayed away, you didn't want anything else to do with me," she said quietly. "But I was going to keep my baby. I wanted him so much! I left the pregnancy kit in the bathroom, I was so shocked by the results, and Valeria found it. She insisted on a termination, but I told her I wouldn't do that. I told her I'd move out, I already even had a job…" She stopped. Her eyes closed on the memory. "She pushed me. I came to in the hospital. The concussion was the least of my sorrow."

"And then I called you and cussed you out, after all that." He stopped, fighting for control. He felt sick to his soul.

She saw the anguish in his face. It seemed so strange, to be sitting here with Cal after all they'd been through, to realize how much he still cared. He'd wanted the child. He'd wanted her. Only now could she understand what he'd been going through six years ago, the terror, the confusion, probably some guilt into the mix.

"At least you had someone to help you through all the trauma," she said.

"If you mean Edie," he said heavily, "her only purpose was to avenge you."

"Excuse me?"

"Rubbing salt into open wounds?" he replied, lifting his head. "She made my life hell. I couldn't touch her. She was physically repulsive to me, and she knew it, but only after she'd coaxed me in a drunken haze to marry her. After that, it was men and booze and drugs for the rest of her life. When she died, it was a relief for both of us. Hell on earth, Amelia," he added softly.

She gaped at him. "Couldn't…touch…her," she stammered.

"She wasn't you," he said simply. He reached into his pocket and pulled out a jeweler's box. He put it on the coffee table and opened it. It was a wedding set of diamond rings. Amber diamonds.

He stared at her. "I bought those six years ago," he said quietly. "Hid them in my travel kit. I was going back to get you. I'd planned to call you the day Valeria called me."

It was too much. Just too much. She started crying. Sobbing. If it hadn't been for Valeria…!

She felt arms around her, holding her, arms that were still familiar after all the years between.

"Don't cry," he whispered at her ear. "Don't. It's over. We found each other again."

Her arms tightened around his neck. "Damn her!" she sobbed. "And damn Edie!"

"And damn me, too, but we can't go back and change a thing. We can only go forward, Amelia." His hands were caressing on her back, slow and tender, like the voice at her temple. He drew in a long, shuddering breath. "I would give an arm to take back what I said to you, what I did. It was my fault, more than anyone's. I refused to listen. If I'd just kept my damned temper…!" He groaned out loud and held her closer. "I'm sorry, honey. I'm so…sorry!"

She felt a wetness at her throat where his face was buried. Tears stung her own eyes. Six long years of agony because of two miserable people who liked to cause trouble. "Me, too," she choked.

He just held her, rocking her, in a silence that finally calmed them both.

He lifted his head and searched her dark eyes with his. "We can't go back," he said sadly. "But we can go forward. We can start over. Just you and me, Amelia, the way we were meant to start over six years ago. And this time, there won't be any interference."

Her face nestled into his throat, and she snuggled close as he lifted her and sat back down with her in his lap. His arms tightened and he sighed with pure delight. He hadn't expected this reaction from her. Not even in his dreams.

"I love you, Amelia," he whispered huskily. "I think I loved you the first time I saw you. But I only knew it when it was too late."

She nuzzled closer. "I loved you, too. It was why I would never have given up my baby."

"I should have known that."

She stilled. "How did you know, about how I lost the baby?"

"Eb told me." He sighed. "I've been drunk for three days. Marquez came this morning and shoved that disgusting vanilla coffee into me to sober me up. I hated being sober. I relived what happened all over again. I was going to buy a new bottle of rum. But I thought maybe I could get you to listen to me if I just came over and stood at your door until you let me in."

She laughed softly. "I didn't mean to."

He kissed her hair. "I know you didn't. Father Eduardo told me just a few hours ago that miracles happen when you expect them. So I expected this one. I'll have to phone him and tell him it worked."

She lifted her head. "Father Eduardo? The priest who faced down seven armed attackers and sent them all to the emergency room, empty-handed?"

"The very one," he said, smiling.

"He's something of a legend in San Antonio."

"He was a legend in Ngawa, as well."

She drew in a long breath and wiped her eyes on a paper towel from her pocket. He caught her hand and kissed it.

"We can get a license at city hall," he suggested. "I already have the rings. We can buy you a really pretty dress. Then we can have a honeymoon. Afterward we can go to Fernando's every Friday night and do the tango!"

She laughed. "I haven't danced in years."

"Dancing is something you never forget how to do. Along with something else that we did very well together," he said, bending to kiss her very gently. "But this time, we wait until after the wedding," he added firmly. His eyes searched hers. "That is, if you'll marry me."

She searched his eyes and saw the years of anguish, of hopeless, helpless love that she'd seen in her mirror for the same length of time.

"Take a chance on me," he said quietly. "Believe in miracles."

She took a long breath. He was absolutely gorgeous. The ice inside her that had kept her going for so long was slowly melting under the warmth of his hunger for her. And not just physical hunger. The love in his eyes was like brown velvet.

But he was tense, waiting. Hoping. Not pressuring. She saw all that, in a flash. Her own love had never wavered, even when she thought he hated her. It never would.

She smiled, finally, and wrinkled her nose at him. "Okay."

"Thank God," he ground out, and bent and kissed her, tentatively at first, and then with such hunger and passion that she moaned aloud.

A long time later, he lifted his head. He took deep breaths. "First, we get married," he said tightly. "We do it right, this time."

She smiled dreamily and reached up to kiss him softly. "Yes." She laid her head on his chest with a sigh.

"And you stop carrying a gun," he added in a teasing tone.

"I will if you will."

"I'm a law enforcement officer. I'm required to carry a gun," he said smugly.

She lifted her head and started to speak.

"Show me your concealed-carry permit," he challenged.

"It's in my wallet."

"Is it?" he purred. "You can't watch it every minute."

"I what?"

He gave her a blithe smile. "One of my officers ate the license of a man who verbally abused him during a traffic stop in town," he pointed out.

She began to see the light. "You wouldn't dare," she exclaimed, reading between the lines, her eyes like saucers.

"I can arrest people, too," he pointed out.

She gaped at him.

"I have handcuffs," he added.

He just stared at her. Until they both burst out laughing.

"You're going to be a lot of trouble," she said.

He nodded and smiled. "Count on it."

Chapter Thirteen

They were married in the Methodist Church in Jacobsville by Pastor Jake Blair, with a building full of friends of both bride and groom. Eb and his family were in the front row as Cal and Amelia said their vows.

There was a huge reception in the fellowship hall with, sadly, no riot, as lamented by Police Chief Cash Grier, who had warm memories of one when local DA Blake Kemp married his secretary, Violet. Liquor had been allowed, and the ensuing mayhem was remembered with humor by most of the participants. Grier, especially.

They honeymooned in Jamaica, in a hotel in Montego Bay. Their room opened onto the beach, where they took a midnight stroll before finally ending the day in the appropriate manner.

It was like six years ago. Amelia was shy at first, but Cal knew how to cope with that. A few kisses later, she was helping him get the fabric out of the way.

"I never forgot…how it felt," she whispered as his mouth lowered to her breasts.

"Neither did I," he groaned. "Not once. Oh, God, this is so…sweet!"

"Sweet," she moaned, holding on tight as she felt him move between her parted legs. "Sweet!"

He wanted to take ages with her, but it had been a long time between women. "I'm truly sorry," he began to apologize as his movements became insistent.

"You don't need to be sorry," she whispered back, shifting as their positions became suddenly intimate and hectic. "Just... hurry!" she said on a laugh and a groan, all at once.

She closed her eyes as the fever burned high and bright, almost incandescent as it brought waves of pleasure, each one taking them higher and higher, until finally, at the culmination, they both cried out at the intensity of fulfillment.

For a long time they stayed like that, just holding each other as the sound of the waves crashing on the shore became audible.

"Was it that sweet before?" he whispered huskily.

"I'm not sure." Her long leg slid against his. "Can we do it again and make sure it was?"

"With pleasure...!"

They stayed for a week, bringing home memories of moonlit nights and feverish passion interspersed with sightseeing and souvenirs.

The ranch house was laden with food the day they came home, courtesy of neighbors and friends.

Rick Marquez and his wife and daughters, and baby son, came to greet them, along with his mother, Barbara, who owned Barbara's Café, and her friend, the ex-mobster and now policeman Fred Baldwin.

"And if that's not enough, you just let me know," Barbara added, hugging them both before they left.

They surveyed the kitchen table with its huge platters of food.

"We can last until Christmas at least," Cal remarked.

"Maybe New Year's," she seconded.

They laughed and started putting away food.

The captain's new wife fascinated his officers. Every time she visited, she was whisked into the canteen to be quizzed about her former job.

A lot of the questions came from Clancey Banks, who had at

one time been Cal's secretary and was still like a young sister to him. Clancey and Amelia got on famously. So did she and Clancey's baby brother, Tad.

Clancey had a new baby boy. She and her husband, Colter, were frequent visitors at Cal's ranch, which gave Amelia a chance to hold the baby. Cal did his share of that, too.

One afternoon, when the Banks had gone home, Amelia sat in Cal's lap on the porch in the rocking chair reminiscing about the baby.

"Babies are nice," he commented.

She smiled. "Yes, and holding Clancey's is good practice for you."

"It is?" he asked, his eyes on one of his prize Santa Gertrudis cattle grazing in the nearby pasture.

She held a plastic stick under his nose.

He looked at it. He looked at her, his eyebrows raised.

"It's the right color," she said mischievously.

"The right…" His brain clicked. One and one made two. "You're pregnant?" he exclaimed, so loudly that the cow raised her head and stared at him.

"Oh, yes, very pregnant," she said, grinning.

He got up with her in his arms, rocking her, fighting tears. "Miracles," he whispered as he bent to kiss her hungrily. "Everyday miracles."

"Yes," she agreed and nuzzled close. "Love doesn't die. No matter how hard you hit it."

He chuckled. "Truly. But we aren't hitting it anymore."

"Never again." She reached her arms around his neck. "I hope you don't mind that I sometimes remember how much fun it was to blow up stuff before I did it for a living?"

"Not if you don't mind if I occasionally remember how much fun it was to dream about being a mercenary."

"The reality is less fulfilling than the anticipation," she agreed. "Except when it comes to having babies."

He grinned. "I agree wholeheartedly." He kissed her warmly. "I'll love you until I die. And then some."

She searched his black eyes. "And I'll love you until I die. And then some. Aren't we the two luckiest people in the whole world?"

He nodded. He kissed her. "And then some," he teased.

* * * * *

GUY

Chapter One

It was a cool autumn day, and the feedlot was full. A good many of these steers were already under contract to restaurants and fast-food establishments, but in these last weeks before they were shipped north, the cowboys who worked for the Ballenger Brothers in Jacobsville, Texas, were pushed to the limit. Guy Fenton hated his job when things were this hectic. He almost hated it enough to go back to flying; but not quite.

He pushed his hat back from his sweaty dark hair and cursed the cattle, the feedlot, people who ate beef and people who bought it in eloquent succession. He wasn't a handsome man, but he still had a way with women. He was lean and lanky, thirty years old, with gray eyes and a tragic past that an occasional date numbed just a little. Lately, though, women had been right off his list of pastimes. There had been too much work here at the feedlot, and he was responsible for mixing the various grains and nutrients to put just enough, but not too much, weight on these beef cattle. He enjoyed the job from time to time, but just lately everything was rubbing him the wrong way. A chance meeting with an old acquaintance several months ago from the days of his engagement had brought back all the bad memories and set him on a weekend binge. That was followed by another, when the man settled nearby and came to visit him occasionally, not realizing the damage he was doing to Guy's peace of mind.

"For two bits," he said out loud, "I'd chuck it all and become a beachcomber!"

"Keep your mind on that conveyor belt and thank God you don't have to climb down in there to inoculate those horned devils," came a drawling voice from behind him.

He glanced over his shoulder at Justin Ballenger and grinned. "You don't mean things could get worse around here?"

Justin stuck his hands into his pockets and chuckled. "It seems that way, from time to time, when we get this much extra business. Come over here. I want to talk to you."

The big boss rarely came out to talk to the hands, so it was an occasion for curiosity. Guy finished the settings on the conveyer belt that delivered feed to the dozens of stalls before he jumped down lithely to stand before one of the two owners of the feedlot.

"What can I do for you, boss?" he asked pleasantly.

"You can stop getting drunk every weekend and treeing Thompson's place," he replied solemnly, his dark eyes glittering.

Guy's high cheekbones went a little ruddy. He averted his gaze to the milling, mooing cattle. "I didn't realize the gossip got this far."

"You can't trim your toenails in Jacobsville without somebody knowing about it," Justin returned. "You've been going downhill for a while, but just lately you're on a bad path, son," he added, his deep voice quiet and concerned. "I hate to see you go down it any farther."

Guy didn't look at the older man. His jaw tautened. "It's my road. I have to walk it."

"No, you don't," Justin said curtly. "It's been three years since you signed on here. I never asked any questions about your past, and I'm not doing it now. But I hate to see a good man go right down the drain. You have to let go of the past."

Guy's eyes met the other man's almost on a level. Both were tall, but Justin was older and pretty tough, too. He wasn't a man Guy would ever like to have to fight. "I can't let go," he replied shortly. "You don't understand."

"No, I don't, not in the way you mean," Justin conceded, his dark eyes narrowing. "But all this carousing and grieving isn't going to change whatever happened to you."

Guy drew in a short breath and stared at the flat horizon. He didn't speak, because if he let the anger out, Justin would fire him. He might hate his job, but he couldn't afford to lose it, either. "Rob Hartford settled up in Victoria and he comes down to see me. He does it too often," he said finally. "He was there—when it happened. He doesn't know it, but he brought all the memories back."

"Tell him. People can't read minds."

He sighed. His gray eyes met Justin's dark ones. "He'd take it hard."

"He'll take it harder if you end up in jail. The one good thing about it is that you've got sense enough not to drive when you're in that condition."

"The only good thing," Guy said wearily. "Okay, boss, I'll do what I can."

Justin followed his gaze. "Winter's coming fast," he murmured. "We'll just get this batch of steers out before we have to buy more feed. It'll be close, at that."

"Only crazy people get into feeding out cattle," Guy pointed out, lightening the atmosphere.

Justin smiled faintly. "So they say."

He shrugged. "I'll try to stay away from Thompson's."

"It doesn't make a hell of a lot of sense to drink up your salary every weekend," the older man said flatly. "Regardless of the reason. But that isn't what I came out here to talk to you about."

Guy frowned. "Then why did you?"

"We've got a beef industry publicist coming tomorrow from Denver. She wants to visit a few area ranches, as well as our feedlot here, to get some idea of what sort of methods we're using."

"Why?" Guy asked curtly.

"The local cattlemen's association—of which Evan Tremayne was just elected president—wants to help punch up the image of the industry locally. The industry as a whole has had some bad press lately over bacterial contamination. There's been even more bad press about some renegade cattlemen and their practices. We don't follow their lead around here, and we're anxious to get the fact across to the beef-eating public. Evan also has an idea about customizing lean beef for a specialized market of buyers."

"I thought Evan was too busy with his wife to worry about business," Guy murmured dryly.

"Oh, Anna's doing his paperwork for him," he mused. "They're inseparable, business or not. Anyway, this publicist is expected in the morning. The Tremaynes are out of town, Ted Regan and his wife are at a convention in Utah and Calhoun is going to be tied up with a buyer tomorrow. You're the only cowboy we've got who knows as much about the industry as we do, especially where feedlots are concerned. We've elected you to be her guide."

"Me?" Guy cursed under his breath and glared at the older man. "What about the Hart boys? There are four of them over at the Hart ranch."

"Two," Justin corrected. "Cag's off on his honeymoon, and Corrigan went with his wife, Dorie, to visit Simon and Tira in San Antonio. They've just had their first child." He chuckled. "Anyway, I wouldn't wish the two bachelor Hart boys on her. We don't know if she can make biscuits, but Leo and Rey may be too desperate to care."

Guy only nodded. The Hart boys were a local legend because of their biscuit mania. Pity none of them could cook.

"So you're elected."

"I know more about rodeo than I know about ranching," Guy pointed out.

"Yes, I know." He searched the younger man's closed face. "I heard someone say you used to fly yourself to the competitions."

Guy's eyes glittered and he straightened. "I don't talk about flying. Ever."

"Yes, I heard that, too," Justin said. He threw up his hands. "All right, clam up and fester. I just wanted you to know that you'll be away from here tomorrow, so delegate whatever chores you need to before the morning."

"Okay." Guy sighed. "I guess you couldn't do it?"

Justin glanced over his shoulder. "Sorry. Shelby and I have to go to the elementary school in the morning. Our oldest son's in a Thanksgiving play." He grinned. "He's an ear of corn."

Guy didn't say a word. But his eyes danced and his lower lip did a tango.

"Good thing you kept your mouth shut, Fenton," he added with a wicked grin. "I hear they're shy a turkey. It would be a pity to volunteer you for *that* instead of the ranch tour."

He walked off and Guy gave in to the chuckle he'd choked back. Sometimes he didn't mind this job at all.

He went back to the bunkhouse after work, noting that it was empty except for one young college student from Billings, who was sprawled on a bunk reading Shakespeare through small rimmed glasses. He looked up when Guy entered the building.

"Cook's off sick, so they're shuttling supper out from the main house," the college student, Richard, remarked. "Just you and me tonight. The other bachelors went off to some sort of party in town."

"Lucky stiffs," Guy murmured. He took off his hat and sprawled on his own bunk with a weary sigh. "I hate cattle."

Richard, who liked to be called "Slim" by the other cowhands, chuckled. He was much more relaxed when he and Guy were the only two men sharing the bunkhouse. Some of the older hands, many uneducated, gave him a hard time in the evenings about his continuing studies.

"They may smell lousy, but they sure do pay my tuition," Slim remarked.

"How many years do you have to go?" Guy asked curiously.

The younger man shrugged. "Two, the normal way. But I have to work a semester and go to school a semester, because it's the only way I can afford tuition. I guess it'll take me four more years to graduate."

"Can't you get a scholarship?"

Slim shook his head. "My grades aren't quite good enough for the big ones, and my folks make too much money for me to qualify for financial aid."

Guy's eyes narrowed. "There should be a way. Have you talked to the finance office at your school?"

"I thought about it, but one of the other kids said I might as well save my time."

"What's your field?"

Slim grinned. "Medicine," he said. "So I've got a long road ahead of me, even after I get my B.S."

Guy didn't smile. "I've got a couple of ideas. Let me think them over."

"You've got problems of your own, Mr. Fenton," Slim told him. "No need to worry about me, as well."

"What makes you think I've got problems?"

Slim closed the literature book he was holding. "You get drunk like clockwork every weekend. Nobody drinks that much for recreation, especially not a guy who's as serious the rest of the week as you are. You never shirk duties or delegate chores, and you're always stone sober on the job." He smiled sheepishly. "I guess it was something pretty bad."

Guy's pale gray eyes had a faraway, haunted look. "Yes. Pretty bad." He rolled over onto his back and pulled his hat over his eyes. "I wish you outranked me, Slim."

"Why?"

"Then you'd get stuck with the publicist tomorrow, instead of me."

"I heard Mr. Ballenger talking about her. He says she's pretty."

"He didn't tell me that."

"Maybe he was saving it for a surprise."

Guy laughed hollowly. "Some surprise. She'll probably faint when she gets a good whiff of the feedlot."

"Well, you never know." Pages in the book rustled as he turned them. "Man, I hate Shakespeare."

"Peasant," Guy murmured.

"You'd hate him, too, if you had to do a course in Elizabethan literature."

"I did two, thanks. Made straight A's."

Slim didn't speak for a little while. "You went to college?"

"Yup."

"Get your degree?"

"Yup."

"Well, what in?"

"In what," Guy corrected.

"Okay, in what?"

"You might say, in physics," he said, without mentioning that his degree was in aeronautics, his minor in chemistry.

Slim whistled. "And you're working on a cattle ranch?"

"Seemed like a good idea at the time. And it's sure physical," he added with a deliberate play on words.

Laughter came from across the room. "You're pulling my leg about that physics degree, aren't you?"

Guy smiled from under his hat. "Probably. Get back to work, boy. I need some rest."

"Yes, sir."

Guy lay awake long into the night, thinking about college. He'd been a lot like Slim, young and enthusiastic and full of dreams. Aviation had been the love of his life until Anita came along. Even then, she was part of the dream, because she loved airplanes, too. She encouraged him, raved over his designs, soothed him when plans didn't work out, prodded him to try again. Even when things were darkest, she wouldn't let him give up on the dream. And when it was in his grasp, she never complained about the long hours he was away from her. She was always there, waiting, like a dark-haired angel.

He'd given her the ring just before they went up together, that last time. He was always so careful, so thorough, about the plane. But that once, he was exhausted from a late-night party the night before, and his mind had been on Anita instead of the engine. The tiny malfunction, caught in time, might have been rectified. But it wasn't. The plane went down into the trees and hung, precariously, in the limbs. They could have climbed down, only bruised, but Anita had fallen heavily against the passenger door and, weakened by the crash, it had come open. He saw her in his nightmares, falling, falling, forty feet straight down to the forest floor, with nothing to break the fall except hard ground, her eyes wide with horror as she cried his name...

He sat straight up on the bunk, sweating, barely able to get his breath as the nightmare brought him awake. Slim was sleeping peacefully. He wished he could. He put his head in his hands and moaned softly. Three years was long enough to grieve, Justin said. But Justin didn't know. Nobody knew, except Guy.

He was half-asleep the next morning when he went down to the feedlot in clean blue jeans and a blue-and-white checked flannel shirt under his sheepskin jacket. He wore his oldest Stetson, a beige wreck of a hat, wide-brimmed and stained from years of work. His boots didn't look much better. He was almost thirty-one years old and he felt sixty. He wondered if it showed.

Voices came from Justin's office when he walked into the waiting room at the feedlot. Fay, J. D. Langley's pretty little wife, smiled at him and motioned him in. She was technically

Calhoun Ballenger's secretary, but today she was covering both jobs in the absence of the other secretary.

Guy smiled back, tipped his hat and walked on in. Justin stood up. So did the pretty little brunette with him. She had the largest, most vulnerable brown eyes he'd ever seen in a human being. They seemed to see right through to his heart.

"This is Candace Marshall, Guy," Justin said. "She's a freelance publicist who works primarily for the cattle industry. Candy, this is Guy Fenton. He manages the feedlot for us."

Guy tipped his hat at her, but he didn't remove it. He didn't smile, either. Those eyes hurt him. Anita had brown eyes like that, soft and warm and loving. He could see them in his nightmares as she cried out for him to help her...

"I'm pleased to meet you, Mr. Fenton," Candy said solemnly and held out a hand toward him.

He shook it limply and without enthusiasm, immediately imprisoning both his hands in the pockets of his jeans.

"Guy is going to show you the ranches in the area, before he familiarizes you with the feedlot itself," Justin continued. He produced two typed sheets and handed one to Guy and one to Candy. "I had Fay type these for you. There's a map on the back, in case you don't recognize where the ranches are located. The local ranches contract with us to custom-feed their yearling bulls and replacement heifers," he explained to Candy. "We do some out-of-state business, too, with consortiums like Mesa Blanco, which Fay's husband, J. D. Langley, operates. Any details you need about daily routine and operation and costs, Guy can give you. He's been with us for three years now, and he's very good at his job. He's in charge of the feeding schedules, which are scientific in the extreme."

Candy studied Guy with new interest. "Scientific?"

"He minored in chemistry," Justin added. "Just what we need here to work out feed concentrates and nutritive combinations, all to do with weight-gain ratios, the bottom line of which is profit."

She smiled softly at Justin, pushing back a long strand of dark hair that had escaped from the French twist at her nape. "My dad was a cattleman, so I know a bit about the business. My mom runs one of the biggest ranches in Montana, in fact."

"Does she, really?" Justin asked, impressed.

"She and J. D. Langley and the Tremayne boys gang up on the others at cattlemen's conventions," she continued. "They're radicals."

"Don't tell me," Justin groaned. "No additives, no hormones, no antibiotics, no pesticides, no herbicides, no cattle prods—"

"You *do* know J.D.!" Candy chuckled.

Guy was trying not to notice her resemblance to Anita. She was very pretty when she smiled.

"Everybody around here knows J.D.," Justin said with an exaggerated sigh. He glanced at the Rolex watch on his left wrist. "Well, I've got a play to catch, so I'll let you two get down to business."

Candy was glancing hurriedly at the list. She grimaced. "Mr. Ballenger, we can't possibly see all these ranches in one day!"

"I know. We figure it will take a week or so. We've booked you into our best motel. The cattlemen's association will pick up the tab, including meals, so don't skimp on food." He frowned, noting her extreme thinness and pallor. "Are you all right?"

She straightened and smiled with something like deliberation. "I'm just getting over a bad case of flu," she said slowly. "It's hard to pick up again."

"So it is. Early for the flu."

She nodded. "Yes, it is, isn't it?"

Justin hesitated, then shrugged. "Take it easy, just the same. Guy, if you don't mind, check in with Harry every morning and give him his instructions. I know they're pretty much cut-and-dried for the next week, but do it just the same."

"Sure thing, boss," Guy said lazily. "Well, Miss Marshall, shall we go?"

"Of course." She started slowly toward her compact rental car when she noticed that Guy was going in the opposite direction.

"Mr....Fenton?" she called, having had to stop and remember his name.

He turned, his hands still deep in his pockets. "This way," he said. "We'll go in one of the ranch trucks. You'll never get that thing down Bill Gately's pasture without a broken axle."

"Oh." She stared at the car and then at the big black double-cab pickup truck with the Ballenger logo in red on the door. "I see what you mean." She went toward the truck in that same, slow gait, a little winded by the time she reached it. She stepped on the running board, displaying a slender, pretty, long leg as her skirt rode up. Catching hold of the handhold just above the door, she pulled herself up and into the seat with a gasp.

"You're out of condition," he murmured. "Bronchitis?"

She hesitated just a second too long before answering. "Yes. From the flu."

"I'll try to keep you out of feed dust on the tour," he said, closing the door tight behind her.

She had to sit and catch her breath before she could struggle into the seat belt. All the while, Guy Fenton sat holding the steering wheel in one gloved hand while he observed her pale complexion and flushed cheeks. She looked unwell.

"I got out of bed too soon," she said finally, pushing back a loose strand of dark hair. "I'm fine. Really." She forced a smile and her big brown eyes softened as she looked at him.

He almost groaned. Memories hit his heart and made his breath catch. He flicked the key in the ignition and put the truck in gear. "Hang on," he said tautly. "We've had a lot of rain and the roads are a mess."

"Muddy, huh?" she asked.

"Muddy. Some are washed out."

"Winter floods," she mused.

"El Niño," he informed her. "It's played havoc with the West Coast, the East Coast and all points in between. I don't think I've seen this much rain in Texas in my lifetime."

"Were you born here?"

"I moved here three years ago," he said tersely.

"Not a native Texan, then." She nodded.

He glanced at her. "I didn't say I wasn't born in Texas. Just that I wasn't born in Jacobsville."

"Sorry."

He looked back at the road, his jaw taut. "No need to apologize."

She was pulling hard at air, as if she couldn't get enough in her lungs. She leaned her head back against the seat and closed her eyes for a minute. Her eyebrows drew together, as if she were in pain.

He put on the brakes and slowed the truck. Her eyes opened, startled.

"You're ill," he said shortly.

"I'm not," she protested. "I told you, I'm still weak from the flu. I can handle my job, Mr. Fenton. Please don't...don't concern yourself," she added stiffly. She turned her head and stared out the window at the bleak winter landscape.

He frowned as he pulled ahead down the rough track that led to the main road. She was prickly when he referred to her health and he'd have bet she was hiding something. He wished he knew what it was.

The first ranch on the agenda was owned by old Bill Gately, on the Victoria road. It wasn't the showplace of most ranches around Jacobsville, a fact which Guy pointed out to her when they arrived.

"Bill hasn't moved with the times," he told her, his eyes on the road ahead. "He grew up in the thirties, when ranching was still done the old-fashioned way. He doesn't like the idea of feeding cattle anything supplemental, but when we were able to prove to him the weight-gain ratios we could get, he caved in." He glanced at her with a wry smile. "Not that he's completely sold. And he's going to have trouble with you, I'm afraid."

She chuckled. "Women don't belong in the cattle industry, I gather, and how could the cattlemen's association be blind enough to let them do publicity—and why do we need publicity, anyway, when everybody loves steak?"

"Pretty good," he said. "He'll trot out all those arguments and a few more besides. He's seventy-five and he can run circles around some of our cowboys." He glanced at her. "We have it on good authority that he knew Tom Mix personally and once, briefly, had charge of grooming Tony."

"I'm impressed," she said.

"You know who Tom Mix is?"

She laughed. "Doesn't everybody? He was as much a showman as a movie star. I have several of his silent films, and even a talkie." She shrugged. "I don't care a lot for most modern films, with the exceptions of anything John Wayne starred in."

He navigated a tricky turn and changed gears as they went down what looked like a wet ravine. "See what I meant about this place?" he asked as she held on for dear life while the truck manfully righted itself at the bottom of the sheer drop.

"I sure do," she agreed, catching her breath. "What does Mr. Gately drive?"

"He doesn't," he informed her. "He goes where he has to go on horseback, and if he needs supplies, he has them brought in." He grinned. "The grocer in town has a four-wheel drive, or I guess old Bill would starve."

"I should think so!"

He shifted back into high gear. "How did your mother become a rancher?"

"My dad was one," she said simply. "When he died, she kept the place going. It was difficult at first. We had ranch hands like your Mr. Gately, who were still living in the last century. But my mother is a law unto herself, and she gathers people in without even trying. People just love her, and they'll do whatever she asks. She's not bossy or sharp, but she's stubborn when she wants her own way."

"That's surprising," he said. "Most women in positions of authority are more like overbearing generals than women."

"Have you known a lot?" she returned.

He pursed his lips and thought. "I've seen plenty in movies."

She shook her head. "Most of which are written by *men*," she pointed out. "What you get in cinema and even in television is some man's idea of a woman authority figure. I've noticed that not many of them are true to life. Certainly they aren't like my mother. She can shoot a Winchester, round up cattle and build a fence—but you should see her in a Valentino gown and diamonds."

"I get the point."

"It's been a long road for her," she said. "I'm sorry Dad died when he did, because she's known nothing but work and business for most of her life. It's made her hard." And as cold as ice, she could have added, but didn't.

"Any brothers or sisters?"

She shook her head. "Just me." She turned her head toward him. "How about you?"

"I have a brother. He's married and lives in California. And a married sister up in Washington State."

"You've never married?"

His face became hard as stone. He shifted the gears again as they approached the rickety old ranch house. "Never. There's Bill."

Chapter Two

Bill Gately was white-headed and walked with a limp, but he was slim and as spry as most men half his age. He shook hands politely with Candy and lifted a bushy eyebrow but made no comment when he was told what her job was.

"Justin Ballenger said that you wouldn't mind letting us look over your place," Candy said. She smiled. "I understand that you've made some amazing progress here in the area of old forage grasses."

His blue eyes lit up as if plugged into an electrical socket. "Why, so I have, young lady," he said enthusiastically. He took her by one arm and led her around to the back of the house, explaining the difficulty of planting and cultivating such grasses. "It wouldn't be feasible on a large scale because it's too expensive, but I've had great success with it and I'm finding ways to bring down the cost with the use of mixing common grasses with cultivated ones. The calves forage on these grasses, on a rest-rotation grazing system, until they're yearlings, and then I send them over to Justin and Calhoun to have them fed out for market." He smiled sheepishly. "I've shown some pretty impressive weight gains, too. I should probably let the Ballengers do my marketing as well, but I like to do my own selling, keep my hand in. I only have about a hundred head at a time, anyway, and that's a small lot for the brothers to want to bother with."

"Where do you usually sell your stock?" she asked curiously.

"To a hamburger chain," he said and named it. It was a local chain that had started on a shoestring and was now branching out to larger cities.

Her eyebrows lifted. "I'm really impressed," she said. "Most hamburger joints were buying all their beef from South America until the news about the dwindling rainforest got out. After that, a number of chain restaurants lost customers because people were upset about South American ranchers cutting down rainforest to make way for pasture for their beef cattle."

He grinned. "That's the very argument I used on them!" he told her with a sweeping gesture. "It worked, too. They're even starting to advertise their hamburgers as the ones that don't come from the rainforest, and if they wanted to, they could advertise it as 'organically grown,' because I don't use anything artificial in their diets."

She sighed. "Oh, Mr. Gately, if only we could package and sell *you!* What a marvelous approach to cattle raising."

He blushed like a young girl. Later, he got Guy to one side and told him that he'd never met anyone as capable as Candy at publicizing the cattle industry.

Guy related the story to his companion as they wound down the road toward Jacobsville. The Gately ranch had taken up most of the afternoon, because Candy checked Bill's research journal for his progress with several other strains of old grasses, like the old buffalo grass, which had largely been destroyed on the Western plains by farmers in the early days of settlement. It had been a productive session.

"You're very thorough," Guy commented.

She was reading her notes but she looked up at his tone. "Did you expect someone slipshod to do such important work?" she asked.

He held up a lean, strong hand. "I wasn't throwing out a challenge," he told her. "I only meant that you seem pretty good at what you do."

She leaned back against the seat with a little sigh. "I take pride in my work," she confessed. "And it hasn't been an easy job from the beginning. There are plenty of cattlemen like Mr. Gately, only less easily convinced, who enjoy making me as uncomfortable as possible."

"How?"

"Oh, they make sure I'm escorted past the breeding pastures when the bulls are at work," she mused, tongue-in-cheek, "and into the barn when the cows are being artificially inseminated. I once had a rancher discuss his cattle weight-gain ratios in front of a stable where a mare was being bred. He had to shout to make himself heard."

He whistled. "I'm surprised. I thought most men in this business had a little respect for the opposite sex."

"They do, as long as she's in a kitchen making biscuits."

"Don't say biscuits around the Hart boys, whatever you do!" he exclaimed. "Rey and Leo are still single, and I could tell you some incredible tales about the lengths they've gone to for a biscuit feast since Corrigan and Simon and Cag got married and moved out of the main house!"

She chuckled. "I've heard those all the way back at our main office in Denver," she confided. "At any cattle convention, somebody's got a story to tell about the Hart boys. They get more outrageous by the day."

"And more exaggerated."

"You mean it wasn't really true that Leo carried a cook bodily out of the Jacobsville café one morning and wouldn't let her go until she made them a pan of biscuits?"

"Well, that one was…"

"And that Rey didn't hire one of the cooks in Houston to make him four whole trays of uncooked biscuits, which he hired a refrigerated truck to take down to the ranch for them?"

"Well, yes, he did…"

"And that when Mrs. Barkley retired from the Jones House restaurant in Victoria, Rey and Leo sent her red roses and truckloads of expensive chocolates for two weeks until she agreed to give up retirement and go work for them last month?"

"She's allergic to roses, as it happens," he murmured dryly, "and she was gaining a lot of weight on those chocolates."

"She's probably allergic to those Hart boys by now, poor soul," she said with a tiny laugh. "Honestly, I've never been around any such people!"

"You must have characters back home in Montana."

She dusted off her skirt. "Sure we do, but only like old Ben who used to hang out with Kid Curry and Butch Cassidy, and served time for being a train robber," she replied.

He grinned at her. "Beats stealing a cook."

"I don't know. I understand one of the Hart boys keeps a giant snake. His poor wife!"

"He had an albino python, but when he married Tess, he gave it to a breeder. He visits Herman occasionally, but he wouldn't ask Tess to live with it."

"That's nice."

"Cag is a lot of things. Nice isn't one of them." He thought for a minute. "Well, maybe his wife likes him."

"No wonder his best friend was a reptile."

"You're sounding a little winded," he remarked. "That wheat straw in the corral wasn't too much for you, was it? The wind was blowing pretty hard."

She stared at him blankly. "Am I supposed to notice a connection between that and my being breathless?"

He lifted a shoulder. "Why don't you use your medicine?"

She stilled. "What medicine?"

"Surely you know you're asthmatic?"

She kept right on staring at him, her eyes turbulent, although he couldn't see them. "I don't—have asthma," she said after a minute.

"No? You could have fooled me. You can't walk ten steps without resting. At your age, that's pretty unusual."

Her jaw clenched and her pretty hands had a stranglehold on her purse as she stared out the window.

"No comment?" he persisted.

"Nothing to say," she returned.

He would have pursued it, but they were already going down the main street in Jacobsville, barely a block from her hotel.

"My rental car," she began.

"I'll pick up Slim. He can drive it over here and ride back with me. Got the keys?"

She handed them to him warily. "I'm perfectly capable of driving. There's nothing wrong with me!"

"I'd do it for anyone," he said, acting puzzled. "You've had a long day. I thought you might be tired."

"Oh." She flushed a little as they reached the hotel and he pulled up in front of it. "I see. Well, thank you, then."

He parked the truck, got out and went around to help her down from the high cab. She seemed to resent that, too.

He frowned down at her. "What put that chip on your shoulder?" he asked. "You're overly sensitive about any sort of help."

"I can get out of a truck by myself," she said shortly.

He shrugged. "I do it for a great-uncle of mine," he informed her. "He's not old, but he has arthritis and appreciates a helping hand."

She flushed. "You make me sound terrible!"

His pleasant tone had been deceptive. The eyes that met hers were ice-cold and completely unfriendly. "You're about that unappealing, yes," he said bluntly. "I like a woman who can command respect without acting like a shrew or talking down to men. You don't like doors opened for you or concern for your health. Fine. I can assure you that I won't forget again." His jaw clenched. "My Anita was worth ten of you," he added roughly.

"Why didn't you marry her, then?"

"She died," he said, his eyes terrible to look into. He took a slow breath and turned away, weary of the whole thing. "She died," he said again, almost to himself, as he went back toward the truck.

"Mr. Fenton..." she called hesitantly, aware that she'd hit a nerve and felt vaguely ashamed of herself.

He turned and glared at her over the hood of the truck. "I'll phone the manager of the hotel in the morning and have him tell you where to meet me for the next stop on the tour. You can drive yourself from now on."

He got into the truck, slammed the door, and took off in a cloud of dust.

She stared after him with conflicting emotions. It was important to stand on her own two feet, not to be babied or pitied. She'd gone overboard here, though, and she was sorry. He was grieving for his lost love. He must have cared very much. She wondered how the mysterious Anita had died, and why Mr. Fenton looked so tormented when he spoke of her.

She went into the hotel with slow steps, feeling every step she took, hating her weakness and her inability to do anything to correct it. She reached the desk and smiled forcibly as she asked for her key.

The clerk, a personable young woman, handed it to her with an indifferent smile and turned away, pointedly disinterested in the breathless, bedraggled guest before her.

Candy laughed to herself. It was such a contrast from Guy Fenton's quiet concern. She hated having been so hateful to him, when he was only being compassionate. It was just that, over the years, she'd had so much pity and lurid curiosity, and so little love.

When she got to her room, she locked the door and fell onto the bed in a collapsed heap, without even taking her shoes off. A minute later, she was sound asleep.

The shots woke her. She sat up in bed, her heart hammering at her throat. She had a hand over her chest and she was shaking. More shots, more...

She was out in the open. There were no trees. There was nothing to hide behind. She felt a blow in her chest and touched it with her hand. It came away red, wet with fresh blood. The pain came behind it, wrenching pain. She couldn't breathe...

She threw herself down onto the ground and held her hands over her head. She saw blood. She saw blood everywhere! People were screaming. Children were screaming. A man in a clown suit went down with a horrible piercing scream. Beside her, she saw her father double over and fall, his eyes closed, closed, closed forever...

Suddenly her eyes opened and she was aware that she'd been sobbing out loud. She was lying on the cold floor, on the carpet, doubled up like a frightened child. She sucked in wind, trying desperately to get enough air in her lungs to breathe. She dragged herself into a sitting position. She was wet with sweat, shivering, terrified. All those years ago, she thought, and the nightmares continued. She shivered once more, convulsively, and dragged herself back onto the bed, to lie with open eyes and a throbbing chest.

The nightmare was an old companion, one she'd managed for a long time. There were, fortunately, not so many maniacs running loose that her injury was a common one. But it did appeal to a certain type of person, who wanted her to recount that horror, to relive it. She couldn't bear the least reference to her breathlessness, because of bad memories about the media, hounding her and the other survivors just after the tragedy that had taken so many innocent lives that bright, sunny spring day ten years ago.

She put her face in her hands and wished she could squeeze her head hard enough to force the memory out of it forever. Her mother had withdrawn into a cold, self-contained shell just after her husband's funeral. Forced to assume control of the family ranch or give it up, she became a businesswoman. She hated cattle, but she loved the money they earned for her.

Candy was an afterthought, a reminder of her terrible loss. She'd loved her husband more than anything on the face of the earth. Somehow she blamed Candy for it. The distance between mother and daughter had become a gap as wide as an ocean, and there seemed no way to bridge it. Candy's job was a life-saver, because it got her out of Montana, away from the mother who barely tolerated her.

Mostly she liked her job as a cattle industry publicist. Unlike her mother, she did love cattle and everything connected with them. She'd have enjoyed living on the ranch, but Ida hated the very sight of her and made no attempt to conceal it. It was better for both of them that Candy never went home these days.

She pushed back her damp hair and tried to think about the next day's adventure. They were going to see a rancher named Cy Parks, from all accounts the most unfriendly rancher in Jacobsville, a man with no tact, no tolerance for strangers and more money than he knew what to do with. She was used to difficult men, so this would be just another check on her clipboard. But she was genuinely sorry that she'd been so unfriendly to Guy Fenton, who was only concerned for her. She should tell him about her past and then perhaps they could go from there. He wasn't a bad man. He had a sense of humor and a good brain. She wondered why he wasn't using it. He didn't seem the sort to tie himself for life to managing a feedlot. Surely he could have struck out on his own, started his own business.

She laid her head back on the damp pillow with a grimace. Only a few more hours to daylight. She had sleeping pills, but she never took them. She hated the very thought of any sort of addiction. She didn't smoke or drink, and she'd never been in love. That required too much trust.

A glance at the bedside clock assured her that she had four hours left to stare at the light patterns on the ceiling or try to sleep. She closed her eyes with a sigh.

* * *

Guy Fenton, true to his word, called the motel and left a message for Candy, giving her directions to the Parks ranch and assuring her that he'd be there when she arrived. She was dreading the meeting after the way she'd acted. He probably thought the worst of her after yesterday. She hoped she could undo the damage.

She drove up to the sprawling wood ranch house. The surroundings were well-kept, the white fences were painted, the corrals looked neat and clean, there was a huge barn out back with a fenced pasture on either side of it, and the paved driveway had obviously been landscaped, because there were flowering plants and shrubs and trees everywhere. Either Mr. Parks had inherited this place or he loved flowers. She wondered which.

He came out onto the porch with Guy to meet her, unsmiling and intimidating. She saw at once that none of her former experiences with difficult men had prepared her to deal with this tiger.

"Cy Parks, Candace Marshall," Guy introduced them curtly. "Ms. Marshall is interviewing local ranchers for a publicity spread in a national magazine to promote new ideas in beef management."

"Great idea," Cy said, but the smile he gave her wasn't pleasant. "The animal rights activists will use the platform for protests and the antimeat lobby will demand equal space for a rebuttal."

Candy's eyebrows lifted at the frontal attack. "We're trying to promote new methods," she replied. "Not start a food war."

"It's already started, or don't you watch daytime television?" Cy drawled coldly.

She let out a slow breath. *"Welll,"* she drawled, "we could just lie down on the highway voluntarily and let the other side pave us over."

The corner of his wide mouth jerked, but there was no

friendly light in those cold green eyes, and his lean face was harder than the tanned leather it resembled. He was Guy's height, but even slimmer, built like a rodeo cowboy with a cruel-looking mouth and big feet. He kept his left hand in his pocket, but with his right, he gestured toward the nearest pasture.

"If you want to see my new bull, he's that way," Cy said shortly. He came down the steps with a slow, lazy stride and led the way to the fenced area. "He's already won competitions."

Candy stared through the fence at the enormous animal. He was breathtaking, for a bull, with his shiny red coat and eye-catching conformation.

"Nothing to say?" Cy chided.

She shook her head. "I'm lost for words," she replied simply. "He's beautiful."

Cy made a rough sound in his throat, but he didn't take her up on the controversial description.

"I thought you might want to mention your, shall we say unorthodox, pest control methods," Guy prompted.

Cy's black eyebrows jerked under the wide brim of his hat. "I don't like pesticides," he said flatly. "They mess up the ground-water table. I use insects."

"Insects?" Candy had heard of this method, and she began to quote a magazine article she'd read recently about the use of beneficial insects to control pest insects on agricultural land.

"That's exactly where I found out about it," he replied, impressed. "I thought it was worth a try, and couldn't be worse than the stuff we were already using. I was pretty surprised with the results. Now I'm going organic on fertilizer, as well." He nodded toward the heifers in a far pasture, safely removed from his bull. "Shame to waste all that by-product of my growing purebred herd," he added tongue-in-cheek. "Especially considering what city folk spend to buy it in bags. I don't even have to waste plastic."

Candy laughed. Her voice was musical, light, and Guy found

himself staring at her. He hadn't heard her laugh, but here was the town's most hostile citizen and he amused her.

Cy didn't smile, but his green eyes did. "You should smile more," he said.

She shrugged. "Everybody should."

He bent his head toward her. "I saw your mother a few weeks ago at a convention. She's turned to ice, hasn't she?"

Her face was shocked. "Well, yes, I suppose…"

"Can't blame her," he said heavily. He searched Candy's eyes. "But it wasn't your fault."

"Everybody says that," she said shortly, all too aware of Guy's intent scrutiny.

"You should listen," he said shortly.

She nodded. "Now about that bull," she said, changing the subject.

Once on his favorite theme, he was good for several minutes. For a taciturn man, he was eloquent on the subject of that bull and all his good breeding points. He expanded until Candy had all she needed and walked quietly beside him while he showed them around the rest of the compound.

She was ready to leave shortly before Guy. She shook hands with Cy Parks, nodded cautiously toward Guy, got in her rental car and drove back to her motel.

Guy wasn't in such a big hurry. He paused by the fender of his pickup truck and turned toward Cy. "What happened to her?"

"Ask her," he said with customary bluntness.

"I could get more by asking the car she's riding in."

Cy shrugged. "I don't guess it's any real secret. About nine or ten years ago, her dad took her to a fast-food joint for lunch. You know, Dad and his little girl, sharing a meal and talking to each other. As it happened, that particular day the manager had fired an employee for drinking on the job. The guy was using drugs, too, but the manager didn't know that. So, there's everybody in the fast-food joint, talking and waiting for orders, including Candy and her dad, when this guy they fired comes in with an AK-47 assault rifle and starts shooting."

Guy caught his breath audibly. "Was she hit?"

Cy nodded solemnly. "In the chest. Destroyed one of her lungs and she almost died. They removed the lung. Her dad wasn't so lucky. He took a round in the face. Died instantly. They say that her mother never stopped blaming her for it. It was her idea to go there for lunch, you see."

"And the mother assumed that if she hadn't wanted to go, Candy's father would still be alive."

"Exactly." He stared toward the small dust cloud Candy's car was making in the distance. "She's real touchy on the subject, they say. The media hounded her and her mother right after the shooting. Even now, some enterprising reporter turns up her name and wants to do an update. Her mother sued one of them for trespassing on her ranch and won. She doesn't get bothered much. I imagine Candy does." He shook his head. "I hear that she and her mother barely speak these days. Apparently she's decided that if Mama doesn't want her around, she'll cooperate."

"What's her mother like?"

Cy pursed his lips. "The sort you can't imagine ever getting married. Most men walk wide around her. No inhibitions about speaking her mind, and that mind is sharp as a knife blade. Nothing like Candy, there," he added thoughtfully. "She's all bluff. Underneath, she's marshmallow."

Guy scowled. "How do you know that?"

"I recognize a fellow sufferer," he said, and took his left hand out of his pocket.

Guy's eyebrows jerked, just a little, when he saw it. It wasn't disfigured, but it had very obviously been badly burned. The skin was slick and tight over it.

"Didn't anyone tell you that my Wyoming ranch burned to

the ground?" he asked the younger man. "I don't suppose they added that I was in it at the time, with my wife and son?"

Guy felt sick to his stomach. It was painfully obvious that the other two members of the Parks family hadn't survived.

Cy looked at his hand, his jaw taut and his face hard. He put it back in the pocket and looked at Guy with dead eyes. "It took three neighbors to drag me back out of the house. They sat on me until the firemen got inside. It was already too late. I'd gotten home late because of bad weather. There was a thunderstorm while I was finishing up some urgent paperwork in the office on one side of the house. The fire started in the other, where they were both asleep. Later, they said a lightning strike caused the fire." He stared into space with terrible eyes. "My boy was five years…" He stopped, turned away, breathed until his voice was steady again. "I left Wyoming. Couldn't bear the memories. I thought I'd start again, here. Money was no problem, I've always had that. But time doesn't heal, damn it!"

Guy felt the man's pain and understood it. "I was flying my fiancée around the county one afternoon," he said evenly. "I thought I'd impress her with a barrel roll…but I stalled out. The plane went down into some trees and hung there by a thread with the passenger side facedown to the ground. I came to my senses and saw Anita there, hanging onto the seat with her feet dangling." His eyes grew cold. "It must have been a good forty feet to the ground. She was crying, pleading with me not to let her fall. I reached down to catch her, and she let go with one hand to grab mine. She lost her hold." His eyes closed. "I wake up in the night, seeing her face, contorted with fear, hear her voice crying out to me." His eyes opened and he drew in a breath. "I know what hell is. I've lived in it for three years. You don't get over it."

Cy winced. "I'm sorry."

"So am I, for you. But it doesn't help, does it?" he asked on cold laughter. He removed his hat, ran a hand through his hair and put it back on again. "Well, I'll go chase up the publicity lady and carry on."

"Sure."

He lifted a hand and got into the truck. There was really nothing more to be said. But commiseration did ease the sting of things. Just a little.

Chapter Three

Guy followed Candy back to the motel and found her car parked in front of one of the rooms on the end of the complex. He parked his truck beside it, got out and rapped on her door.

She opened the door, looking pale and worn. She wasn't breathing very well, either.

"We can go out to Matt Caldwell's place tomorrow," he said at once. "If you don't mind," he added carefully, trying not to let his concern for her health show too much. "I've got a few things I need to do at the feedlot this afternoon, but if you're determined to carry on…?"

"No, it can…wait." She searched his face. "He told you about me, didn't he?" she added without preamble.

There seemed little reason to hedge. "Yes," he replied, with no trace of expression on his face. He continued as if he hadn't paid much attention to the subject. "I'll phone you in the morning. I've got a client coming to look over his cattle, and he'll want details about our feeding program that I'll have to explain to him. He's a lot like J. D. Langley—he doesn't like feedlots but he's working for a corporation that does. We're expecting him when we open for business, but if he comes later, I may have to let you go to Matt's place alone. If that happens, I'll email a map over to the motel office and you can pick it up before you leave. His ranch is almost a half hour out of town on some real back roads. Some of them don't even have road signs!"

She was surprised that he didn't mention her past. She relaxed a little. "That will be fine," she said.

He watched her struggle for breath, and she began to cough rather violently. "Have you ever been tested for asthma?" he persisted.

She held a tissue to her mouth while she fought the weakness that was making it hard for her to talk at all. "No."

"Well, you should be," he said bluntly, eyes narrow with concern. "Everybody says asthma makes you wheeze, but it doesn't always. I dated a girl last year who had it real bad, but she didn't wheeze, she just coughed until it sounded like her lungs might come up."

She leaned heavily against the door casing. "Why aren't you still dating her?" she asked.

"I let another woman flirt with me when we went on our first date," he replied. "We didn't have a lot in common, but I felt ashamed. I'm not usually that inconsiderate."

"Did she find somebody else?"

He chuckled. "She married her boss, one of our local doctors. My loss, but I think he was sweet on her from the beginning. He gave me hell about letting her go home alone from the theater."

She searched his eyes quietly. "Why do you get drunk every weekend?" she asked.

He was shocked, and looked it. "Who told you?" he asked impatiently.

"Mr. Gately, while you were looking at the horses," she replied. "He said to stay away from you on weekends, and I asked why."

He rammed his hands in his pockets and looked unapproachable. "My fiancée died in a plane crash. I was flying the plane. I stalled out the engine showing off, and I managed to get it down into the trees without killing us. But the tree we landed in was forty feet off the ground. Her seat belt came loose and she fell out before I could catch her." His eyes darkened with the memory. "I drink so I won't have to see her face as she fell out the door, or hear her scream for me to help her."

She crumpled the tissue in her hand. "I'm so sorry," she said gently. "So very sorry."

"I wouldn't have told you if I hadn't known what happened to you," he replied. "Some people love to hear about violent deaths. Maybe it makes them feel alive. It just makes me feel like getting drunk."

"I can understand that. But she wouldn't have wanted you to mourn that way, would she?"

He hesitated. "No. I don't suppose she would."

"Or live your life alone, either," she persisted. She smiled. "My father was like that, always doing for other people, bringing us little presents, taking care of us. He was much more nurturing than my mother ever was. Of course, now she hates me. I killed him, you see," she added tightly. "I was the one who suggested that we go to that particular place for lunch."

"It could have happened anywhere," he said.

She shrugged. "Sure it could, but it happened there. These days, I spend as little time at home as I can manage. I suppose I'm tired of paying for my sins." She laughed hollowly. "I run. You run. And they're still dead, aren't they?"

Her voice broke on the last word. He couldn't understand why it affected him the way it did, but he couldn't stand there and watch her cry.

He eased her into the motel room and closed the door behind them. He drew her into his arms and held her hard, tight, close against the length of him while his lean hand stroked her soft hair. She'd left it loose today, and it fell to her shoulders like dark silk. It smelled of flowers.

"I don't need..." she began, in just a token protest.

He smoothed the hair back from her face. "You do," he corrected. "So do I. It's human to want comfort."

"Do I?" she asked miserably.

"Yes. And I do, too."

He wrapped her up again and just stood there holding her while she clung to him, more at peace than he'd been in years. He liked the way she felt in his arms, warm and soft and vulnerable.

She sighed after a minute and nestled closer.

"Didn't your mother ever hug you?" he asked.

"Not really. She wasn't affectionate, except with Dad, and that was rare. She still isn't a touching person."

"Neither am I, as a rule." His chest lifted and fell against her. "What a hard little shell you wear, Ms. Marshall," he murmured against her temple.

"I don't want pity."

"Neither do I," he said. "But I could get used to being comforted."

She smiled against his shirt. "So could I."

"Suppose we give up fighting and declare a truce?"

Her heart jumped. "Isn't that cowardice under fire?"

"Not between two old troopers like us."

She smoothed her hand over his soft shirt. "I suppose I could try not to be on the defensive so much if you'll try not to get drunk."

He was still. His eyes went past her head to the big oak tree beside the motel. Absently, he wondered how old it was. "I haven't tried going without alcohol in a long time," he confided. "Even if just on weekends. But I'd have to have an alternative."

Her fingers toyed with a pearl button midway down his chest. "I don't suppose you like fishing."

He lifted his head. "You're kidding, of course."

"Do you or don't you?" she asked, perplexed.

"I won the bass rodeo last year."

Her eyebrows went up and she chuckled. "Only because I wasn't competing with you," she said. "I love to fish for bass!"

A soul mate, he was thinking. He almost said it aloud. "I'll bet you didn't bring your tackle with you."

She grimaced. "I had to fly here. I couldn't carry everything I wanted to."

"I'll kit you out. I've got spinning reels and cane poles, everything from sinkers to hooks to floats. We'll spend Saturday at the lake."

"I'd love to!" She smiled up at him with her soft eyes, and he wondered why he'd ever thought she was cold.

"I'll try to get somebody to substitute for me so I can go with you to Matt's in the morning. About nine suit you? I'll arrange it with him, too."

"That will be fine. Is he like Cy Parks?" she asked, curious.

He shook his head. "Matt's easygoing most of the time, unless he's really mad and then people get out of his way. He likes women. As a rule," he added.

"There's an exception, I gather?"

"Only one." He smiled at her. "I'll see you tomorrow. You might try some strong coffee," he suggested. "They say it helps an asthma attack—if that's what you're having. If you don't get better, call the doctors Coltrain or Dr. Morris. They're all great."

"Okay. Thanks."

He let her go with a sigh. "It's not a weakness to get help when you're sick," he mused. "I just thought I'd mention that."

"I wasn't allowed to be sick at home," she told him. "Some lessons are hard to unlearn."

He searched her wan face. "What a childhood you must have had," he said sadly.

"It was all right, until my dad died."

"I wonder," he mused, unconvinced.

She coughed again, holding the handkerchief to her mouth.

He scowled. "That wheat straw dust gets to you, doesn't it?" he asked with concern. "You need to stay out of enclosed places where it's bad. If you really do have asthma, it's dangerous."

"I have one lung," she said huskily. "It's sensitive to dust, I guess."

He wasn't buying it. "I'll call you tonight, just to make sure you're okay. If it doesn't get better, call the doctor or get to the hospital."

"I will. You don't need to worry."

"Somebody does," he said curtly. "If you're not better in the morning, we might put Matt off until you are. He lives in town, but his ranch is about twenty-five minutes out of town. If you had a life-threatening attack out there, I'd never get you to town in time in the truck."

"Mr. Caldwell has an airplane," she pointed out.

"He has two—a Learjet and a little Cessna Commuter," he replied, "but he's only going to be at the ranch long enough to introduce us to his ranch manager. He's flying himself to Fort Worth in the Learjet for a conference."

"I'll be fine by the morning," she said doggedly. "I know I will." She ruined the stoic image with another choking cough.

"Go drink some coffee, just to humor me, will you?"

She sighed. "Okay."

"Good girl." He bent abruptly and put his mouth gently against hers.

She jumped and a shocked breath pulsed out of her.

He searched her eyes curiously. "You aren't afraid of me, are you?" he asked gently.

"I don't…think so."

Her attitude was surprising. She seemed confident and self-assured, until he came intimately close. She didn't seem to know a lot about men.

"Don't people kiss you, either?" he asked.

"Not a lot."

"Pity," he said, glancing down at her mouth. "You've sure got the mouth for kissing—soft and warm and very sweet."

She put her hand to it, unconsciously. "I don't like sports," she said absently.

"What's that got to do with kissing?"

"Most of the men I meet are married, but the ones who aren't want to take me to football or baseball games. I like fishing."

"I like sports," he mused. "But mostly rodeo and fishing."

"I like rodeo, too."

"See? Two things we have in common, already," he said with a smile. He bent and brushed his mouth against hers again, feeling the same faintly electric sensation as before. He grinned as his lips teased hers. "I could get addicted to this."

She put her hands on his chest. "I can't…breathe very well," she whispered. "I'm sorry."

He lifted his head and stared down at her. "Is that why you don't get involved? You can't get your breath and when you mention it, men think you're giving them the brush-off?"

"How did you know?" she asked, surprised.

"It's the obvious answer to your lack of marriageable suitors," he said simply. "It certainly isn't due to a lack of looks. Why didn't you tell them you only had one lung?"

She grimaced. "It wouldn't have mattered very much. They wanted a lot more than a few kisses."

"And you didn't."

She shook her head. "I've been dead inside since my father died. The psychologist they sent me to afterward said it was guilt because he died and I didn't. Maybe it's still that way." She looked up at him. "But regardless of the guilt, I just don't feel that way with most men. Well, I haven't…before."

She was flushing and he knew why. He grinned, feeling ten feet tall. "It's like little electric shocks, isn't it?" he mused.

She smiled shyly. "Sort of."

He pursed his lips. "Care to try for a major lightning strike?"

She laughed. "Not today."

"Okay." He pushed back a stray strand of her hair, admiring its softness. "I'll see you in the morning, then."

"I'll look forward to it."

He sobered. "So will I." There was an odd little glitter in his eyes. It grew as he looked at her. It was almost as if he had to jerk his eyes away from hers and force himself to move away. In fact, that's exactly how it was. He liked women, and from time to time he was attracted to them. It hadn't been like this. He wanted this woman in ways he'd never wanted any other.

He hesitated as he reached the truck. "I meant it about the doctor," he said with genuine concern. "If that cough doesn't stop, see someone."

"All right." She smiled, waved and closed the door.

He drove away, but not without misgivings. He didn't like the way she looked when that cough racked her. She was fragile, but she didn't realize it or just plain ignored it. She needed someone to take care of her. He smiled at the random thought. That was certainly an outdated notion. Women didn't like being taken care of. They wanted to be independent and strong. But he wondered if they didn't secretly like the idea of being nurtured by someone—not controlled, dominated or smothered, but just…nurtured.

He thought of her as an orchid that needed just the right amount of attention—a growth mixture of bark, a little careful watering now and then—to make it grow. Orchids needed lots of humidity and cool nights. He smiled at the thought of Candy letting him put her in a pot and pour water over her. But it was the sort of thing he wanted, to take care of her and never let her be hurt again. He scowled, because the things he was thinking were very much against his nature. He was a loner. He'd never thought much about nurturing anything, much less a woman. He couldn't think of Candy any other way, and he'd known her only a matter of days.

It was too soon to be thinking of anything permanent, he assured himself. All the same, it wouldn't hurt to keep an eye on her. He had a feeling that she was going to form a very large part of his future happiness.

* * *

Back in the motel, Candy had finally gotten the best of the raging cough by stifling it with a large pot of strong black coffee. She hadn't expected results, despite Guy's assurances about coffee being good for asthma, but apparently he was right. She frowned. If she did have asthma, it was going to complicate her life. Working around ranches and wheat straw dust and grain dust was going to constitute a major challenge, even if there was a reliable treatment for it.

She sipped her coffee and thought about Guy's concern, about the way he took care of her. She was a modern woman, of course she was. But it felt nice, having somebody care what happened to her. Her mother didn't. Nobody had cared what happened to her since her father died. She couldn't help being touched by Guy's concern—and wasn't that an about-face from his first attempts at it, she asked herself wryly.

Later, just before she went to bed, the phone rang. It was Guy, just checking on her. She told him that she was all right and he told her that he'd found someone to handle the visiting cattleman for him. He'd see her in the morning.

He hung up and she held on to the receiver for a long time before she put it down. It wasn't bad, having somebody care about her. It wasn't bad at all.

The next morning dawned bright and beautiful. Candy dressed in a neat beige pantsuit and suede boots for the trip, leaving her hair loose. She felt younger and happier than she had in years. She had a whole new outlook on life because of Guy.

She reviewed her few facts on the Caldwell ranch. It was only one of a dozen pies Matt had his finger in. He was an entrepreneur in the true sense of the word, an empire-builder. If he'd been born a hundred years ago, he'd have been a man like Richard King, who founded the famous King Ranch in southeastern Texas. Matt was an easygoing, pleasant man to most people. She'd heard that he was hell in boots to his enemies. There were always rumors about such a powerful man, and one of them was that he had it in for a female friend of his cousin's and had caused her to lose her job. It was a glaring black mark against a man who was generally known for fair play, and people talked about it. She was a very young woman, at that, not at all the sort of female the handsome tycoon was frequently seen with.

Matt's taste ran to models and Hollywood stars. He had no use for high-powered career women in his private life, although he employed several in executive positions in his various companies. Perhaps that was why the young woman had run afoul of his temper, Candy speculated. She was rumored to be very intelligent and sharp at business.

A rap on the motel door startled her. She went to answer it and found a smiling Guy on the doorstep.

"Ready to go?"

"Oh, yes!" she said brightly. The day had taken a definite turn for the better.

Matt's sprawling ranch lay about twenty-five minutes out of town, and it was truly out in the boondocks.

Guy took a road that wasn't identified in any way and flashed a grin at Candy. "I'm afraid even a good map wouldn't have helped much. Matt says he likes being someplace where he's hard to find, but it's hell on people who have to go out here on business."

"He must not like people," she commented.

"He does, in fact, but not when he's in a black mood. That's when he comes out here. He works right alongside his cowhands and the newer ones sometimes don't even realize he's the boss until they see him in a suit and boarding the Learjet. He's just one of the boys."

"How rich is he?" she asked.

He chuckled. "Nobody knows. He owns this ranch and a real estate franchise, two planes, he has property in Australia and

Mexico, he's on the board of directors of four companies and on the board of trustees of two universities. In his spare time, he buys and sells cattle." He shook his head. "I've never known a man with so much energy."

"Does he do it to get his mind off something?" she wondered aloud.

"Nobody's ever had the nerve to ask. Matt's very pleasant, but he isn't the sort of man you question."

She bumped along beside him in the truck and something nagged at the back of her mind.

"You said you were flying the plane. Did you own it?" she asked carefully.

He drew in a slow breath. He didn't want to talk about it, but then, she was entitled to know something about him. He glanced at her. "I did. I have an air cargo company."

Her eyes widened. "And you're working for wages at a feed-lot?"

"They don't know I own the company," he told her. "I wanted someplace to… I don't know, hide out maybe." He shrugged broad shoulders. "I couldn't cope with the memories there, and I didn't want enough spare time to think. I got the most demanding job I could find. I've been here three years and I like it. My manager is doing great things with the air cargo company. I'm considering making him a full partner."

"Is it a profitable company?"

"I'm not in Matt Caldwell's league," he said. "But I suppose I'm pretty close." He glanced at her and smiled. "I could afford to live high if I liked. I don't. I was too fond of the fast lane. It's what cost me Anita." His face tautened as he stared ahead at the long, winding road. "I'd been on the road all of the day before, and I hadn't slept that night because someone had a party and I was enjoying myself. Anita wanted to go up for a few minutes, so I took her. If I'd had a good night's sleep, I wouldn't have done such a sketchy walk-around and I'd have noticed the problem in the engine before it caused a tragedy. That was when I looked at my life and decided that I was wasting it. I came down here to decide what to do." He shook his head. "It's been three years and I still haven't decided that."

"What do you want to do?" she asked.

His eyes held a faraway look. "I want to settle down and have a family." He saw the expression on her face and chuckled. "I can see that you hadn't considered that answer as a possibility."

"You don't seem the sort of man to want to settle," she said evasively. She twisted her purse in her lap.

"I wasn't, until recently. I'm not that old, but I'm beginning to see down the road further than I used to. I don't want to grow old and die alone."

"Most people don't."

He grinned. "Including you?"

She hesitated. "I'd never really thought about marrying and having a family," she said seriously.

"Because you only have one lung? That shouldn't worry you."

"It might worry a prospective husband," she pointed out. "Most men want a whole woman."

"You're whole, in every way that matters," he said firmly. "With or without two lungs."

She smiled. "Thanks. That was nice. But marriage is a big step."

"Not really. Not if two people have a lot in common and if they're good friends. I've seen some very happy marriages since I moved to Jacobsville. Marriage is what you make of it," he said pensively.

"So they say."

The road dead-ended at a long, winding gravel driveway with a huge black mailbox at the fork which read Caldwell Double C Ranch.

"We're almost there," Guy told her, pulling into the ranch road. "Matt runs some of the prettiest Santa Gertrudis cattle in the state. It's a purebred herd, which means they aren't slaughter cattle. He sells seed bulls and heifers, mostly, and he does a roaring business."

"I like Santa Gerts," she remarked.

"So did my father," he told her. "He worked on the King Ranch. I grew up with cattle and always loved them. I just loved airplanes more. Now I'm caught between the two. That tickles my parents."

"They're still alive?"

He chuckled. "Very. He still works on a ranch, and she's gone into real estate! I go to visit them every few months." He glanced at her. "As I mentioned before, I have a brother in California and a sister in Washington State. She has a little boy about four. Her husband's a lawyer."

"Quite a family," she mused.

"You'd like my family," he told her. "They're just plain folks, nothing put on or fancy, and they love company."

"My mother screams about uninvited guests," she recalled. "She's not really fond of people unless they come to buy cattle. She's pretty mercenary."

"You aren't."

She laughed. "Thanks for noticing. No, I'll never make a businesswoman. If I had a lot of money, I'd probably give it all away. I'm a sucker for a lost cause."

"That makes two of us. And here we are."

He indicated a sprawling white two-story ranch house with a porch that ran two-thirds of the way around it. There was a porch swing and plenty of chairs and gliders to sit in. The pasture fences near the house were all white, and behind them red-coated cattle grazed on green grass.

"Improved pasture," she murmured, taking notes. "You can always tell by the lush grass."

"Matt's a stickler for improvements. There he is." He nodded toward the front steps, where a tall, darkly handsome man in a suit and a white Stetson was coming down to greet them.

Chapter Four

Matt Caldwell was attractive, and he had a live-wire personality to go with his lean good looks. He helped Candy from the truck with a charm that immediately captivated her.

"Glad you got here before I had to leave," Matt said, greeting Guy as he came around the truck. "I'm going to have Paddy show you the place. I wish I could, but I'm already late for a meeting in Houston." He glanced at his watch. "I never have a minute to spare these days. I think I need to slow down."

"It wouldn't hurt," Guy chuckled. "Candy Marshall, this is Matt Caldwell."

"Glad to meet you," Candy said with a smile and an extended hand.

Matt shook it warmly. "Publicists are getting neater by the day," he mused. "The last one we had here was twenty-five, unshaven and didn't know a Santa Gert from a Holstein."

"I shaved my beard off just this morning," she said pertly.

Matt chuckled. "Glad to know that you have good personal hygiene," he drawled. "Paddy will show you anything you want to see. If you need to talk to me, I should be back by tomorrow morning. If that's not soon enough, you can email me the questions, I'll answer them and send them back to you." He handed her a business card with Mather Caldwell Enterprises, Inc. in raised black lettering.

"Impressive," she told him.

He chuckled. "Not very." He glanced at Guy with a calculating gleam in his eyes. "If you wanted to give her a bird's-eye view of the ranch, the Cessna Commuter 150's gassed up and ready to fly."

Guy's face went hard just thinking about the small, two-seater plane. It was the type he'd crashed three years ago taking Anita for a ride. "I don't fly anymore."

Matt exchanged a complicated glance with him. "Pity."

"She wants to see cattle on the hoof, anyway."

"I bought a new Santa Gertrudis bull from the King Ranch. Paddy will show him to you. He's a looker." Matt shook hands with them both. "Got to run," he said. "Paddy should be out here any minute. He was with me when you drove up, but he got held up in the office. Have a seat on the porch and wait for him."

"Nice porch," Candy remarked.

He grinned. "I bought the place for the porch. I like to sit out there on warm summer evenings and listen to Rachmaninoff."

He piled into his Mercedes and gunned the engine as he drove out to the small hangar and airstrip that were barely visible in the distance.

"Does he do that often? Offer you his airplane, I mean?" Candy asked when they were comfortably seated in the porch swing.

"Every time he sees me," he said with resignation. "I suppose I'm getting used to it. Which doesn't mean I like it," he added.

She didn't quite know how to answer that. It was a good thing that Paddy Kilgraw chose that moment to come out onto the porch. He was a wizened little man with skin like leather and twinkling blue eyes. He took off his hat, revealing pale red hair on either side of a huge bald spot, and shook hands warmly with them both. He led them out to the barn and Candy got down to business.

Matt's operation was enormous, but it still had the personal touch. He knew each of his bulls by name, and at least two of them were tame. Candy enjoyed the way they nuzzled her hand when she petted them. To her mother, cattle were for slaughter, nothing else. Candy much preferred a ranch that concentrated on keeping them alive, where the owner liked his animals and took proper care of them. Even cantankerous Cy Parks, who did run beef cattle, was concerned for their welfare and never treated them as if they were nothing more than an investment.

But the barn, while neat and clean for such a structure, was filled with wheat straw, and it was strictly an enclosed space. They'd barely entered it when Candy started coughing. She bent over double and couldn't stop.

Guy asked Paddy for a cup of coffee, which the little man went running to get. Meanwhile, Guy lifted Candy and carried her out of the barn, to where the air was less polluted by wheat straw dust. But once outside, seated on the running board of the truck, she was still coughing. Tears were running down her face, which was red as fire.

Paddy appeared with a cup of coffee. "It's cold, will that do?" he asked quickly.

"Cold is fine. It's the caffeine we want." Guy held it to her lips, but she was coughing so hard that she couldn't even drink in between spasms. His face contorted with fear. He looked up at Paddy from his kneeling position beside Candy. "I think it's a bad asthma attack," he said abruptly.

"Has she got an inhaler on her?" Paddy asked.

Guy shook his head worriedly. "She hasn't been diagnosed by a doctor yet. Damn!"

She bent over again, and this time she was definitely wheezing as she coughed. It was getting worse by the second and she looked as if she was struggling to get a single breath of air.

"It's twenty-five minutes to Jacobsville!" Guy said harshly. "I'll never get her there in time!"

"Take the Commuter," Paddy said. "I've got the keys in my pocket. Boss said you might like to fly her while you were here."

Guy's eyes were haunted. "Paddy, I can't!" he bit off, horror in his expression at the memory of his last flight.

Paddy put a firm hand on his shoulder. "Her life depends on it," he reminded the younger man solemnly. "Yes, you can! Here. Go!"

Guy took another look at Candy and groaned. He took the keys from Paddy, put Candy in the truck, swung in beside her and gunned the engine out to the airstrip, with Paddy hanging on in the truck bed.

He pulled the truck to a stop at the hangar. Leaving Candy in the cab of the truck, Guy and Paddy got the little Cessna pulled out onto the apron. Then Guy carried Candy and strapped her into the passenger side. She was barely conscious, her breath rasping as she tried desperately to breathe.

"You'll make it," Paddy said firmly. "I'll phone ahead and have an ambulance and EMTs waiting at the airport in Jacobsville with the necessary equipment. Get going!"

"Thanks, Paddy," Guy called as he ran to get inside the plane.

It had been a long time since he'd flown, but it was like riding a bicycle, it came right back to him. He went over the controls and gauges and switches after he'd fired up the engine. He taxied the little plane out onto the runway and said a silent prayer.

"It's going to be all right, honey," he told Candy in a harsh tone. "Try to hang on. I'll have you to the hospital in no time in this!"

She couldn't manage a reply. She felt as if she were drowning, unable to get even a breath of air. She gripped the edge of the seat, crying silently, terrified, as Guy sent the little aircraft zipping down the runway and suddenly into the air.

He circled and turned the plane toward Jacobsville, thanking God for his skill as a pilot that had made this trip even possible. He could see that Candy was slowly turning blue and losing consciousness.

"Just a little longer, sweetheart," he pleaded above the noise of the engine. "Just a little longer! Please hold on!"

He kept talking to her, soothing her, encouraging her all

the way to the Jacobsville airport. He was so preoccupied with her welfare that his horror of flying took a backseat to his concern for Candy. He called the tower and was immediately given clearance to land, which he did, faultlessly. An ambulance pulled onto the tarmac, lights flashing, and came to a halt as he taxied onto the apron and cut the engine.

Seconds later, they had Candy out of the plane and on oxygen. They loaded her into the ambulance, with one EMT and a worried Guy in the back with her. They roared away to the hospital, with Guy holding her hand and praying silently that he wasn't going to lose her, when he'd only just found her.

Her color was better and she was breathing less strenuously when the ambulance pulled up sharply at the emergency entrance. The physician on duty came running out behind the nurses and supervised Candy's entrance.

Guy was gently put to one side while Candy was wheeled right into the emergency room, into a cubicle.

"You can sit here in the waiting area," a nurse told him with a gentle smile. "Don't worry. She's going to be fine."

Easy to say, he thought worriedly. He jammed his hands into the pockets of his jeans and paced, oblivious to the other people also waiting and worrying nearby. He couldn't remember the last time he'd been so upset.

He glanced toward the swinging doors through which Candy had been taken and sighed. She'd looked a little better after the oxygen mask was put into place, but he knew it was going to take more than that to get her back on her feet. He was almost certain that they'd keep her overnight. He hoped they would. She was stubborn and unlikely to follow instructions.

Just when he was contemplating storming the doors, the physician came and motioned him inside.

He pulled him into an empty cubicle and closed the curtain. "Is she your fiancée?" he asked Guy.

He shook his head. "She's a visiting publicist for the cattlemen's association. I was deputized by our local association to escort her around the area ranches."

"Damn!" the doctor muttered.

"Why? What's wrong?"

He glowered. "She's got the worst case of asthma I've come across in years, and she won't believe it. I've got her on a nebulizer now, but she's going to need a primary care physician to evaluate and treat her, or this isn't going to be an isolated incident. She needs to see someone right away. But I can't convince her."

Guy smiled wryly. "Leave it to me," he murmured. "I think I'm beginning to know how to handle her. Is this a long-standing condition, do you think?"

"Yes, I do. The coughing threw her off. Most people don't associate it with asthma, but while it's not as common as wheezing, it is certainly a symptom. I've prescribed a rescue inhaler for her to carry, and told her that she needs to be on a preventative. Her own doctor can prescribe that."

"She lives in Denver," Guy said. "I'm not sure she goes to a doctor regularly."

"She'd better," the young man said flatly. "She almost got here too late. Another few minutes and it would have been touch and go."

"I figured that," Guy said quietly.

"She owes you her life," he continued.

"She owes me nothing, but I'm going to make sure that she takes care of herself from now on."

"I'm glad to hear it."

"May I see her?"

He smiled and nodded. "Sure. She won't be able to talk. She's very busy."

"Good. She can listen better. I've got a lot to tell her."

The doctor only chuckled. He led the way into a larger cubicle where a worn-looking Candy was inhaling something in a mask that covered part of her face. She glanced at him and looked irritated.

"Asthma," Guy said, plopping down onto a stool nearby. "I told you, didn't I?"

She couldn't speak, but her eyes did. They were eloquent.

"He says you need to see a doctor and get the asthma treated."

She tugged at the mask. "I won't!"

"You will," he replied, putting it firmly back in place. "Committing suicide is not sensible."

She struck the side of the examination couch with her hand.

"I know, you don't want any more complications," he said for her. "But this could have cost you dearly. You have to take precautions, so that it doesn't happen again."

Her eyes seemed to brighten. She shifted and shook her head.

"Hay and wheat and ranches sort of go together," Guy said. "If you're going to spend any time around them, you have to have proper care. I'm going to make sure you get it."

She gave him a look that said him and what army?

He chuckled. "We'll go into that later. Getting easier to breathe?"

She hesitated, and then nodded. She searched his eyes and made a flying motion with her hand. She tugged the mask aside for a second. "I'm sorry…you had to do that. Are you… all right?"

He put the mask back in place again, touched by her concern for him at such a traumatic time for herself. "Yes, I'm all right," he said. "I didn't have time to think about myself and my fears. I was too busy trying to save you. It wasn't as bad as I thought it would be. Of course," he added with a faint smile, "I was pretty preoccupied at the time."

"Thank you," she said in a ghostly, hoarse tone.

"Don't talk. Breathe."

She sighed. "Okay."

The nebulizer took a long time to empty. By the time she'd

breathed in the last of the bronchodilator, she was exhausted. But she could get her breath again.

The doctor came back in and reiterated what he'd said about seeing a physician for treatment of her asthma.

He gave her a sample inhaler and a prescription for another, plus another prescription. "This one—" he tapped it "—is for what we call a spacer. It's a more efficient way of delivering the medicine than a pocket inhaler. You're to follow the directions. And as soon as possible, you get treatment. I don't want to see you back in here again in that condition," he added with a smile to soften the words.

"Thank you," she said.

He shrugged. "That's what we're here for." He frowned. "You never knew you had asthma. I find that incredible. Don't you have a family physician?"

"I only go to the clinic when I'm sick," she said shortly. "I don't have a regular doctor."

"Find one," the physician recommended bluntly. "You're a tragedy waiting to happen."

He shook hands with Guy and left them in the cubicle.

Guy helped her to her feet and escorted her to the clerk, where she gave her credit card and address to the woman in charge.

"No insurance, either?" he asked.

She shrugged. "It never seemed necessary."

"You need taking in hand."

She shook her head. "Not tonight. I'm too tired to fight. I want to go back to the motel."

He didn't like that idea at all. He worried about her, being alone at night. "You shouldn't be by yourself," he said uneasily. "I could get a nurse to come and stay with you."

"No!" she said vehemently. "I can take care of myself!"

"Don't get upset," he said firmly. "It won't help matters. It could even bring on another attack."

She drew in a shaky breath. "I'm sorry. It scared me."

"That makes two of us," he confided. "I've never moved so fast in my life." He caught her hand in his and held it tight. "Don't do that again," he added in a strained tone.

She turned to him as they made it into the sunlight. "How do we get to the motel?" she asked worriedly. "And what about your truck?"

"Paddy will take good care of the truck. We have a taxi service here. We can use it," he added with a smile. "Come on. I need to make arrangements to return the plane and then I'll see that you get where you want to go. Eventually," he added under his breath.

Candy expected the cab to take them to the motel, but the address Guy gave the driver wasn't the motel after all. It was a doctor's office.

"Now see here…!" she began.

Her protests didn't cut any ice. He paid the driver and frog-marched her into Drew Morris's waiting room. The receptionist who'd replaced Drew's wife, Kitty, smiled at them.

Guy explained the problem, and the receptionist had them take a seat. But only a couple of minutes later, they were hustled into a cubicle.

Drew Morris came right in. He ignored Candy's protests and examined her with his stethoscope. Seconds later, he wrapped the stethoscope around his neck, sat back on the couch and folded his arms.

"I'm not your physician, but I'll do until you get one. I'm going to give you a prescription for a preventative medicine. You use it along with the inhaler the emergency room doctor gave you."

"How did you know about that?" Candy asked, aghast.

"Guy called me before he called the cab," Drew said nonchalantly. "You use both medicines. If the medicines stop working, for any reason, don't increase the dosage—call me or get to the emergency room. You had a life-threatening episode today. Let it be a warning. You can control asthma, you can't cure it. You have to prevent these attacks."

She gave in gracefully. "Okay," she said. "I'll do what I'm told."

"Have you had problems like this before?"

She nodded. "Quite a bit. I thought it was just a mild allergy. Nobody in my family has any sort of lung problem."

"It doesn't have to be inherited. Some people just get it— more today than ever before, especially children. It's becoming a major problem, and I'm convinced that pollution has something to do with it."

"What about my job?" she asked miserably. "I love what I do."

"What do you do?" Drew asked.

"I go around to ranches and interview people on their production methods. There's always a grain elevator, a storage silo, a barnful of hay or wheat straw—they're unavoidable."

"Then wear a mask and use your inhalants before you go near those pollutants," Drew said. "No reason you can't keep doing your job. People with asthma have won Olympic medals. It won't get you down unless you let it."

She smiled at him. "You're very encouraging."

"I have to be. My wife, Kitty, is asthmatic."

"How is Kitty?" Guy asked.

He chuckled. "Pregnant," he murmured, and his high cheekbones colored. "We couldn't be happier."

"Congratulations," Guy said. "And thanks for having a look at Candy."

"My pleasure," Drew replied, and not without a noticeable speculation as his gaze went from one of them to the other.

"He seems to know you very well," Candy mentioned when the cab was carrying them back to her motel.

"He does. I used to date his wife, before she was his wife," he said. "I told you about her. She coughed instead of wheezed."

"Oh, yes, I remember." She didn't like the memory. Guy had apparently done a lot of dating locally, despite his grief at losing his fiancée.

"Kitty was sweet and gentle, and I liked her a lot," he continued. "But she loved Drew. I'm glad they made it. He was grieving for his late wife. People around here never thought he'd marry again. I guess Kitty came up on his blind side."

"He's nice."

"Yes, but like all our doctors around here, he's got a temper." He glanced at her pocketbook and leaned forward and told the cabdriver to stop at the nearby pharmacy. "You need to get those filled. We'll wait for them and call a cab when they're filled."

"I could do it tomorrow," Candy began.

"No," he said, leaning over the seat to talk to the cabdriver.

They stopped and got the prescriptions filled and then went on to the motel. Guy left Candy in her room reluctantly and made sure that she had a bucket of ice and some soft drinks before he left, so that she wouldn't have to go out to get them.

"Try to get some rest," he said.

"But we didn't get to see all of Matt's ranch," she protested, frowning. "How will I ever write the story?"

"Matt said he could email you the answers to any questions you didn't get answered at the ranch," he replied. "I'll explain the situation to him and you can work up some questions. I'll make sure he gets them."

"That's really nice of you," she said.

He smiled down at her, feeling protective and possessive all at once. "This could be habit-forming, too, you know."

"What could?"

"Taking care of you," he said softly. He bent and brushed his mouth tenderly against hers. "Lie down and rest for a while. I'll come back and get you and take you out to eat, if you're up to it."

She grimaced. "I want to," she said. "But I'm so tired, Guy."

She did look tired. Her face was drawn and there were new lines around her mouth and eyes. He traced one of them lightly.

"Suppose I bring something over to you?" he asked. "What would you like?"

"Pork lo mein," she said at once.

He grinned. "My favorite. I'll see you about six."

"Okay."

He finished his chores at the feedlot, having had Paddy drive his truck back to town. He drove Paddy home and then went to get supper for Candy. He took the food to the motel. They ate silently and then rented an action film on the pay per view channel and piled up together on one of the double beds to watch it.

In no time at all, Candy was curled up against him sound asleep. He held her that way, marveling at the wonder of their closeness, at her vulnerability and his own renewed strength. He hadn't thought seriously about getting involved with anyone since he'd lost Anita, but Candy had slipped so naturally into his life that he accepted her presence with no misgivings at all.

He looked down at her with soft, possessive eyes. He didn't want to go back to the feedlot. He wanted to stay here with her, all night long. But if he did that, he'd compromise her. He couldn't risk that. She might not want commitment so soon. He wondered about the sanity of getting mixed up with a woman who lived several states away, but he couldn't talk himself out of it.

He knew at that moment that she had a hold on him that no distance, no circumstance, could break. And he was afraid.

Chapter Five

Guy bent and kissed Candy's closed eyes, brushing his lips against them until they fluttered and lifted.

She looked up at him drowsily, but with absolute trust. Involuntarily, her arms snaked up around his neck and she pulled him down to kiss him slowly, tenderly, on his hard mouth.

He groaned, and she felt him move, so that his body shifted next to hers. The kiss grew in pressure and insistence until one long leg slid right between both of hers and his mouth demanded.

She pushed at his chest, frightened by the sudden lack of breathable air.

His head lifted. He breathed roughly, but he understood without her speaking why she'd drawn back. "Sorry," he whispered. His mouth moved to her chin, her neck and into the opening her blouse left. His lean fingers unfastened buttons, so that his mouth could move down past her collarbone and onto even softer flesh.

Her hands picked at his shirt, hesitated, as new sensations lanced through her. She loved the feel of his mouth. She didn't protest as he eased the lacy strap off her shoulder, and his mouth trespassed on flesh that had never known a man's touch before.

She yielded immediately, arching up to meet his lips, pushing the fabric aside to make way for it. She felt his mouth over her hard nipple and its sudden moist pressure made her moan with pleasure.

He lifted his head and looked where his mouth had touched. He traced the firm rise sensually and bent to kiss it once more, lovingly, before he righted the lacy strap and buttoned the blouse again.

Her eyes asked a question.

He smiled and bent to kiss her tenderly. "We have all the time in the world for that," he whispered. "Right now, you're a little wounded bird and I have to take care of you."

Tears stung her eyes. She'd never had tenderness. It was new and overpowering.

He kissed the tears away. "Don't cry," he murmured. "You're going to be fine now. Just fine. Nothing bad is ever going to happen to you as long as I'm around."

She clung to him hard, burying her face in his throat as the tears fell even more hotly.

"Oh, Candy," he murmured huskily. He held her close, rocked her in his arms, until she had her self-control back. Then he got up from the bed and pulled her up beside him, to hold her carefully close.

"Sorry," she murmured on a sob. "I guess I'm tired."

"So am I." He brushed his mouth against her pert nose. "I'm going back to the feedlot. Can I get you anything before I go?"

She shook her head. She smiled hesitantly. "How about that fishing trip tomorrow?"

He smiled. "I'm game if you are."

"I'll use my medicines," she said without enthusiasm.

"You sure will, or we won't go," he assured her.

She wrinkled her nose at him. "Spoilsport."

"I hate emergency rooms," he said simply. "We have to keep you out of them."

"I'll try."

"Good."

"Thank you for saving my life," she said solemnly. "I know

it must have brought back some terrible memories for you, having to fly again."

He wouldn't admit that. He wasn't going to think about it. He only smiled at her, in a vague, pleasant way. "Get some sleep. I'll see you bright and early tomorrow. If you feel like going, we'll go. If not, we'll find some other way to pass the time. Okay?"

She smiled wearily. "Okay."

He left her and went back to the bunkhouse at the feedlot, but he didn't sleep. Over and over again he saw Anita's face. He groaned as he finally just got up and forgot trying to make the memories go away. It was useless.

The next morning, Guy and Candy went fishing on the river, with cane poles and a bait bucket. It was, she muttered, absolutely primitive to try to catch a fish in such a manner.

He only grinned. He'd made a small fire and he had a frying pan heating. He was going to treat her to fresh fish for lunch.

It was a good idea, except that they sat on the riverbank for three hours and at the end of it they had yellow fly bites and mosquito bites, and not one fish between them.

"It must have been this prehistoric fishing gear," Candy remarked with a glowering look. "The fish probably laughed so hard that they sank to the bottom!"

"It isn't prehistoric," he said. "It gives fish a sporting chance."

She waved her hand at the river. "Some sporting chance! And whoever uses worms to catch a self-respecting bass?"

"You just wait until the next bass rodeo, pilgrim," he said with a mocking smile. "And we'll see who can catch fish!"

She grinned at him. The word play was fun. He was fun. She'd smiled and laughed more in the past few days than in her whole recent life. Guy made her feel alive again. He'd knocked the chip off her shoulder about her past and led her into the light. She put down the pole, sighed and stretched lazily.

He watched her covetously. "A woman who likes to fish," he mused, "and who doesn't worry about getting her hands dirty."

"I like to garden, too," she remarked. "I used to plant flowers when I lived at home. Nobody does, now."

He pursed his lips and stared at the ripples on the river as it ran lazily past the banks. He was thinking about flower beds and a small house to go with them, a house just big enough for two people.

She looked up at him with soft, warm brown eyes. "I've really enjoyed being here," she said. "I'm sorry I have to leave tomorrow."

Reality came crashing down on him. He turned his head and looked at her, and saw Anita's eyes looking back at him. He blinked. "You have to leave?"

She nodded sadly. "I have to write up all these articles and get back to my desk. I expect I've got a month's work piled up there."

"In Denver."

"Yes. In Denver." She pulled in her line and put the pole down beside her. "It's been the most wonderful week I can remember. Thank you for saving my life."

He frowned. He was staring at his line, but he wasn't seeing it. "Couldn't you stay for another week?"

"I couldn't justify the time," she said miserably. "I can't just chuck my job and do what I please. I don't depend on my mother for my livelihood, you know," she added. "I work for my living."

He was more morose than he'd felt in years. He pulled in his own line and curled it around the pole. "I know how that is," he said. "I work for my living, too." He turned his head and looked down at her. He wanted to ask her to stay. He wanted to tell her what he was beginning to feel for her. But he couldn't find the words.

She saw the hesitation and wondered about it. He got to his feet and gathered the poles silently, placing them back in the truck. He glanced deliberately at his watch.

"I've got another group of cattlemen checking in at the feedlot later," he said, lifting his eyes to hers. "I'd offer you lunch, but I'm not going to have time."

She smiled. "That's okay. I enjoyed the fishing trip. Even though we didn't catch any fish," she added.

He wished he could make some humorous reply, but his heart was heavy and sad. He put out the campfire, gathered up the frying pan and the bottle of vegetable oil and put everything in the truck.

He drove her back to the motel in silence, his whole manner preoccupied and remote.

She got out at the door to her room, hesitating with the passenger door of the truck open. "I don't guess you ever get to Denver?" she asked.

He shook his head. "Not much reason to."

"And this is the only time I've ever been to Jacobsville. I guess they won't send me back."

He searched her face and it hurt him to see the sadness in her dark eyes. He was remembering Anita again, he thought irritably, remembering how it had felt to lose her.

"It's been fun," he said with a forced smile. "I'm glad I got to know you. Keep up with that medicine," he added firmly.

"I'll take care of myself." She hesitated. "You do the same," she added gently.

He hated the concern in her eyes, the softness in her voice. He didn't want to love someone who was in such a hurry to leave him.

He leaned over and closed the door. "Have a safe trip home," he said. He threw up a hand and gunned the truck out of the parking lot.

Candy stared after him, perplexed. She'd thought they were building toward something, but he seemed anxious to get away from her. She bit her lower lip and turned to go into her room. Amazing how wrong her instincts were lately, she thought as she opened the door and went inside. She seemed to have no judgment whatsoever about men.

* * *

Guy, driving furiously back to the feedlot, was feeling something similar. He couldn't bring himself to beg her to stay, after all. If her job was so important, then who was he to stop her? Perhaps he'd been too hasty and she didn't want him on any permanent basis. That made him irritable, and the more he thought about it, the more frustrated he got.

By early evening, he was boiling mad. He had supper in the bunkhouse and then drove himself out of town to the most notorious bar in the county and proceeded to drink himself into forgetfulness.

He realized the stupidity of it, so he drank more. In no time at all he was bleary-eyed and spoiling for a fight.

Cy Parks, usually unsociable and rarely seen around town, had stopped by the joint for a beer and saw him. He had a good idea why Guy was there, and he knew just the person to do something about the situation. He walked right back out the door and drove himself to the motel where Candy was staying.

He rapped on the door with his good hand. She came to open it, still wearing jeans and a tank top, with her long hair around her shoulders. She gaped when she realized who was standing at her door.

"Mr. Parks!" she exclaimed. "Did you come to tell me something else about your operation, for the article?" she asked, voicing the most likely reason for his presence here.

He shook his head. "I phoned Justin Ballenger from my car and asked where you were staying." His black eyes glittered, and not just with impatience. He almost looked amused. "I thought you might like to know that Guy Fenton is getting tanked up at the local dive. He looks in the mood to break something. I thought you might like to try your hand at keeping him out of jail."

"Jail?" she exclaimed.

He nodded. "Rumor is that the sheriff won't give him a second chance if he wrecks the bar again."

"Oh, dear," she murmured. She sighed. "Can you drive me out there?"

He nodded again. "That's why I came."

She didn't hesitate. She all but jumped into the passenger seat of his luxury car and fastened her seat belt before he climbed in behind the wheel.

"I made him fly," she said heavily. "I had an asthma attack at the Caldwell place and he had to get me back to town in a hurry, so he had to fly Matt's plane. I brought back all the memories of the girl who died in the plane crash. Poor Guy."

He glanced at her. "Are you sure that's what sent him out to the bar?"

"I can't think of anything else."

He smiled to himself. "Justin says you told him you'll be leaving tomorrow."

"That's right," she said with resignation. "The boss only gave me a week to do these articles. I can't stay any longer."

He didn't reply to that. But his whole look was speculative as he drove. He pulled up at the bar and switched the engine off.

"Want me to go in with you?" he asked.

She glanced at the sheer size of him, and almost said yes. He looked tough, and she knew that having a damaged hand wouldn't save any man who challenged him. But it would be cowardly to take protection in with her, she considered.

"Thanks, but I think I'll go in by myself," she said.

"I'll wait out here, then," he replied. "Just in case."

She smiled. "Thanks."

She got out and walked warily into the bar. There was a hush, nothing like the regular sounds of clinking glasses and conversation and loud music. The band was sitting quietly. The customers were grouped around a pool table. As she watched, a pool cue

came up and went down again and there was an ominous crack-
ing sound, followed by a thud and a louder bump.

Following her intuition, she pushed through the crowd. Guy
was leaning over a cowboy with a bleeding nose, both big fists
curled and a dangerous look on his face.

She moved right up to him, without hesitation, and caught
one of his big fists in her hands.

He jerked upright and stared at her as if he was hallucinating.

"Candy?" he rasped.

She nodded. She smiled with more self-confidence than she
felt. "Come on, Guy."

She tugged at his fist until it uncurled and grasped her soft
hand. She smiled shyly at the fascinated audience and tugged
again, so that Guy stumbled after her.

"Don't forget your hat!" a cowboy called, and sailed Guy's
wide-brimmed hat toward them. Candy caught it.

There were murmurs that grew louder as they made it to
the front door.

Guy took a deep breath of night air on the steps and almost
keeled over. Candy got under his arm to steady him.

"My God, girl, you shouldn't…be here," he managed to say,
curling his arm closer. "Anything could have happened to you
in a joint like this!"

"Mr. Parks said they'd arrest you if you broke it up again,"
she said simply. "You rescued me. So now I'm rescuing you."

He began to chuckle. "Do tell?" he drawled. "Well, now that
you've got me, what are you going to do with me?" he asked
in a sensuous tone.

"If she had any sense, she'd lay a frying pan over your thick
skull," Cy Parks muttered. He moved Candy out of the way
and propelled Guy to the car. He shoved him headfirst into the
backseat and slammed the door after him.

"We'll drop him off at the feedlot and then I'll take you
home. Justin can send somebody for the truck."

"What are you doing here?" Guy asked belligerently. "Did she bring you?"

"Sure," Cy said sarcastically as he cranked the car and pulled it out of the parking lot onto the highway. "She drove my car to my house and tossed me in and forced me to come after you."

Guy blinked. That didn't sound quite right.

"I'm sorry I made you fly," Candy said, leaning over the backseat to look at Guy. "I know that was what did this to you."

"What, flying?" he murmured in some confusion. He pushed back sweaty hair. "Hell, no, it wasn't that."

"Then what was it?" she asked hesitantly.

"You want to go home," he said heavily. He leaned back and closed his eyes, oblivious to the rapt stare of the woman in the front seat. "You want to walk off and leave me. I had a job I was beginning to like, but if I can't have you, I have nothing worth going on for."

Cy exchanged an amused glance with a shocked Candy. "What if she stayed?" Cy asked. "What good is a man who gets stinking drunk every Saturday night?"

"If she stayed I wouldn't have any reason to get drunk every Saturday night," Guy muttered drowsily. "Could get a little house, and she could plant flowers," he murmured on a yawn. "A man would work himself to death for a woman like her. So special…"

He fell asleep.

Candy felt her heart try to climb right out of her body. "He's just drunk," she rationalized.

"It's like truth serum," Cy retorted. "So now you know." He glanced at her. "Still leaving town?"

"Are you kidding?" she asked, wide-eyed. "After a confession like that? I am not! I'm going to be his shadow until he buys me a ring!"

Cy Parks actually threw back his head and laughed.

* * *

Guy came to in a big bed that wasn't his own. He opened his eyes and there was a ceiling, but it didn't look like the ceiling in the bunkhouse. He heard soft breathing. Also not his own.

He turned his head, and there, beside him in the bed with just a sheet covering her, was a sleeping Candy Marshall. She was wearing a pink silk gown that covered only certain parts of her exquisite body, and her long dark hair was spread over the white pillow like silk.

He looked down and found that he was still wearing last night's clothing, minus his boots. He cleared his throat and his head began to throb.

"Oh, boy," he groaned when he realized what had happened. The question was, how had he gotten here, in bed with Candy?

She stirred. Her eyes opened, dark velvet, soft and amused and loving.

"What are we doing here in bed together?" he asked dazedly.

"Not much," she drawled.

He chuckled softly and grabbed his head.

"How about some aspirin and coffee?" she asked.

"How about shooting me?" he offered as an alternative.

She climbed out of the bed, graceful and sensuous, and went to plug in the coffeemaker that was provided with the room. She had cups, and she went to her purse and pulled out a bottle of aspirin. Before she shook them out, she paused to use the preventative inhalant Dr. Morris had prescribed.

"Good girl," Guy murmured huskily.

She glanced at him and smiled. "Well, I have to take care of myself so I can take care of you." She brought him the aspirin and a glass of water. "Take those," she directed. "And if you *ever* go into a bar again on Saturday night, I really will lay an iron skillet across your skull!"

"They'll arrest you for spousal abuse," he pointed out.

"Put your money where your mouth is," she challenged.

He chuckled weakly as he swallowed the aspirin. "Okay. Will you marry me, warts and all?"

"We've only known each other a week," she stated. "You might not like me when you get to know me."

"Yes, I will. Will you marry me?"

She smiled. "Sure."

He laughed with pure delight. "Care to come down here and seal the bargain?"

She hesitated. "No, I don't think so. You're in disgrace. First you can get over the hangover and clean yourself up a bit."

He sighed. "I guess I do look pretty raunchy."

She nodded. "And you still smell like a brewery. By the way, I don't drink. Never."

He held up a hand. "I've just reformed. From now on it's coffee, tea or milk. I swear."

"Good man. In that case, we can get married next week. Before Saturday night," she added with a smile.

He opened his eyes wide and studied her with possessiveness. "It wasn't flying at all," he said softly. "It was losing you. I couldn't bear the thought that you were going to go off and leave me. But this time the alcohol didn't work. I've lost my taste for bars and temporary oblivion. If you'll marry me, I won't need temporary oblivion. I'll build you a house where you can plant flowers." His gaze dropped down over her slender body. "We can have children, if it's safe for you."

She beamed. "I'd like that."

"It might be risky."

"We'll go ask Dr. Morris," she assured him. "Since I'm going to be living in Jacobsville, he can be my doctor."

He just stared at her, his heart in his eyes. "I didn't know it could happen like this," he said aloud. "I thought love died and was buried. It isn't."

She smiled brilliantly. "I never even knew what it was. Until now."

He opened his arms and she went down into them, and they lay for a long time just holding each other tightly in the shared wonder of loving.

He lifted his head finally and looked down at the treasure in his arms. "I suppose, if you want, I can go back to my air cargo company and run it."

"Do you want to?"

He thought about that for a minute before he answered her. "Not really," he said finally. "It was a part of my life that I enjoyed at the time, but there will always be bad memories connected with it." He put his hand over her lips when she started to speak. "I'm not still grieving for Anita," he added quietly. "I'll always miss her a little, and regret the way she died. But I didn't bury my heart with her. I want you and a family and a home of our own. I enjoy managing the feedlot. In many ways, it's a challenge." He grinned. "And if you'd take over publicity for the local cattlemen's association, we'd have a lot more in common."

She beamed. "Would they let me?"

"They'd beg you!" he replied. "Poor old Mrs. Harrison is doing it right now, and she hates every word she writes. She'll make you cakes and pies if you'll take it off her hands."

"In that case, I might enjoy it," she replied.

"And we'd get to work together," he murmured, bending to kiss her gently. He lifted his head. "Oh, Candy, what did I ever do to deserve someone like you?" he asked huskily. "I do love you so!"

She pulled him down to her. "I love you, too."

Neither of them questioned how love could strike so suddenly. They got married and spent their honeymoon in Galveston, going for long walks on the beach and lying in each other's arms enjoying the newness of loving in every possible way.

"My mother wants us to come and visit her when we're back

from our honeymoon," she mentioned to Guy after a long, sweet morning of shared ecstasy. She curled closer to him under the single sheet that covered them. "She said she hoped we'd be happy."

"We will be," he mused, stroking her long hair with a gentle hand. "Do you want to go?"

"I think it's time I made my peace with her," she replied. "Maybe I've been as guilty as she has of living in the past. Not anymore," she added, looking up at him with love brimming over in her eyes. "Marriage is fun," she said with a wicked grin.

"Is it, now?" He threw off the sheet and rolled over onto her with a chuckle. "Was that a hint?" he whispered as he began to kiss her.

She slid against him with delight and wrapped a soft, long leg around his muscular one. "A blatant hint," she agreed, gasping as he touched her gently and his mouth settled on her parted lips.

"Anything to oblige," he whispered huskily.

She laughed and gasped, and then clung to him as the lazy rhythm made spirals of ecstasy ripple the length of her body. She closed her eyes and gave in to the pleasure. Love, she thought while she could, was the most indescribable of shared delights.

Outside the window, waves crashed on the beach and seagulls dived and cried in the early-morning sunlight. Somewhere on the boundary of her senses, Candy heard them, but she was so close to heaven that the sound barely registered.

When the stormy delight passed, she held an exhausted Guy to her heart and thought of flower gardens in a future that was suddenly sweet and full of joy. She closed her eyes and smiled as she dreamed.

Guy felt her body go lax. He looked down at her sleeping face with an expression that would have brought tears to her eyes. From a nightmare to this, he was thinking. Candy had made him whole again. She'd chased away the guilt of the past, and the grief, and offered him a new heart to cherish. He knew without a doubt that his drinking days were over. Candy would make his happiness, and he'd make hers.

He settled back down beside her and drew the sheet over them both. In his mind, before he fell asleep, he was already working on plans for that small house where he and Candy would share their lives.

* * * * *